GOING ROGUE

A STEPHANIE PLUM NOVEL

GOING ROGUE

RISE AND SHINE TWENTY-NINE

JANET EVANOVICH

THORNDIKE PRESS
A part of Gale, a Cengage Company

Thorndike Press® Large Print Basic.
The text of this Large Print edition is unabridged.
Other aspects of the book may vary from the original edition.
Set in 16 pt. Plantin.

LIBRARY OF CONGRESS CIP DATA ON FILE.
CATALOGUING IN PUBLICATION FOR THIS BOOK
IS AVAILABLE FROM THE LIBRARY OF CONGRESS.

ISBN-13: 979-8-8857-8363-7 (hardcover alk. paper)

Published in 2022 by arrangement with Atria Books, a Division of Simon & Schuster, Inc.

Printed in Mexico
Print Number: 01   Print Year: 2023

GOING ROGUE

Going Rogue

CHAPTER ONE

My name is Stephanie Plum. I'm a bail bonds enforcement agent, working for my cousin Vinnie, and I'm currently locked out of the bail bonds office. It's nine in the morning in Trenton, New Jersey. It's October. It's Monday. Everything is good in my world except the office is closed and the lights are off. This is a first because the office manager, Connie Rosolli, is always at her desk by now.

A red Firebird pulled to the curb behind my blue Honda CR-V. Lula got out of the Firebird and walked over to me. Lula is a former hooker who now works for Vinnie doing whatever the heck she wants. At five feet five inches she's two inches shorter than I am. She's a smidgeon younger, her skin is a lot darker, and she's a bunch of pounds heavier. Her hair was yellow today, with braided extensions that hung halfway down her back. She was wearing a black sweater that was two sizes too small and fuchsia spandex tights.

I was wearing jeans, and a sweatshirt over a T-shirt, and because I was wearing sneakers and Lula was wearing six-inch stiletto heels, she had me by a couple inches.

"What the heck?" Lula asked.

"The office is locked," I said, "and Connie's car isn't here."

"Did you check the lot in the back?"

"Yeah."

"Well, this is just wrong," Lula said. "She's supposed to be here. She brings the doughnuts. What am I supposed to do without my doughnuts?"

Connie is in her midthirties and lives with her widowed mother. The living arrangement isn't ideal for Connie, but she's a good Italian Catholic girl and family takes care of family. I called Connie's cell phone and didn't get an answer, so I called her house phone.

Mama Rosolli answered on the second ring. "Who's this?" she asked.

"It's Stephanie Plum," I said. "Is Connie there?"

"She's at work. She left extra early today so she could get gas and some lottery tickets. I was still in my robe and nightgown when she was going out the door."

"Okay," I said. "Thanks."

"And?" Lula asked when I hung up.

"She's not home. Her mother said she left early to get gas and lottery tickets."

I dialed Vinnie.

"Now what?" he asked.

"Connie isn't here. Have you heard from her?"

"No. She's supposed to be there. She's always there."

"Not today," I said. "The office is locked, and the lights are off."

"You're calling me, why?"

"I thought you might want to open the office for us."

"You thought wrong. I'm in Atlantic City with Big Datucci and Mickey Maroney. We're waiting on Harry."

Harry the Hammer is Vinnie's father-in-law. He owns the agency, and he owns Vinnie.

"Go to the back door," Vinnie said. "There's a key under the brick by the dumpster."

The bail bonds office is a one-story storefront on Hamilton Avenue. It's squashed between a dry cleaner and a mystery bookshop, and it's across the street from the Burg. I grew up in the Burg, and my parents still live there. Houses are small. Cars and televisions are large. Most of the residents are hardworking, overfed, and underpaid. They're staunch believers in the First and Second Amendments, the sanctity of football and baseball, a first-class funeral, homemade marinara, stuffed cabbage, white bread, grilled anything, and cannoli from Italian Peoples Bakery.

Lula and I walked around the block to the alley behind the bonds office. We found the key under the brick, opened the back door, and entered the storeroom.

For the most part, bail bonds are secured by real estate, vehicles, bank accounts, and pawnable items like weapons, electronics, and jewelry. Vinnie has been known to accept other items of questionable value that appeal to his own personal interests — such as unusual sex toys, high-quality pot, whips of any sort, desirable seats for the Mets or the Rangers, and nooners from fancy ladies, and he once took possession of an aging racehorse. All these odds and ends find their temporary homes in the storeroom. Small items are kept in multi-drawered metal cabinets. Medium-sized items are tagged and crammed onto rows of shelves. The racehorse was kept in Vinnie's backyard until the neighbors complained.

Lula walked through the storeroom to the

small alcove that served as a kitchenette.

"There's no coffee brewing," she said. "I'm not supposed to start my day like this. I got a routine. My morning has expectations, if you see what I'm saying."

I was more concerned about the storeroom than the coffee machine. Some of the cabinet drawers weren't completely closed and the items stashed on the shelves had been shoved around.

"Were you looking for something in the storeroom over the weekend?" I asked Lula.

"Nuh-uh, not me," Lula said. "I only was here for a couple hours on Saturday."

I told myself that Connie was probably in a rush to find something, but I only halfway believed it. It wasn't normal behavior for Connie to leave the storeroom like this.

"I know the gas station Connie uses," I said to Lula. "You stay here and man the desk, and I'll see if I can track her down."

"Get doughnuts on your way back," Lula said. "Make sure you get a Boston cream for me."

Connie lives on the outskirts of the Burg and gets gas on State Street. I took Hamilton to State and turned left. I pulled into the gas station, bypassed the pumps, and parked in front of the gas station minimart. I didn't see Connie's car, so I went inside

11

and asked the cashier if she'd seen Connie.

"A couple inches shorter than me," I said to the cashier. "Lots of dark brown hair, lots of eyebrows, lots of mascara, about my age. She was going to get lottery tickets this morning."

"Yeah, she was here," the cashier said. "She's chesty, right?"

"Right. I was supposed to meet her, but she didn't show up," I said. "Did she say anything about where she was going?"

"No. She got her lottery tickets and left."

I drove to the bakery, got a box of doughnuts, and returned to the office.

"Did you find her?" Lula asked.

"No." I set the doughnut box on Connie's desk. "She got lottery tickets at the gas station. And I found out that she got doughnuts at the bakery."

"What? She got doughnuts? I don't see no Connie's doughnuts. I don't even see no fresh powdered sugar or chocolate icing smudges anywhere on her desk. Where'd she go with my doughnut after she left the bakery? There's something wrong here." Lula looked in the box I had just put in front of her. "There's no Boston cream."

"They were sold out."

"Damn."

We hung out in the office eating doughnuts and drinking coffee. An hour went by and there was still no Connie.

"Maybe you should check her email," I said to Lula.

"Why me?" Lula asked.

"You're sitting in her chair."

"Okay, I guess that makes sense, but how am I going to do that? She's got a password."

"She keeps all her passwords in a notebook in the bottom drawer with her office gun."

Lula opened the drawer and pulled the book out. "She's got a lot of passwords," Lula said, paging through. "I could see where her life is unnecessarily complicated. I only have one password. I use it for everything, so I don't need a book like this."

"That's frowned on in the world of cybersecurity."

Lula blew out a raspberry. "That's what I think of cybersecurity." She found the password, typed it in, and the computer came alive. She opened email and scrolled through a bunch of messages. "Here's a court report," she said. "It looks like three idiots failed to appear for their hearings on Friday. I'll print them out for you."

The deal is that when someone is arrested and doesn't want to sit around in a cell until his court date, he's required to post a cash bond. If he doesn't have the money, he gets it from a bail bondsman like Vinnie. If he fails to appear when his hearing is scheduled, Vinnie is out big bucks unless I can find the FTA and bring him back into the system.

I took the printouts from Lula and paged through them. Brad Winter was a no-show on a blackmail charge. It carried a high bond. Carpenter Beedle tried to rob an armored truck and accidentally shot himself in the foot. Also a high bond. Bellissima Morelli was charged with arson, resisting arrest, and assaulting a police officer.

"Holy cow," I said. "This last one is Joe's grandmother."

Lula leaned forward to get a better look at the file. "Say what? I wasn't paying that close attention."

When I was five years old and Joe Morelli was six, we played choo-choo in his father's garage. This wasn't an entirely rewarding experience because I was always the tunnel and I wanted to be the train. When I was seventeen, I volunteered my virginity to Morelli in a moment of passion and prurient curiosity. The outcome was only marginally better than choo-choo, and Morelli walked away from it without so much as a follow-up

14

phone call. Two years later I saw him strolling down the sidewalk in Trenton. I jumped the curb and clipped him with my father's Buick, relieved that I finally had a satisfying encounter with the jerk. Our relationship has improved since then. He's a Trenton cop now, working plainclothes in crimes against persons. He's a good cop, he's become a good friend, and he's made a lot of progress on the choo-choo game. I suppose you could say that he's my boyfriend, although the term seems insufficient for our relationship.

"Isn't Bella the one who dresses in black like an extra in a Mafia movie about Sicily?" Lula asked.

"Yes."

"And she puts *the eye* on people and makes their teeth fall out and they poop their pants?"

"Yes."

"Well good thing I'm working the desk this morning and you're the bounty hunter," Lula said. "I wouldn't want to be the one who has to haul her bony ass back to jail. She creeps me out."

I left Lula at the office, and I drove to my parents' house. The easiest and most reliable way for me to get information on

15

anyone in the Burg is to talk to my Grandma Mazur. She shops at Giovichinni's Deli and the Italian Peoples and Tasty Pastry bakeries. She goes to bingo twice a week, and she regularly attends Mass at the Catholic Church and viewings at Stiva's Funeral Home. The Burg gossip mill is in full force at all these gatherings. Several years ago, Grandpa Mazur succumbed to a full-fat diet and two packs of Lucky Strikes a day, so Grandma moved in with my parents. My father survives this invasion by spending a lot of time at his lodge, and my mom has developed a relationship with Jack Daniel's.

My parents still live in my childhood home. It's a small duplex that's attached to another duplex. The inside of the house is packed with comfortable, overstuffed furniture and a lot of memories. Three tiny bedrooms and one bath upstairs; living room, dining room, kitchen downstairs. The front door opens to a small foyer that leads to the living room. There's a back door in the kitchen, and beyond the back door is a small, rarely used backyard and a single-car garage.

It was midmorning, and I knew I would find my mom and Grandma in the kitchen. I look a lot like my mom, but my brown hair is longer and curlier than hers, my blue eyes are a shade deeper, and my body is a little slimmer. Grandma looks like my mom and me, but gravity has taken its toll on Grandma. It's as if she was partially melted and then got frozen into a new semi-gelatinous shape where things like breasts and cheeks hang a lot lower than they used to.

My mom was mixing something in a big bowl, and Grandma was at the little kitchen table, doing the day's Jumble. I looked in the bowl and grimaced.

"Meatloaf," my mom said. "Turkey, sirloin, and pork. Giovichinni ground it up for me fresh this morning."

"It's mostly turkey," Grandma said, "on account of your father's cholesterol is high. He had to cut back on either beef or full-fat ice cream, and he didn't want to give up the ice cream." She leaned to the left in her seat and looked behind me. "Where's your sidekick, Lula?"

"Connie isn't in the office this morning, so Lula's manning the desk." I dropped my messenger bag on the floor and sat at the table with Grandma. "Remember when Manny Tortolli's garage burned down last month?"

"Yeah, it was a beauty of a fire," Grandma said. "I was watching TV and I heard the trucks go past our house, so I went out to look. You could see the flames shooting up into the sky."

"Morelli's Grandma Bella was charged with arson for that fire," I said.

"She was standing on the sidewalk holding an empty one-gallon metal can that used to have kerosene in it. And she was yelling, 'Burn, baby, burn!' at the garage," Grandma said. "I got it all straight from Emily Mizner. Her boy was one of the first cops to get there. He tried to calm crazy Bella down, and she hit him with the empty can and gave him *the eye.* Now he's got boils all over him, even on his private parts."

"Vinnie posted Bella's bail bond, and she didn't show up for her court appearance on Friday," I said. "The failure-to-appear notice came into the office this morning."

My mother stopped mixing and stared at me. "Don't even *think* about going after her. She's a lunatic. Let Joseph bring her in."

My mom is the only one on the planet who calls Morelli by his first name. Sometimes I call him Joe, but never Joseph.

"It's hard to believe she could give someone boils just by pulling her lower eyelid down and glaring at him," I said to my mom.

"Emily told me they weren't ordinary

boils," Grandma said. "According to Emily, they're huge. *Gigantic* and oozing pus. She called them the Devil's boils."

"Forget the boils," my mother said to me. "Crazy Bella set fire to Manny Tortolli's garage! She's dangerous. You don't want to get anywhere near her."

Truth is, I've gone after people who were a lot more dangerous than Bella. I've taken down killers, rapists, and serial mooners. Not that I wanted to trivialize Bella. I mean, who's to say if she's for real? What I knew was that I didn't want to have to tackle my boyfriend's grandmother and wrestle her to the ground so I could cuff her, and I didn't want boils on my private parts.

"That Bella is a mean one," Grandma said. "She thinks she owns the Burg. If you have any problems with her, let me know. I'm not afraid of her. She's just a big bag of wind with no fashion sense. She's been wearing that same dumpy black dress for twenty years. Who else are you looking for? Anybody interesting?"

"Brad Winter. Lives in North Trenton. And Carpenter Beedle."

"I read about Carpenter Beedle. He's the one who shot himself while he was trying to rob an armored truck. I wouldn't mind seeing what he's about."

"Are you staying for lunch?" my mom asked.

I stood up. "No. Gotta go. Work to do."

"If you're leaving now, you can give me a ride," Grandma said. "Your mother's up to her elbows in meatloaf and I need shampoo. I like the kind they sell at the hair salon. I just need to get my purse and a jacket."

Three minutes later we were in my car.

"Okay," Grandma said. "I'm all set. I say we go after Beedle first. It's not like he can outrun us since his foot got shot up."

"I thought you needed shampoo."

"That was a ruse to get out of the house. You're missing your wingman, so I'm gonna fill in."

Just when you think your day can't get any worse, there it is, yet another disaster. Not of the magnitude of Connie going missing, but a disaster all the same.

CHAPTER TWO

I like Grandma a lot but having her ride shotgun doesn't have a lot of appeal. It's hard to be taken seriously as a bounty hunter when you're partnered with your grandmother. Not to mention, my mother would have a cow if she knew.

"Mom isn't going to be happy about this," I said.

"Yeah, she'll be nuts, so you better get a move on before she figures it out." She searched my messenger bag. "Here's Beedle's file," she said. "He's thirty-one years old and he lives at Ninety-Three Brill Street."

I looked over at Grandma. I could stun gun her and leave her on the front lawn, but my mom wouldn't like that either.

"Okay," I said, "but I get to do all the talking and you have to leave your gun in the car."

"What gun?"

"The gun you've got in your purse. The gun you're not supposed to have."

"There's a crime wave going on," Grandma said. "A woman has to protect herself. Besides, I'm a responsible gun owner. And anyways, someone on this team has to have a gun, and we all know it's not going to be you."

"I don't need a gun."

Grandma hefted her purse. "Plus, there's an added advantage to packing. My forty-five gives me the right amount of weight in case I have to smack someone in the face with my handbag."

I couldn't argue with that one. I pulled away from the curb, made a U-turn, and headed for Hamilton Avenue. I wanted to drive by the office and check to see if Connie's car was there.

"I never heard of Brill Street," Grandma said. "You're gonna have to GPS it."

I turned onto Hamilton and parked across the street from the office. I could see Lula at the desk. No Connie. No Connie's car at the curb. I called Lula.

"Have you heard from Connie?" I asked.

"No. Nothing. Nada. And I got a empty bakery box. I had to compensate for not getting the Boston cream by eating all the other lame-ass doughnuts. And now I'm getting acid reflux from drinking so much coffee without nothing more to soak it up."

"Anything else going on?"

"A moron phoned in on account of he wanted to be bonded out. I told him he was gonna have to keep his ass in jail or find some other sucker to fork over the money. I mean it's not like I can just jump up and run off to the courthouse to bail him out. Who's gonna sit at the desk if I go to the courthouse?"

"Not to mention, we aren't authorized to write a bail bond."

"Say what?"

"Vinnie and Connie are the only ones who are authorized to write a bond."

"Hunh," Lula said. "I bet I could if I wanted to."

"Gotta go," I said. "Call me if you hear from Connie."

I tapped 93 Brill Street into my iPhone map app, and it took me to a sketchy area by the train station. The street was narrow and lined with two- and three-story grimy brick row houses. I suspected most of them had been converted into multifamily units. I was able to park a couple houses down from Beedle's address.

"This is just the sort of place you'd expect an armored-car robber to live," Grandma said. "I bet this neighborhood is filled with criminals."

It looked to me like it was filled with people who couldn't afford to live anywhere else. If they were criminals, they weren't very good ones.

There were three buzzers alongside the door to number 93. The names on the buzzers were Goldwink, Thomas, Warnick. No Beedle. I tried the door. Locked. I pushed the buzzer for Goldwink. No answer. No answer for Thomas. Warnick opened his connection with static.

"What?" Warnick yelled when the static died down.

"I'm looking for Carpenter Beedle," I said.

"He's not here," Warnick said. "He moved back with his mother." The connection cut out.

Grandma and I returned to my car, and I paged through Beedle's file.

"We're in luck," I said. "His mother signed for his bond. She secured it with her car. She lives on Maymount Street."

"That's off Chambers," Grandma said. "Your cousin Gloria used to live there when she was married to husband number one. He turned out to be a real stinker."

I cut back to State Street and got a hollow feeling in my stomach when I drove past

Connie's gas station. No word from Lula. No text message or phone call from Connie. I took Chambers to Maymount and parked in front of the Beedle house. I called Connie and didn't get an answer. Her voice mail didn't kick in.

"If she was in an accident and was in the hospital we would have heard by now, so I don't think that's it," Grandma said. "There's been a lot of aneurisms going around lately, but we would have heard about that too. That leaves two possibilities. The first is that she got fed up with everything and she's on her way to Hawaii. The second is that she got taken to the mother ship by aliens. I just saw a special on UFOs, and it was real convincing."

My possibilities were just as irrational, and I hoped just as unlikely. I couldn't shake the feeling that something bad had gone down and Connie was in the middle of it.

The Beedle house was a small, pale yellow bungalow with a red front door. A rusted Nissan Sentra was parked in the driveway. Grandma and I went to the red door, and I rang the bell.

"Should I draw my gun?" Grandma asked. "How's this gonna happen?"

"No gun," I said. "We're going to politely request that Carpenter goes with us to get rebonded."

"What if he doesn't want to go?"

"I'll try to persuade him."

"Is that when I get to draw my gun?"

"No! No gun."

A woman in her midfifties opened the door and looked out at us.

"Mrs. Beedle?" I asked.

"Yes."

I gave her my nonthreatening, casually pleasant bounty hunter smile. "I'm looking for your son, Carpenter. I work for his bail bonds agent."

"Such a nice man," she said. "He was so helpful. He personally came to the police station to see that Carpenter was released. He walked him out the door and made sure we safely got into our car." She stepped aside. "Come in. Carpenter is in the kitchen. He's getting ready to go to work. He's a bum."

"Panhandler," Carpenter yelled from the kitchen. "It's the second-oldest profession."

Carpenter was at the kitchen table. His brown hair was pulled back into a ponytail, and he had a three-day-old beard. He was wearing a wrinkled, washed-out flannel shirt and baggy sweatpants. He had a filthy sneaker on one foot and an orthopedic sandal on the other. He clutched a coffee mug in his right hand.

Grandma looked down at the orthopedic-sandaled foot. "I read where you shot yourself in the foot," Grandma said. "Where'd the bullet go in? Did you lose any toes?"

"No," Carpenter said. "I took a chunk out of the side and broke a bone."

"At least it's not your gas pedal foot," Grandma said.

"I told him over and over not to carry a gun," Mrs. Beedle said. "Does he listen to me? No. So, this is what happens."

"It was an accident," Carpenter said. "It could have happened to anybody."

"*Anybody* doesn't try to hold up an armored car," Mrs. Beedle said.

"Yeah, I didn't think that one through," Carpenter said. "It was a spur-of-the-moment thing. I saw them unloading all that money and I thought, there I was on the corner panhandling for spare change when I could be robbing an armored car."

"Why don't you have a job?" Grandma asked.

"I have a job," Carpenter said. "I panhandle. I was doing okay at it until I got shot in the foot. This will be my first day back at my corner."

"You don't just panhandle," his mother

said. "You pick people's pockets. You're a disgrace."

"I only do that on lean days," Carpenter said. "And I'm selective. I don't go after senior citizens."

"He's a CPA," Mrs. Beedle said. "He had a good job downtown. He was moving up in the company."

"I hated that job," Carpenter said. "It gave me eczema. I spent all day in a cubicle, staring at numbers. Panhandling is better. I'm my own boss and I'm out in the fresh air all day."

"Good for you for figuring that out," Grandma said.

"You're a bum," his mother said. "And now you're an armored-car robber."

"Technically I'm not an armored-car robber," he said. "I only *attempted* to rob it."

"How'd you shoot yourself in the foot?" Grandma asked.

"The guard handed me a bag of money, and it was heavier than I thought it would be. I dropped it on my foot and when I went to pick it up, I guess I squeezed the trigger on the gun."

"I could see that happening," Grandma said. "You don't look like you've got a lot of muscle. You should work out when you get sent to the big house."

"While we're on the subject," I said. "You missed your court date. You need to come with us to get rebonded."

"He never used to miss a date," Mrs. Beedle said. "He kept a calendar, and he always knew everyone's birthday. And he was right on time with filing taxes."

"I'm a new man now," Carpenter said. "I don't pay taxes. I don't make enough money. I lead a simple life."

"His wife left him, and he snapped," Mrs. Beedle said.

"Good riddance," Carpenter said. "She was just one more encumbrance."

"You might like prison," Grandma said. "I don't think you got a lot of encumbrances there as long as you don't mind being locked up."

Carpenter pushed back from the table. "This won't take long, will it?" he asked me. "I don't want to miss the lunch crowd. I have some regulars at lunchtime."

"No problem," I said.

So, here's the thing about being a bounty hunter. You do a lot of fibbing. Especially to first-time offenders who don't know anything about the system. If you told them the truth, they might not cooperate. The truth in this case wasn't good. Carpenter was going to have to sit in jail until Vinnie got back in town. An alternative was to find another bail bondsman. And even worse news, his mother would have to guarantee a new bond and she probably didn't have a second car.

I left Grandma in the car and walked Carpenter into the municipal building that housed the police department. I handed him over to the desk lieutenant and told him I would have Vinnie get in touch as soon as he got back in town. I left the building and ran into Morelli in the parking lot. On a good day, Morelli is six feet of lean muscle and Italian charm dressed up in a button-down shirt, jeans, and running shoes. This morning he was six feet of bad attitude. His wavy black hair was soaking wet and slicked back. The rest of him was equally wet and splattered with mud. His shirt was in tatters. His face looked like it had been clawed by a panther. His right eye was almost swollen shut.

"Omigod," I said. "What happened to you? Are you okay?"

"Road rage incident on the Stark Street bridge. I was stuck in traffic, two cars back from the scene. Two women, out of their cars, beating the crap out of each other. I got between them, and they both attacked me. A second motorist came to help, we got the women separated, and one of them jumped off the bridge."

"So, you jumped in after her?"

"It was more like I dangled and dropped. It was close to the bank on the Trenton side. I grabbed her and dragged her out."

"Was she all right?"

"She broke her leg. The water was only about ten feet deep. She's lucky she didn't go off headfirst."

"Is there something I can do? You're bleeding and your eye is swelling. Do you want to see a doctor?"

"I'm okay. I'm going in to collect some things and then I'm headed home. What brings you here?"

"I dropped off Carpenter Beedle. FTA. He's the guy who tried to rob the armored car and ended up shooting himself in the foot."

I wanted to talk to Morelli about his grandmother and about Connie, but he was dripping river water and the scratches were still oozing blood.

"I need to talk to you when you're dry and not bleeding," I said. "How about dinner? I'll get takeout."

"Sounds good."

I crossed the lot to my car and slid behind

the wheel.

"Was that Morelli you were talking to?" Grandma asked. "I could hardly recognize him with his hair slicked back."

"He hauled a woman out of the Delaware."

"He's such a hero," Grandma said. "And he looks good even when he's wet."

This was all true.

"Now what?" Grandma asked.

"I'm going to the office to see how Lula is managing."

Lula was at Connie's desk when Grandma and I walked in.

"It took me a couple hours to figure it out, but this is where I belong," Lula said. "There's almost nothing to do. All I have to do is sit here and look important. And I got a lot of authority now that I'm behind Connie's computer. I already ordered some new magazine subscriptions. And I'm thinking about getting a new couch."

"Connie's only been gone for a couple of hours," I said. "It's not as if she's not coming back."

"Sure, I know that," Lula said, "but I figure I should put myself to good use while I'm here. I'm a born organizer. I'm one of those take-charge people. And I look excellent behind a desk."

"You do look pretty good," Grandma said. "And the yellow braids brighten up the room and give a good contrast to your skin."

"It's like I'm an M&M," Lula said. "Chocolate on the inside and a splash of color on the outside."

"Have you heard from Connie or Vinnie?" I asked Lula.

"Nothing," Lula said. "I've been listening to the police calls, but no one's mentioned Connie, and I don't want to hear from Vinnie. I don't see where we even need him. I got everything under control here. I'm so organized I've got my lunch ordered already. And it's getting delivered so I don't have to leave my desk. Turns out this desk comes with petty cash."

"We're doing good, too," Grandma said. "We already made a recovery. Carpenter Beedle."

"How's his foot?" Lula asked.

"It's okay," Grandma said. "He has it in one of those orthopedic-sandal things."

"Pull up Connie's calendar on her computer," I said to Lula. "See if she has anything on there for today."

"I already did that," Lula said. "There's nothing for today, but she has a dentist appointment tomorrow at four o'clock."

"Maybe it got switched to this morning at the last minute," Grandma said. "Maybe she's at the dentist."

"I guess that could be it," Lula said.

I nodded.

No one said anything. Grandma fidgeted with her purse and Lula stared blank-faced at the computer screen. No one believed Connie was at the dentist. Connie would have told us that she wouldn't be in until later.

"Bummer," Grandma finally said.

I nodded again.

My mother called me. "Where are you?" she asked. "Is your grandmother still with you? Are you coming home for lunch?"

"I'm at the office," I said. "Grandma's with me, and we'll be home for lunch."

I hung up and Grandma started for the door. "Let's not waste a lot of time on lunch. We still got two more felons to catch."

"There's no rush," I said. "I'm not going to go after Bella until I talk to Morelli."

"Well, I want to be there when you do the takedown. That woman's been a thorn in my side for as long as I can remember. And she thinks she owns the funeral home. She scuttles around, threatening to give everybody the eye if they get in her way. People are afraid to take a cookie when she comes over to the refreshment table."

"How about you?" Lula asked. "Are you afraid to take a cookie?"

"Heck no," Grandma said. "I know the cookies she likes. She goes after the pignoli. So, if I see her at a viewing, I shove all the pignoli into my purse before she can get to them."

CHAPTER THREE

My mom was setting the kitchen table when we walked in. "I made minestrone soup this morning and we have bread from Italian Peoples," she said.

Butter and the bread slices were already on the table.

"It's a good day for soup," Grandma said. "There's a chill in the air."

"Did you get your shampoo?" my mom asked Grandma.

"They were all out," Grandma said. "Stephanie's going to take me to the mall after lunch."

My mother looked at me. Slitty-eyed. "I'm holding you responsible," she said. "Don't let her shoot anybody and keep her out of the strip clubs."

I nodded. "Understood."

"I don't hardly ever go to strip clubs," Grandma said. "Although I do like to look at the men dancers. Some of them have real good moves."

I saw my mother's eyes cut to the over-the-counter cabinet alongside the sink where she keeps her whiskey stash. No doubt debating if it was too early to have a nip.

Grandma took a bowl of soup to the table and checked email on her smartphone while she ate.

"Look at this," she said. "Len Leoni died. Margie Wisneski says they think he threw a clot. He's having a viewing on Wednesday. That's going to be a good one. He was a big deal in the Knights of Columbus." Grandma took a piece of bread and dunked it into her soup. "Crazy Bella will be there. The Morellis and the Leonis are neighbors. And one of the Leoni girls married into the Morelli family. A second cousin, I think. You should go to the viewing with me, and we'll take Bella down at the cookie table."

My mother sucked in some air. "You wouldn't!"

"Of course not," I said.

"I'd do it in a heartbeat," Grandma said.

"You have no authority," my mother said to Grandma. "You don't work for Vinnie. And even if you did work for Vinnie, it would be a horrible thing to do. It would be disrespectful to the deceased."

"Okay," Grandma said. "How about if we get Bella in the parking lot before or after?"

"There will be no *getting* Bella," my mother said to me. "For goodness' sake, get someone else. Someone we don't know. I'm sure you have a whole laundry list of people to get."

"Not so many," I said. "They skip town. They die. They get picked up by other bounty hunters. And a surprising number of the accused actually show up for court."

Grandma finished her soup and brought the cookie jar to the table. "I always like to have a sweet after a meal," she said. "We didn't do cookie baking this weekend, but we've got Oreos."

Twenty minutes later, I was back in my Honda CR-V with Grandma.

"I don't suppose I could talk you into tracking down Bella?" she said.

"Not today."

I wound my way out of the Burg to State Street, took State for two blocks, and turned onto Connie's street. I drove to her house and idled at the curb. Her car wasn't in the driveway. I called Lula and asked if she'd heard from Connie.

"No," Lula said. "Nothing from Connie. Only person called was some loser who wanted Vinnie. Said he had to talk to him.

So, I told him I was the only one here, and he could talk to me or no one. So, he hangs up and then ten minutes later he calls back. He tells me that Vinnie is gonna want to talk to him on account of he has something that belongs to Vinnie. So, I ask him what it is, and he says it's none of my business and that it's between him and Vinnie. He said Vinnie has something of his, and he's gonna keep this thing of Vinnie's until he gets his own thing back. So, I tell him I don't give a rat's ass about any of this. Honest to goodness, as if I haven't got anything better to do than to waste my time on someone who doesn't listen to what I'm saying. Vinnie isn't here to talk to you. How hard is that to understand?"

An alarm went off in my brain. What if the something this person has is Connie?

"Did you get a phone number?" I asked Lula.

"Hell no. It was probably one of those scam calls that turns out to be for phony car insurance."

The thought stuck with me. The storeroom looked like it had been searched. And Connie was missing. *Vinnie has something that's mine and now I have something that belongs to him,* the caller had said. Yes, but some*thing* is different from some*one,* I told myself. Too early to panic. And even if Connie had been snatched, it wasn't death and destruction. Vinnie would simply have to return whatever it was that the man wanted. Most likely something that had been posted for bail.

"If he calls again hand him over to me," I said to Lula.

"Whatever," Lula said. "Lord knows I got more important things to do. I gotta pick out fabric for the new couch. And I need a new desk chair. This chair I'm in has no personality, you see what I'm saying?"

"You should run all this by Vinnie before you order," I said to Lula.

"Like heck," Lula said. "He'll say no. He's a big cheapskate and he has no taste."

This is true. He's also a sexual deviant who cheats on his wife, cheats at cards, and is a compulsive gambler, and his pants are too tight. As Grandma puts it, he's a festering pimple on our family's behind. Setting all this aside, he's a good bail bondsman. And our boss.

"What was that phone call all about with Lula?" Grandma asked.

"She hasn't heard from Connie and she's busy redecorating the office. She also had a phone call from someone who said Vinnie has something that belongs to him, and now he has something that belongs to Vinnie."

"Probably one of those scam calls about phony car insurance," Grandma said. "They've got all kinds of gimmicks to suck you into signing up."

"I thought it might have been about Connie."

"That would have been my second guess," Grandma said. "Now what?"

"We wait for him to call back."

"That's uncomfortable. Don't you think we should go proactive?"

"I have no starting point. I ran down the few leads I had. And I have no real proof that Connie is in trouble."

I dialed Vinnie.

"Now what?" Vinnie said.

"Connie is still missing."

"Maybe she's having a hot flash somewhere."

"Lula is taking her place in the office and —"

"Hold on. Are you shitting me?"

"Someone has to take phone calls, so Lula is in the office."

"Okay, now you have my attention. Get her out of the office and lock the door so she can't get back in."

"I can't do that. It's important that someone answers the phone. A man called in asking to talk to you. He said you have something that belongs to him and now he has something that belongs to you. Lula told him you weren't there and to call back."

"And?"

"And it's possible that he has Connie."

"And you've figured this out, how?"

"When we let ourselves in through the back door, I noticed that the storeroom looked messy. Like someone had been looking for something. And then Connie never showed up for work. She stopped at the bakery and got the usual box of doughnuts, but she hasn't been at her desk."

"No doughnuts left on the desk?" Vinnie asked.

"No doughnuts left on the desk," I said.

"Maybe it's that time of the month, she ate all the doughnuts before she got to the office, and she's sleeping it off in some parking lot."

"When are you getting back?"

"Tonight. *Late* tonight."

"And you'll be in the office in the morning?"

"Yeah. What are you, my wife?"

"I'm not even happy that I'm your cousin."

Grandma looked at me when I hung up. "How'd that go?"

"As expected," I said.

"Are we going after another FTA slime-ball?"

"Yup. Brad Winter. Wanted for blackmail."

"Classy."

"Afraid not. He slept with a bunch of married women, videoed their encounters with a hidden camera, and blackmailed them."

"That's a real clever crime," Grandma said. "If you press charges against him, you know people are going to be looking at the videos. And your husband isn't going to be happy."

I thumbed through Winter's file. "He lives on Oak Street."

"That's a nice part of town," Grandma said. "Mostly new townhouses from where they tore down the toilet factory. It was called the porcelain factory, but everyone knew they made toilets. Not that there's any shame in making toilets."

I plugged the address into my GPS system and ten minutes later we were parked across the street from Winter's red brick and white vinyl clapboard townhouse. Postage-stamp front yard that was neat grass with a perfectly shaped row of small shrubs bordering the house. Two steps led to a large stoop and mahogany-colored front door.

"This is real classy," Grandma said. "You

could tell he's got money. I bet his bushes were shaped by a gardener. What's he look like?"

"Forty-two years old. Five foot ten. Brown eyes. Brown hair cut short. Average build. Nice looking."

I rang the bell and Winter answered. Naked.

"Here's something I don't get to see every day," Grandma said, staring at his privates.

"Catch you at a bad time?" I asked.

"Nope. I was just hanging out," he said. "What can I do you for?"

I introduced myself, showed him the badge I got on Amazon, and explained that he'd missed his court date and needed to reschedule.

He looked surprised. "Really? I didn't know I had a court date. No one told me."

"It's not a problem," I said. "Happens all the time. Get dressed and I'll drive you downtown to get a new date."

"Thanks, but that's not necessary. I can drive myself. Thanks for stopping by to tell me."

"Unfortunately, you're officially a felon now and I need to accompany you to the courthouse. Get dressed."

"A felon? Whoa, where'd that come from?"

"Not my idea," I said. "It's the law. You

failed to appear for a court date and that makes you a felon."

"That's harsh."

"Are you going to get dressed or are we taking you downtown naked?"

He smiled wide, showing perfect white teeth and dimples. "Really? Would you really take me in naked?"

"Yes," I said. "I've done it before, and I'll do it again."

"I have a better idea," he said. "Why don't you and your sister come in and we'll socialize a little. Have a glass of wine. Get to know each other. Then I'll get dressed and we can all go wherever you want."

"I'm not actually her sister," Grandma said, all smiles.

He winked at Grandma, and I clapped a cuff on his right wrist.

He turned his attention to the handcuffs. "Kinky."

"You're a sick person," I said, cuffing his other wrist.

"I'm not sick," he said. "I'm fun."

"You're also a blackmailer."

"I prefer to think of myself as a businessman. I provide a service and then I expect compensation."

"Go to his bedroom and get something that will cover him," I said to Grandma.

Grandma came back with a sheet. "You should see his bedroom," she said. "His bed is huge. One of those king-sized ones."

"Room for three, if you're into that sort of thing," Winter said.

I wrapped the sheet around him and tugged him to the door and down the steps. Grandma closed the door behind us, and we were about to cross the street when a Mercedes sedan slid to a stop in front of us. Four women got out and rushed at Grandma and me. They were in their late thirties to early forties. All had blond hair that was perfectly cut and colored. Minimal makeup. Diamond studs in their ears, and the diamonds didn't look fake. All wearing gym clothes. Lycra leggings and warm-up jackets. One of them drew a gun and the other three grabbed Winter and shoved him into the backseat of the Mercedes.

"Sorry," the woman with the gun said to me. "You're going to have to wait your turn. You can have him when we're done with him."

"I'm bail bond enforcement," I said, handing her my card.

"Whatever," she said. "We'll gift wrap him and bring him back here tomorrow. I'll make sure you get your cuffs back."

She jumped into the front passenger seat

and the car sped away.

"That was weird," Grandma said.

"Yeah, welcome to my world."

"I could see where the ladies like him," Grandma said. "He's a cutie pie. He has dimples. And he has a way with words. He thought I was your sister. I think the new moisturizer I'm using must be working." She thought for a couple beats. "He was sort of kidnapped. Should we tell the police?"

Reporting a kidnapping would involve time and paperwork. I'd have to explain to multiple people how I took my grandmother with me to make a capture and then gave him up at gunpoint to four women. And when I told the police that the women had promised to give him back to me tomorrow, they'd just grimace and file the paperwork away in a bottom drawer.

"It wasn't exactly a kidnapping," I said. "I mean, they promised to bring him back."

I took Grandma home and then went to the office.

"Have you heard anything from Connie?" I asked Lula. "No," she said. "I called all the hospitals, and I called her mama. It's like she vanished."

"How's her mother doing?"

"She didn't sound all that worried. She's not used to seeing Connie all day like we are. She doesn't have a sense that this isn't normal Connie behavior."

"Maybe we're overreacting. Maybe Connie needed to get away. Have a moment. She carries a lot of responsibility between her mother and her job."

"I guess that could be it," Lula said. "Sometimes I feel like I want to get away from my responsibilities. Not to do with my mama, though, on account of she's real independent. A bunch of years ago she retired and went to live with my Aunt Sue in Georgia. They've got a dog-sitting business there and Aunt Sue works part-time at a nail salon. She specializes in acrylics. My responsibilities are to do with my appearance. I have high standards. I gotta keep my wardrobe organized and make sure I'm accessorized properly. And hair and nails like I got don't just happen. It's all responsibility, you see what I'm saying? What about you?"

The first thing that came to mind was my job. I barely made enough money to pay my rent and buy food. I spent a lot of time in smelly, bad neighborhoods chasing down smelly, bad people. And there was no prestige attached to it. Bail bond enforcement was on a level with cesspool maintenance and grave robbing when it came to public opinion.

"Don't you ever want to run away?" Lula repeated.

"Yeah. All the time, but only for a couple minutes and then I get over it."

"I hear you. That's my problem too. I looked it up one time. It's that we have too much inertia because we only got short-term dissatisfaction. It's on account of we're too well adjusted. We got self-esteem and it's what's keeping us from being super-models or entrepreneurial billionaires. You gotta have some deep-seated feelings of inferiority to be a real big success. Like it helps if you have a little dick. Going with that line of reasoning, we should have been the ones to invent Google bein' that we got no dick at all, only it don't work like that since we got balls. If you got balls, you don't necessarily feel inferior even if you haven't got a dick. Course I'm speaking metaphorically."

I thought Lula was right about the inertia, but I suspected my disinclination to flee had less to do with my self-esteem and more to do with a lack of lofty aspiration. Somewhere in my preteen years it became apparent that I was not destined to be an Avenger, and it was all downhill after that. Everything else seemed lackluster. So, I aimlessly drifted through college and ended up in retail selling bargain-basement ladies' undies. And now I'm a bounty hunter and I still haven't found a lofty aspiration. So, what's the point of running away if you have nowhere you want to go?

Or here's a scary thought — maybe I've come to like being a bounty hunter. Omigod!

"What is it?" Lula asked. "You look like you just found Jesus, only he turned out to be Donald Duck."

I waved it away. "I was just thinking about my job . . . and about Connie."

"Yeah, thinking about Connie could give you the grimaces. I'm staying here until four o'clock and then I'm going home and watch some happy movies and eat a couple pizzas so I can get rid of this scary feeling. This is like when you're walking down a dark street at night and you get the feeling someone's waiting ahead, behind a bush, and he's gonna jump out and stab you forty-five times with a butcher knife. And you can't get rid of the feeling and you have to keep walking 'cause that's the only way to get home."

I was walking down that same street right

now, with the same horrible sense of foreboding. Connie and Lula and I had been through a lot together, and it was understood that we would always be there for each other. It was unthinkable that Connie would be out of our lives for a day or, God forbid, forever. I hiked my messenger bag higher up on my shoulder. "I'm going to ride around and look for Connie's car. I'll call you if I find anything."

I cruised all of Connie's haunts. Her neighborhood, including all the back alleys. Her favorite restaurants. Her nail salon and hair salon. Food stores, delis, the liquor store, and the train station. I checked out mall parking lots and the chop shop on Stark Street. I drove past the bail bonds office one last time and continued on to Pino's Italian Bar and Grille to pick up dinner.

Connie's car was parked in Pino's lot. It was at the far side by the dumpster. I parked on the opposite side of the lot and walked to the car. No one inside. Not locked. No bloodstains. No bullet holes. I popped the hatch. No one in there. I felt the hood. Cold. The car had been sitting there for a while. I went inside Pino's and looked around. No Connie. Morelli and I ate here a lot. We knew everyone. Ditto for Connie.

I found the manager, Carl Carolli, and asked if he'd seen Connie.

"Not in a couple days," he said. "She comes here on Thursdays with her mama sometimes. It's after bingo. They get calamari with marinara."

"Is there anyone here that's new? That you don't know?"

"There's always people I don't know." He looked around. "The family in the corner booth. I don't know them."

I looked at the family. Mother, father, two kids. Didn't look like kidnappers.

"I have your order ready," Carl said. "You must be taking it to Morelli. Meatball sandwiches, extra pickles, fries, and the twelve-layer chocolate cake. I'm guessing one of you had a bad day."

"This morning he had to jump into the river to drag a crazy lady out. It wasn't pretty."

Carl grinned. "He's a good cop."

I took my bag of food and walked around the parking lot, looking for signs of a struggle, looking for Connie or something that might belong to her. I didn't see any feet sticking out from under a car. I didn't hear anyone yelling from inside a trunk. I returned to my Honda, got behind the wheel, and locked the doors. My heart was bouncing around inside my chest. I called Morelli and gave him the short version.

"It hasn't been twenty-four hours," Morelli said.

"I know Connie's in trouble," I said. "I absolutely know it."

"I'll make some phone calls. I can't do anything officially, but I can put the word out to keep an eye on the car and to look for Connie."

Morelli lives in a neighborhood that backs up to the Burg. The values and economics are the same in both neighborhoods. The houses are the same. The only difference is an imaginary line that someone drew seventy years ago. Morelli's house is a lot like my parents' house, with a shotgun-style living room, dining room, kitchen. There are three bedrooms upstairs, a powder room downstairs, and a full bath upstairs. Morelli shares the house with a big, orange, overly friendly dog named Bob. There's a large flat-screen television in the living room, a billiard table in the dining room, and a king-sized bed in the upstairs master. I keep a few essentials at his house, and he has a few essentials in my apartment.

Bob rushed at me when I walked in the front door. I braced myself against the impact and did the *good boy, good boy* thing, holding the bag of food over my head. Morelli sauntered over, took the bag, and gave me a friendly kiss.

"You look better," I said. "Okay, so your eye is almost swollen closed, but you're not wet anymore and the scratches on your face aren't oozing blood."

"I'm a fast healer," he said. "It's my Sicilian DNA. My relatives wouldn't have survived if they'd been bleeders."

I went to the kitchen, got Bob's bowl, and brought it to the living room. We emptied the bag of food onto Morelli's big square coffee table, divided it up between Bob, Morelli, and me, and we all ate dinner in front of the television.

"Connie isn't my only problem," I said, adding extra red sauce to my meatball sandwich. "Your grandmother is FTA."

"Seriously?"

"Yes!"

Morelli grinned. "Well at least you know where to find her."

"It's not funny. She's scary. If I go after her, she'll put the eye on me."

He opened two bottles of beer and passed one to me. "Do you believe in the eye?"

"No, of course not. Maybe. Just a little. Even without the eye, she's still scary."

"And?"

"And I was hoping you'd bring her in for me."

"No way," Morelli said. "She's my grandmother. I can't arrest my own grandmother."

"You're afraid of her too, aren't you!"

"I'm not afraid of my grandmother. I'm afraid of my mother. She'll make my life a living hell, and she'll cut me off from lasagna deliveries."

I did a mental eye-roll. "Talk to your grandmother, *please.* Explain to her that she needs to make another court date."

"We could cut a deal here," Morelli said.

"What kind of deal?"

"It would involve you getting naked."

"What about you?"

"I'd get naked too."

"What about your injuries?" I asked. "Your eye is totally shut."

"I can still see with my other eye. And my deal would involve body parts that are functioning perfectly."

This seemed like an okay deal since I'd assumed we'd both get naked eventually anyway. It was one of the benefits of bringing Morelli dinner.

I looked over at the bedside clock. It was

1:00 a.m. Morelli was asleep beside me, and I was wide awake. My mind was running in circles, thinking about Connie. I was having gruesome thoughts of Connie kidnapped, locked in the trunk of someone's car, held hostage in a basement cell, or even worse, left for dead alongside a road somewhere. I should have done a more thorough search of her car, and I should have done an inventory of the storeroom. My phone was on the nightstand next to me in case a call or a message came in from Connie.

She'll show up in the morning and have a perfectly logical explanation, I told myself. After all, this is Connie. Connie isn't the sort to be a victim. Connie is the office security. She's the guard dog in front of Vinnie's inner sanctum. She's good with a gun, she's always armed, and she's street smart. It wouldn't be easy to kidnap her. I told myself this in an effort to relax and fall asleep. Unfortunately, while I knew it all to be true, I also knew from my own experience that bad things could happen to good people no matter how careful or skilled they were.

CHAPTER FOUR

I struggled out of sleep, sensing Morelli moving around in the dark room. He was an early riser, anxious to get on the job, solving mysteries and bringing order to chaos. He'd been a wild kid who'd managed to turn into a responsible adult. The transformation hadn't been easy, but here he finally was, protecting the rights and dignity of Trenton residents both good and bad. Go figure.

I switched my bedside light on and propped myself up on an elbow. "Have you heard anything from dispatch about Connie?" I asked him.

"No. Sorry. I'll ride by Pino's on my way to work and check on her car." He strapped his watch on and took his gun out of the top drawer in his nightstand. "Are you getting up or are you going back to sleep?"

"I haven't decided."

"If I'm gone by the time you get downstairs, there's cereal in the cupboard and yogurt in the fridge."

"Yogurt?"

"It's healthy. It compensates for the junk that I eat the rest of the day."

He gave me a kiss and headed out with Bob on his heels. I didn't think I was ready to face yogurt, so I turned the light off and tried to go back to sleep.

I gave up on sleep at six o'clock. I took a fast shower, got dressed, and followed the aroma of coffee to the kitchen. I ate a bowl of cereal and looked at my watch. It was six thirty. It was dark outside. No one would be at the office. The mall was closed. My parents didn't get up and moving around until seven thirty. The bakery might be open.

"What on earth do people do at this time of day?" I asked Bob.

Bob wagged his tail and looked toward the front door, so I hooked Bob up to his leash and took him for a walk. It was seven o'clock when I got back to Morelli's house. I checked my email, shot some pool, and thought about going home to my apartment. I decided that I would go to the office instead.

On the way to the office, I detoured to Pino's to see if Connie's car was still there.

I got a chill when I saw that it was parked alone in the lot. I drove past Connie's house. Lights were off. I wanted to call her mother, but I didn't know what to say and I didn't want to wake her. I drove past the office. No lights on inside. No cars parked at the curb. No activity in the area. Some morning traffic on Hamilton Avenue. I parked behind the office and sat for a couple minutes, trying to work up enough nerve to get out of the car.

A kidnap scenario was running through my mind. The chances that Connie had parked her car in Pino's lot were just about zero. Connie always parked her car in this lot, I thought. She parked it right where I was currently sitting. She'd gotten out of her car with a box of doughnuts, and when she approached the back door to the office, somebody grabbed her.

My hands were sweating on the steering wheel. It was dark in the alley. Lots of places for a man to hide. There used to be a light over the back door, but someone had shot it out a year ago and it had never been replaced.

Now or never, I thought. Just do it. Get out of the car and into the office. Pretend you're Ranger.

Ranger was the other man in my life. Riccardo Carlos Manoso, a.k.a. Ranger. Formerly Special Forces and now owner of a high-tech security firm in downtown Trenton. He was dark, inside and out. He was fearless. He was perfectly toned and supremely skilled in just about everything. Okay, he didn't cook, at least not in the kitchen, but he was magic in all the other rooms.

I slipped out of the car, got the key from under the brick, and let myself into the office. I locked the door behind myself and turned the lights on. My heart was thumping in my chest, and I had to admit to myself that I was no Ranger. Still, I'd gotten myself into the office and that was pretty good.

I hit the power button on Connie's computer and found the file detailing all the items held as security against a bond. I printed the list and took it to the storeroom. The items were organized by date received. Nothing recorded yesterday. Two bonds had been issued over the weekend. One was secured by a Harley. One was secured by a promissory note from a third party. Three bonds had been issued last Wednesday. They were low monetary bonds secured by a watch, a man's ruby pinky ring, and a DVD player. I found all of the items, including the registration for the Harley. The week before had been a decent week for Vinnie. Twelve bonds had been issued. Carpenter Beedle was one of the bailouts. Two other men had also been bailed out with Carpenter — Sydney Bowler and Paul Mori. Everyone checked out but Paul Mori. He had a low bond and had used a coin as security. No details were given on the coin and there wasn't a coin in the storeroom. I suspected the coin had gone to Atlantic City with Vinnie.

It was almost eight thirty when Lula banged on the front door to the office and woke me up. I'd fallen asleep on the fake leather couch and was disoriented for a moment before getting my act together. I stumbled to the door and unlocked it, and Lula bustled in.

"I saw the light was on in here when I drove up. How come you were sleeping on the couch? Did something happen to your apartment? Did it get firebombed again?"

"I came in early to check on the bond inventory. I thought I might find something that would lead to Connie."

"And?"

"Nothing jumped out at me," I said.

"I guess you're thinking about the guy who called yesterday and said Vinnie had

61

something of his that he wanted back. Personally, I think it's a long shot that it's something stuffed away in the storeroom. I mean it could be anything. This is Vinnie we're talking about. This guy could be talking about his wife or a barnyard animal." Lula set a bakery box on Connie's desk. "I stopped to get the doughnuts this morning. The people at the bakery said they hadn't seen Connie. Have you talked to her mama this morning?"

"Not yet. I didn't want to wake her."

"For all we know Connie could be sound asleep in her bed."

I dialed Connie's number. No answer on her cell phone. No prompt to leave a message. This wasn't a good sign. I dialed the number of their house phone and Connie's mother answered.

"Hello," she said. "Who's this?"

"It's Stephanie Plum," I said. "Is Connie there?"

"No. She didn't come home last night. She didn't call me or anything. She never just doesn't come home. I know something terrible happened to her. I can feel it. The Margucci boy didn't come home one night, and they found him in the river a week later. I'm going to call the police and tell them to look in the river."

"I'm sure she's okay, Mrs. Rosolli. Tell her to call me when you talk to her."

"Well?" Lula asked when I hung up.

"She's not there. She never came home."

Lula opened the box of doughnuts and took a Boston cream. We didn't have to fight over it because they were all Boston cream. She got herself a cup of coffee, sat in Connie's chair, and scanned through the email.

"Here's something interesting," she said. "It's a court bulletin. One of our bondees turned up dead. Self-inflicted gunshot wound. Twelve of them. Paul Mori. It says that we bonded him out two weeks ago."

"I know that name. He was bonded out the same day as Carpenter Beedle. Vinnie took a coin as security, and I couldn't find it."

"What kind of coin?"

"His bond application didn't say."

I called Vinnie.

"Now what?" Vinnie said.

"When are you coming into the office?"

"I don't know. I'm still in AC. Harry's having a board of directors meeting, if you know what I mean."

"I need to talk to you about Paul Mori."

"The dry cleaner? He turned out to be a real pain in the ass. I was at the courthouse to write a bond for Beedle and I ran into

Mori. We take our dry cleaning to him. He needed to get bailed out, so he gave me a deal on dry cleaning and a commemorative coin for security. The dry-cleaning deal was sweet. I didn't care about the coin. I just took it to humor him. And then a couple days ago he came in and said he wanted the coin back. He was going to give me a big bag of money for it, but I didn't have the coin. I told him I lost it and he went nuts. Almost ripped my shirt off, yelling that I was lying. Connie stun gunned him and dragged him out of the office. A car drove up; two guys shoved him into the backseat and drove off with him."

"How did you lose the coin?"

"I don't know. I wasn't paying a lot of attention to it. I bonded Mori out and then I had to turn around and right away bond Beedle out. Beedle's mother was there. Nice lady. She was upset. I had to walk them to her car."

"What did the coin look like?"

"It was supposed to be old. Knights Templar. Like in *Indiana Jones*. I don't think it was real, but it was cool anyway. I gotta go. Harry's giving me the sign."

"What sign?"

"Like he's gonna kill me if I don't get off the phone."

The line went dead.

"Pull up the Paul Mori file," I said to Lula. "Print it out for me."

The front door opened, and Grandma walked in. She was dressed in tight jeans, motorcycle boots, a white T-shirt, and a black leather jacket.

"I thought I'd stop by in case you still needed some extra muscle," she said.

"Did my mother see you leave the house dressed like this?" I asked her.

"No. I sneaked out when she was cleaning up in the kitchen," Grandma said. "I left her a note. I said I was at church."

"Girl, you look bitchin'," Lula said.

"I wore this getup to a Halloween party last year," Grandma said. "I was hoping I'd get a chance to use it again. What's up for today? I was at the bakery earlier and Eleanor said Connie is still missing."

"Her car is parked in Pino's lot, but no one's seen Connie, and her mother hasn't heard from her," I said.

"That's terrible," Grandma said. "That's real worrisome."

I took the Mori printout from Lula. "Paul Mori was seventy years old. Owned Mori Dry Cleaning. He was charged with indecent exposure. Got into an argument with a female customer and mooned her. She got a picture of him on her cell phone and reported him to the police."

"He's dead," Grandma said. "They were talking about it at the bakery. Eleanor's son, Jimmy, is a paramedic, and he was at the scene last night. Someone found Mori by the dumpster behind Smart's Tavern. Jimmy said Mori looked like Swiss cheese."

"The report says twelve shots," Lula said. "And it said they were self-inflicted."

"That's got to be a typo," Grandma said. "Hard to self-inflict Swiss cheese."

"Are there any rumors about him being involved in anything other than dry cleaning?" I asked Grandma.

"You mean something shady? Not that I know. He was just a grouchy bachelor. Never married. Didn't even have a dog. Lived in a row house on Marbury Street for his whole life. Inherited it when his parents passed. I imagine he was sitting on a chunk of money. He had a good business going and he was a real tightwad."

"Vinnie bonded him out and Mori used a commemorative coin as security," I said.

"That sounds like him," Grandma said. "Probably lifted the coin from someone's jacket pocket when it came in to get cleaned. He had a sign up in his place that said anything he found he'd keep. He meant it

66

too. We don't take our dry cleaning to Mori. We take ours to Tide at the strip mall."

"You got a thing about that coin," Lula said to me. "I don't see how it ties to Connie, if that's what you're thinking."

"The coin was valuable. Mori offered Vinnie money for it."

Lula took a second doughnut. "So, then why'd Mori give it to Vinnie if it was so valuable? And why's Mori so dead? And I still don't see what it's got to do with Connie."

"When I talked to Vinnie just now, he said a couple days ago Mori came into the office to get his coin back. Vinnie told Mori that he didn't have the coin. Somehow the coin got lost. Mori went gonzo, grabbing Vinnie and yelling that he was lying. Connie stun gunned Mori and dragged him out of the office. A car came and picked Mori up and drove away with him. Now Mori is dead.

"I think Mori lifted the coin from the wrong pocket, thinking it was a fun trinket. The owner came back looking for it, and Mori said he gave it to Vinnie. The original owner couldn't get in touch with Vinnie, so he forced Connie to let him into the office. He searched the storeroom, couldn't find the coin, and he took Connie as a hostage."

"Well, I didn't know none of that," Lula

said. "That's real suspicious."

A worse scenario was that they'd disposed of Connie just as they'd disposed of Mori, but I didn't want to say it aloud.

The office phone rang, and we all stared at it.

"Someone should answer it," Lula said.

I put it on speakerphone. "Vincent Plum Bail Bonds," I said. "This is Stephanie speaking."

"I want to talk to Vinnie."

Lula waved her arms in the air and mouthed, *It's him. It's him!*

"Vinnie is out of town. I'm Stephanie Plum, and I'm in charge of the office in his absence. How can I help you?"

"Oh jeez, you're the disaster bounty hunter, right? You're in the news all the time."

"Not *all* the time," I said.

"This is personal between me and Vinnie. He has something I want, and I have something he wants."

"Unfortunately, he isn't here, so you're going to have to deal with me. Let's start by telling me what it is that you want."

"It's a coin that was given to Vinnie as security. The coin was stolen, and the rightful owner wants it returned."

"I'll be happy to check our inventory. Who

gave Vinnie the coin?"

"Paul Mori."

I put the caller on hold.

"I knew it!" Lula said. "I knew it was all about that coin. And he's got Connie too. Mark my words."

I returned to the caller. "I'm sorry, but the coin isn't in our inventory. You must be mistaken."

"Here's the deal," he said. "I need that coin and you need to find it for me. That's what you do, right? You find people. So now you can find a lousy coin. Personally, I think you know where it is. And if you don't know where it is, I'm sure Vinnie knows where it is."

"Why is this coin so important? Is it worth a lot of money?"

"It's junk. It's a trinket. It's worth nothing."

"Then why all this trouble to get it back?"

"It's got sentimental value, okay? It don't matter why I want it. What matters is that I'm not a nice guy. I can inflict pain and death and still sleep at night. And as you've probably guessed by now, I have something from your office. I thought it would give incentive if I had something to trade."

"Is it a box of doughnuts? We were short a box of doughnuts yesterday."

"Yeah, very funny. You want to hear a doughnut scream?"

"No," I said. "Not at all."

"Then find the coin. Twenty-four hours."

"What does it look like?"

"It looks old, but it isn't old. It's got a symbol on it. Knights Templar. When you have the coin, hang a sign in your office window. If you don't have it in twenty-four hours, there's gonna be more pain and death. And if you go to the police there's gonna be *a lot* more pain and death."

He disconnected.

"Do you think Vinnie has the coin?" Lula asked.

"No," I said. "But I might know someone else who has it. Carpenter Beedle. He's a panhandler and a pickpocket and he was with Vinnie when Vinnie lost the coin. An alternative theory would be that Vinnie dropped the coin in the parking lot and didn't notice."

"I like the pickpocket version," Grandma said. "Where do we find Carpenter Beedle?"

"In jail," I said. "His mother won't bond him out again, and even if she wanted to bond him out there's no one here who's authorized to write a bond."

"Hunh," Lula said. "I could write his bond. I'm the official replacement office manager. I got rights and duties. I've seen Connie bond out lots of assholes. I got it down."

Grandma and I exchanged glances.

"Worth a try," Grandma said. "I'll stay here and babysit the phone."

Lula took a bond application form out of Connie's desk file and filled it in, using Beedle's previous application. "Easy peasy," she said. "Now I just have to use this stamp that says I'm allowed to do this." Bam. Lula stamped the form. "Now we take this downtown and have Beedle sign it and he's all ours."

I knew it wasn't this simple. Beedle had a high bond. We'd just bought him an expensive get-out-of-jail card that was now guaranteed by Vinnie's surety company. If this got screwed up, Vinnie could lose his license.

I checked my watch. Ten o'clock. I had twenty-four hours to find the coin.

CHAPTER FIVE

Carpenter Beedle looked like the walking dead when we bonded him out.

"It was horrible in there," he said, shuffling to my car. "There was snoring and groaning all night long. And the lights were on. And I had to sleep on a thin mattress on a slab. And the blanket was itchy. And there wasn't a seat on the toilet."

"Yeah, but I bet they gave you a Big Mac and fries for dinner last night," Lula said. "And what'd you get this morning? Did you get a breakfast sandwich?"

"The food was okay," he said. "I just couldn't sleep with the snoring. I thought jail would be better. I didn't think there'd be snoring. Are you taking me home now?"

"We need to talk first," I said. "I'm looking for a coin. Paul Mori gave it to Vinnie as security just before Vinnie bailed you out. Somehow, Vinnie immediately lost it."

"Gee, bummer," Beedle said.

I did my best impression of Morelli interrogating a suspect. Steely eyes. Calm demeanor with just a hint of *don't try to shit me.* "Where's the coin?"

"How would I know?"

"You picked Vinnie's pocket, and you took the coin."

"No way."

"Do you want us to send you back to jail?"

"No!"

"Then tell me about the coin."

"I sold it."

I did a mental double take. I hadn't expected it to be this easy. Truth is, I'd thought chances were zero to slim that he had taken the coin. This questioning went under the category of no stone left unturned.

"My understanding is that it was worthless," I said. "Just a commemorative coin."

"True, it was a commemorative coin, but it wasn't worthless. It was a collectible. It came with a board game that's no longer being produced, The Treasure of Gowa. It was huge back in the day. Not so much now."

"Who did you sell it to?" Lula asked.

"Benji at the comic book store downtown."

Lula grinned. "For real? That store is awesome."

"Yeah," Beedle said. "He gave me twenty bucks. Do I get to go home now?"

"Not yet," I said. "We need to get the coin back, and you need to identify it."

"What's the big deal about the coin?" Beedle asked.

"It has sentimental value," I said, opening the back door for Beedle.

The comic book store was on a side street, minutes away from the municipal building. I found a parking place and we all marched in. Benji came out from behind the counter and did a complicated geek high-five thing with Beedle. Lula went straight to the action figure collection.

"What's up?" Benji said to Beedle. "What's with the ladies?"

"They're interested in that coin I brought in. The Knights Templar one."

"I sold it. I knew I would. I knew this dude would want it. He's in all the time. He goes nuts over anything that's got mummies or knights. Almost messed himself when he saw the coin."

"Do you have his name?" I asked. "His address?"

"That's all confidential," Benji said. "We

take our customer information real serious here."

Lula came over with a box in her hand. "How much is Thor?" she asked.

"Forty-nine ninety-five," Benji said.

"That's robbery," Lula said. "I could get him online for half that price."

"This is collectible quality," Benji said. "The box has never been opened."

"I don't care about that," Lula said. "Do you have a cheaper Thor?"

"You might try the toy department at Target," Benji said. "They usually have a good selection of Avengers."

"About the coin," I said to Benji. "I need a name and an address."

"No can do."

"What do you mean by *no can do*?" Lula said. "Are you telling us you aren't going to cooperate with the police?"

"Are you the police?" Benji asked.

"We're almost the police," Lula said. "We're technically law enforcement. Especially me since I'm a temporary replacement office manager."

"Well, I sell comic books and collectibles and I've got a code of conduct to uphold. Customer confidentiality is paramount here," Benji said.

Lula leaned in so that their noses were

almost touching. "Comic books don't require confidentiality. Nobody cares who buys Donald Duck or who buys Spider-Man. And anyway, we aren't even talking about a comic book. We're talking about a stolen coin that you fenced."

"I didn't know it was stolen," Benji said.

"Don't matter," Lula said. "You did it all the same. Seems to me you should cooperate with us law enforcers so we can return it to its rightful owner."

Benji looked over at Beedle, and Beedle shrugged.

"The dude's name is Melvin Sparks," Benji said. "I don't have an address or anything. He pays in cash."

"Do you know why someone would really, really want this coin?" I asked him. "What's special about it?"

"Not a lot's special about it except that they aren't making any more of them," Benji said. "Sparks wants it because he's a collector. That's what collectors do. They collect things."

"Okay, I get that," I said. "Can you give me a description of the coin?"

Benji went to a small office in the back corner of the store and located the coin on the internet. He printed a picture of it and gave it to me.

"There's a knight Templar on one side in classic pose with his sword," Benji said. "There's a cross and some writing on the other side. If you look close you can see the writing says 'The Treasure of Gowa. Made in Hoboken.'"

"Good enough," I said to Benji. "Appreciate the help."

We returned to my car, and I typed "Melvin Sparks, Trenton, New Jersey" into my smartphone. We had search engines on the office computer that would tell me if Sparks aced math class in seventh grade. I couldn't get that kind of detail on my smartphone, but I could get his address and some other basic information.

"He's at 1207 Kerry Street, apartment 5B," I said.

"I know where that is," Lula said. "That's a mediocre neighborhood. It's not horrible and it's not great. You see what I'm saying? It's mostly safe because the cars aren't interesting enough to steal."

I took State Street to South Central, drove one block on South Central, and turned onto Kerry. Sparks's building was on the corner. It was six floors of unadorned masonry and double-hung windows. THE IVY had been chiseled in big block letters over the front door.

"That's a nice name for a building," Lula said, "except there's no ivy anywhere around."

I parked at the curb, and we entered the small foyer. There were rows of mailboxes on one wall and two elevators on the opposite wall. We took the elevator to the fifth floor, and I rang the bell at 5B. A man answered and squinted out at us. He was about five feet ten inches, in his forties, had thinning sandy blond hair and a soft, squishy-looking body.

Lula elbowed me and mouthed, *mediocre*.

"Melvin Sparks?" I asked.

I introduced myself and explained that I needed to reclaim the coin.

"No way," Sparks said. "Never gonna happen. Finders keepers." And he slammed the door shut and locked it.

"You're supposed to put your foot in the door before he gets to close it and lock it," Lula said to me.

"He caught me by surprise," I said.

"That's lame. You're lucky you don't get your fake bounty hunter badge revoked."

"What about you? Why didn't you put your foot in the door?"

"Look at my shoes. Do they look like foot-in-the-door shoes? These shoes are Manolo knockoffs. Notice the pointy toe and five-inch stiletto heel. I could spear an olive out of a martini with these shoes but I sure as hell wouldn't chance ruining them by going all bounty hunter."

I rang the doorbell a couple hundred times and pounded on the door, but Sparks didn't respond.

"We need someone to kick the door down," Lula said to me. "Obviously I can't do it in my Manolos. And we know you're inept at door kicking."

Beedle was standing behind us. We turned and looked down at his foot in the orthopedic boot.

"It's made out of foam and plastic," Beedle said. "And that looks like a metal fire door."

"He might be right about the door," Lula said. "We need a blowtorch. Anybody got a blowtorch?"

Connie was being held hostage somewhere. I didn't know the circumstances. They could be awful. She could be injured. She could be scared . . . although who knew with Connie. Connie didn't scare easily. I'd done okay with finding a lead on the coin, but I was at a temporary dead end.

I called Morelli when we got back to my car. "I heard about Paul Mori and I'm curious," I said. "Are there any persons of interest?"

"Approximately two hundred thirty people hated him. Aside from that, no."

"How about video? Were there cameras at his dry-cleaning shop?"

"I don't know. Schmidt is the principal on the case. I imagine he's looking into it. Why are you asking?"

"There might be a connection with Connie's disappearance."

I sat through a moment of silence on Morelli's end. "And?" he finally said.

"And I'll tell you about it later. It's complicated."

I imagined Morelli was staring down at his shoe, making an effort to keep his composure. He knew I was withholding information.

"You aren't going rogue on me, are you?" he asked.

"Who, me?"

Lula looked at me when I disconnected from Morelli. "I bet he loved that conversation."

"He accused me of going rogue."

"Who, you?"

I dropped Beedle at his parents' house with strict instructions that he wasn't to leave, and I headed for the office.

■ ■ ■ ■

Grandma was slumped in Connie's chair with her mouth open and her eyes closed when Lula and I walked in.

"I hope she's not dead," Lula said. "I hate when people are dead."

Grandma gave a snort and sat up. "I was just resting my eyes."

"Anything happen while we were gone?" I asked her.

"Nope. It's been real quiet. Did you get the coin?"

"No," I said, "but we know where it is. I came back so I could use Connie's computer. I want to do a search on Melvin Sparks."

Grandma got up, and I sat down. I cleared the screen of bingo and poker apps and fed Sparks into one of Connie's search engines. All the usual stuff appeared. Age, address, education. There was nothing derogatory. No arrests. No wife. No children. A sister. Occupation was listed as a merchandise stocker at Scoopers. That's why he was at home on a Tuesday afternoon, I thought. He works the night shift stocking shelves.

I called Scoopers employment and asked about jobs stocking shelves. I was told that the night shift started at nine o'clock and ran until three in the morning.

I called Ranger.

"I have a situation," I said. "I could use some help."

"Babe," Ranger said.

Depending on the inflection, *babe* means many things in Ranger-speak. It can be as simple as *hello* or as complex as *take off your clothes.* In this case it meant that he was listening.

I gave him the short version of Connie's kidnapping.

"You realize that paying ransom doesn't always guarantee a happy ending," Ranger said.

"It's all I have right now. We don't know for sure how Paul Mori got the coin. The caller said he stole it. It's most likely that Mori found it in something brought in for dry cleaning. He had a reputation for keeping found objects."

"Have you checked security cameras?"

"The cameras at the bail bonds office aren't operational, and I haven't personally checked for cameras at the dry-cleaning store. Even if Mori had cameras, I have no way to access them. And if I could access them, combing through hours, probably days, of files would take more time than I have."

"So, you're concentrating on the coin."

"Unfortunately, Sparks isn't cooperating. I could have Lula sit on him or have you throw him out a window, hoping to get him to change his mind, but that feels wrong. It isn't as if he's a bad guy. I mean he's not dealing drugs or mugging old ladies."

"Does he know the circumstances?"

"No."

"That might make a difference," Ranger said.

"He might also blab it all over town. I can't risk it. That's why I need to get into Sparks's apartment."

"You're going to steal the coin," Ranger said.

"Yes. There's only one door to his apartment and it's a metal fire door. There are double-hung windows but he's on the fifth floor of an eight-story building. It's a corner building. Very visible. I need help getting in."

"No problem," Ranger said. "When do you want to do this?"

"Tonight. He stocks merchandise at Scoopers on the night shift. Night shift starts at nine o'clock."

"I'll pick you up at nine o'clock," Ranger said.

"Where?"

"Wherever you are." And he was gone.

Ranger and I have a complicated relationship. There's a lot of attraction between us that has on occasion been satisfied. Currently there's no satisfaction. At least not sexual. He was my mentor when I started working at the bail bonds office and his role in my life has expanded since then. Early on he decided if he wanted to continue to enjoy my company, he needed to help keep me alive, so he started placing tracking devices on my cars. I found them annoying at first, but I've gotten used to them, and the truth is they've come in handy multiple times.

"I'm available if you need help with the B & E," Grandma said. "I'm good at sneaking around in the dark."

"Thanks for the offer," I said, "but this should be a simple operation. Ranger will get me in, we'll find the coin and lock up after ourselves."

My phone buzzed with a text.

"What's it say?" Grandma asked.

"It says, *We're done with him. He's all yours.* I imagine this is referring to Brad Winter."

"The cute blackmailer," Grandma said.

"What with everything else going on, I'd completely forgotten about him."

I checked my watch. It was almost one o'clock. "Does Mom know you're here?" I asked Grandma.

"Yep. I called and told her that after church I had to fill in for Vinnie. She's bringing sandwiches."

Ten minutes later, Lula and I were on our way to Winter's house on Oak Street. I had one hand on the wheel and the other hand wrapped around a ham and cheese sandwich.

"It was real nice of your mom to bring these sandwiches," Lula said. "You've got a helpful family. Everybody pitches in. That's the way it should be. And this is an excellent sandwich. Not that I would expect any less from your mom. She has everything in just the right order. Mustard on one side, then ham, then cheese, then there's a second deli meat. I think it might be turkey. And she ends with mayo. And she doesn't ruin it with healthy bread. This is fresh white bread. I bet it's from the bakery. What do you think?"

"I don't know," I said. "I didn't notice any of those things."

"That's your problem," she said. "You don't notice these things because you aren't mindful. I do mindful eating. I got mindfulness up my ass. I could coach you to be mindful, if you want. You just let me know when."

"I'm not sure I have time to be mindful."

"I hear you. I mostly do the speed version. I'm mindful in a hurry. Like noticing the mustard on the sandwich didn't slow me down from eating it."

"Smart," I said.

"Fuckin' A."

CHAPTER SIX

Oak Street was quiet at this time of the day. No people or cars in sight. I parked in front of Winter's well-kept townhouse and sat there for a couple minutes, making sure no one was lurking in the bushes or rushing down the street in a Mercedes.

"I must be missing something about Brad Winter," Lula said. "I got his file information here, but I don't understand about somebody being done with him."

"Grandma and I had Winter in cuffs. We were walking him to my car and a Mercedes with four women inside roared up and snatched him away from us."

"And now they're giving him back to you?"

"Looks that way."

"You gotta love this job. There's always crazy shit happening."

"And you like that."

"Damn skippy. Who doesn't like crazy shit?"

"I don't. I like when things are safe and sane."

"Yeah, but you got a job that's almost never safe or sane. That's ironic. You're messed up."

"I don't feel messed up."

"Then maybe it's that you're full of doody when you say you like safe and sane. Maybe you really like crazy shit but don't want to admit it. You could be in denial about the crazy-shit side of you. Not that denial is always a bad thing. It's one of them mental health tools. Like procrasterbation. I'm not necessarily a big procrasterbator myself, but I could see where it serves a purpose."

"Procrastination."

"Yeah. I mean, everybody does it at one time or another."

I nodded. "True."

We left my CR-V and walked to the front door. I rang the bell. No answer. The door was unlocked so we let ourselves in and found Winter in the middle of the living room. He was on the floor, naked, gagged, and hog-tied, completely hairless, head to toe. And newly tattooed. His sheet had been laundered, neatly folded, and placed beside him.

"Damn," Lula said. "Was he like this when you saw him last?"

"He was naked, but he wasn't tattooed. And he had hair."

"Mmmmf!" Winter said. "Grrrrr."

Pervert and *Blackmailer* had been tattooed across his forehead in fancy script. The words were surrounded by swirls that eventually ended in Devil's tails. I thought it probably cost the ladies a fortune.

"I like that they inked him in a lot of bright colors," Lula said. "Makes it more interesting. And it makes the black ink stand out more. Like you can really see the message saying he's a pervert and blackmailer."

I took the gag out of his mouth.

"I'm going to kill them," he said. "All of them."

"I wouldn't do that if I was you," Lula said. "They'll throw you in prison forever and you might not be happy there." She turned to me. "Now, this is what I'm talking about. Crazy shit. Not everybody gets to see stuff like this. The tattoo artist showed some talent and a real steady hand."

I was caught between bursting out laughing and losing my lunch. I would be happy to live the rest of my life without seeing anything like this ever again. Still, I had to give the women credit for a job well done.

89

And from the condition of the house, it was clear that they'd done a search.

"Did they get everything?" I asked Winter.

"They got enough," he said.

"How are we going to get him out to the car?" Lula asked. "You want me to cut the ropes?"

"Yes. He's already wearing my cuffs."

We got him standing, wrapped him in the sheet, and helped him hobble to the car.

"So, I'm thinking you knew the women who snatched you," I said to Winter. "And I'm curious because they all looked alike. They were all blond. In fact, they looked like they had their hair done at the same salon. They all had diamond studs, and they were wearing Lululemon."

"I've got a type," Winter said. "I like blond trophy wives."

"These wives must have got the memo about how to dress for a revenge party," Lula said.

"They're trophy wives," Winter said. "They all dress like that."

"You're an idiot," I said to Winter, and I shoved him into the backseat.

My grandmother was alone in the office when Lula and I returned.

"Your mother had to go to the market and

then home to get dinner started," Grandma said. "We're having chicken parm tonight in case you want some."

"Count me in," Lula said. "I'd just as leave not be alone, thinking about Connie. This is when you want to be with friends and family, and I think about you as being both."

"Sure," I said. "I'll be there, too. Were there any calls while we were gone?"

"None," Grandma said. "I didn't check the email. It's got a password on it."

"No problem," I said. "Lula can check it, and I'll give you a ride home. There's nothing else I can do until Ranger and I get the coin back tonight."

"Perfect," Grandma said. "I'll get home in time to help your mother with dinner. Sometimes she has too much hooch and pounds the bejeezus out of the chicken."

I dropped Grandma off and drove to Pino's. Connie's car was still there. It had a red-and-black police sticker on it. I called Morelli.

"I'm sitting in Pino's lot, looking at Connie's car," I said. "It has a police sticker on it."

"I had the crime lab go over it, but they didn't find anything unusual. You might want to move the car, so it doesn't get vandalized. There's nothing about Connie on my end. Do you know anything?"

"I have some ideas."

"You had ideas earlier," Morelli said.

"I still have the same ideas. I thought I would try to talk to Bella today. I don't suppose you want to come with me?"

"I can't. I'm up to my eyeballs in paperwork and I'm the only one here if a call comes in. Two guys are out with the flu."

"Is this the blue flu?"

"No, this is flu like the plague."

I drove to Connie's house and got an extra set of car keys from her mother.

"Are you doing okay?" I asked her. "Do you need help with anything?"

"No, but it'll be good to get the car back. Have you seen it? Were there bloodstains? Did it look like it had been in the river?"

"The car looks like Connie just parked it at Pino's. It's not damaged at all. I'm sure Connie is fine and will turn up any day now."

Mrs. Rosolli nodded and wiped a tear away.

I gave her a hug and left.

I'd wanted to give Mrs. Rosolli some comfort, some reassurance that Connie was okay. I didn't entirely believe what I'd said to her. It was more that I hoped it was true.

I was feeling a lot of pain over Connie. I couldn't imagine what it must be like for her mom.

I drove deeper into the Burg and idled in front of Morelli's mother's house. It was slightly larger than my parents' house. Four bedrooms upstairs. Living room, dining room, kitchen downstairs. Single-car detached garage sitting in the back corner of the small backyard. I'd been in the house on several occasions and was always terrified of Joe's mother and grandmother. They were stern matriarchs who protected their family no matter the circumstances. And they put up with no nonsense from outsiders. Joe's father had been an abusive drunk. No one was sorry when he passed. On the surface the grandmother looked flat-out crazy, but I suspected she was actually very crafty and enjoyed playing the role. I honestly didn't know what to think about her ability to give someone the eye. It was a little like my position as a Catholic. I was lacking true faith, but the fear of God was strong.

So now what? I thought. Are you going in or are you going to procrasterbate? I took my foot off the brake. I was going to procrasterbate. I didn't want to confront Grandma Bella. It was going to be unpleasant at best and hideous at worst. Even if I managed to get her to go with me, without Connie or Vinnie, I couldn't legitimately bond her out. I'd have to do another *emergency* bond, or even worse, leave her in jail overnight. The thought sent a shiver of horror down my spine. If I left Bella in jail overnight, she wouldn't just give me the eye . . . she'd come after me with a hatchet.

I drove to the office, picked Lula up, and dropped her at Pino's. Lula drove Connie's car to Connie's house, parked it in her driveway, gave the keys to Connie's mother, and jumped into my car.

"It was creepy being in Connie's car without her," Lula said when she buckled herself in next to me. "I don't think Connie drove her car to Pino's. The seat was pushed way back like a man with longer legs was driving it." Lula put my air-conditioning on full blast. "I need air. I'm having a moment, here."

I felt myself choking up and I pushed the emotion away. Don't get overwhelmed, I told myself. It's unproductive. Keep making an effort to remain normal so you can think. It's important to stay sharp.

I was relieved when Lula and I walked into my parents' house, where normalcy rules supreme. Maybe not normalcy by others' standards, but there would be normalcy by Plum standards.

My father was in front of the television in the living room. He gave up a small sigh and slouched lower in his chair when he saw Lula. Bad enough that he had to live with my grandmother. Now he had Lula at his dinner table. It wasn't that he disliked Lula. He just hated additional drama while he forked in his chicken parm.

"Hey, Mr. P," Lula said. "Looking good. Long time no see. How's it going?"

My father mumbled something and I hurried Lula out of the living room and into the kitchen. My mother was heating extra red sauce and Grandma was slicing bread from the bakery.

"You're right on time," Grandma said. "The table's all set and we're only waiting for your father."

Four minutes later the five o'clock news show ended, my father turned the television off precisely at six o'clock and took his place at the head of the table, and we brought the food out. Chicken Parmesan, spaghetti, a gravy boat filled with red sauce, extra grated cheese, bread, butter, broccoli, wine.

Grandma poured wine and my father shoveled chicken onto his plate.

"This is an excellent meal," Lula said. "I wouldn't mind knowing how to cook like this. Lately I've been thinking about going to one of them culinary institutes. I might change my job and be a chef."

"You'd be a good chef," Grandma said. "You know all about eating."

"My other idea is to go to tattoo school," Lula said. "I just got the idea this afternoon when I came into contact with some original art."

My father had his head down, concentrating on his spaghetti, working hard to ignore the conversation.

"The FTA we picked up today had *Pervert* and *Blackmailer* tattooed on his forehead," Lula said. "It was a work of art."

That caught my father's attention. He stopped eating and looked at Lula. "On his forehead?" my father asked.

"Yeah," Lula said. "He was naked and shaved and had this brand-new tattoo when we got to him."

My father gave his head a small shake and went back to eating. My mother went into the kitchen to refresh her iced tea, which we all knew was whiskey. Who could blame her?

"I get it about wanting a new profession," Grandma said to Lula. "Sometimes you need to shake things up and move in a different direction. I've been thinking about becoming an astronaut. They're taking old people now."

My father paused for a moment with his bread halfway to his mouth. Probably liking the idea of sending Grandma to the moon.

Morelli called and I stepped away from the table to talk to him.

"Lula and I are at my parents' house," I said. "We just sat down to chicken parm, if you want to join us."

"I'd love to join you, but I'm on my way to carnage on Stark Street. It's going to be a long night."

"Gangs?"

"Probably. I'll know more when I get there. I called to tell you that Connie is officially a missing person. Her mother reported it. If you have any information, you should pass it along."

"Are you the principal?"

"No. Johnny Krick is the principal. I mostly get cases that involve a lot of blood."

"Thank goodness there's no blood involved in Connie's disappearance."

"Not yet," Morelli said. "Make sure you keep Krick in the loop."

I returned to my seat at the table and all eyes were focused on me.

"Anything important?" Grandma asked.

"No," I said. "He was just checking in. Connie's mother filed a missing person report."

"That poor woman," my mother said. "She must be beside herself."

"Red sauce," my father said. "I need more marinara."

My mother passed him the gravy boat. "I worry all the time about Stephanie and her job, and now it's Connie who goes missing."

"You never know about these things," Lula said. "I had a daddy who went missing and never came back. At least my mama thought he might be my daddy."

"Men," Grandma said. "You can't count on them. You get to be my age and just when you think it's going to work out, they drop dead."

"I hear you," Lula said.

At ten minutes to nine I left my apartment and went outside to wait for Ranger. Five minutes later, headlights appeared at the entrance to my building's parking lot and Ranger's black Porsche 911 Turbo S rolled into the lot and stopped in front of me.

Ranger was a bounty hunter when I first met him. He had a ponytail and a diamond stud in his ear. His address was a vacant lot, and his methods of apprehension were questionable. He's a successful businessman now. The diamond stud has disappeared. His brown hair is expertly trimmed. His clothes are tailored to a perfect fit.

He's still governed by a moral code that doesn't entirely conform to the norm, and his body is as toned as it was during his Special Forces days. For as long as I've known him, he's worn only black. His parents are Cuban, and the black is a good look for his Hispanic coloring. Wearing all black also allows him to disappear in the dark of night.

He lives in a professionally decorated and maintained apartment at the top of his office building. A small silver plaque at the seven-story building's front door simply says RANGEMAN. The first six floors contain state-of-the-art security gizmos and a loyal workforce of men with special skills that were acquired in a number of ways, some legal and some not.

I slid onto the passenger seat and made eye contact with Ranger. On the surface it was *Hello, long time no see.* Below the surface there was more than a smidgeon of desire. I'm sorry, but the man is hot. And

I'm fond of him. Okay, let's get it all out there. I love him. Problem is that I also love Joe Morelli. And my love for Morelli is different from my Ranger love. I have a long history with Morelli. Morelli has a house, a dog, a toaster. He isn't perfect but he's close to normal. I could have a future with him. He's fun. He's comfortable. And he's sexy. Ranger is perfect in many ways, but he will never be comfortable or close to normal. Ranger is the wind. Exciting and sensual and mysterious. A future with Ranger would be uncharted territory.

"Babe," Ranger said, and he leaned across the console and kissed me.

It was a friendly kiss. No lingering. No tongue. It gave me a rush all the same. When he moved away there was a hint of a smile on his lips.

"Welcome to the dark side," Ranger said.

No kidding.

He put the Porsche in gear and drove out of the parking lot. "Do you have an address?" he asked.

"Twelve oh seven Kerry Street."

"Are we looking for anything other than the coin?"

"Nope. Just the coin."

Even without the kiss, riding in the Porsche at night with Ranger is a sexy deal.

The interior is dark and intimate, barely lit by colored lights on the dash. The contoured seats are low. The leather is soft and smooth. The car is powerful and flawlessly engineered. Like Ranger.

Ranger parked in front of the Ivy and cut the engine. The disadvantage to the 911 is that it's not your average car and is noticed. The advantage to the 911 is that in Trenton only drug lords and Ranger can afford one, so it will never be stolen or vandalized.

We sat for a moment, taking the temperature of the surroundings. There was minimal traffic on the street. No activity around the Ivy. We left the Porsche and entered the lobby. I was in jeans and a sweatshirt. I was looking very pleasant with my ponytail and tasteful makeup. Ranger was wearing black cargo pants, a black T-shirt, and a black windbreaker. Not exactly the boy next door but not a gangbanger either.

We entered the elevator and Ranger looked around and checked his cell phone. "No cameras," he said. We exited the elevator on the fifth floor and Ranger checked his cell phone again. "No cameras here either. Whoever owns the Ivy isn't putting money into it."

We went directly to 5B. Ranger worked his magic with the lock, and we were in. He flashed a penlight around the dark apartment. "Not good," he said. "This guy is a hoarder. Turn the lights on. We can't do this in stealth mode."

I flipped the switch at the door and sucked in some air. There were collectibles everywhere. Stacks of unopened boxes containing action figures. Stacks of books and games. Racks of knight costumes. Creepy life-sized mummies in gruesome poses. An entire wall of cabinets with shallow drawers. Furniture was mixed in with the clutter. A small couch facing a television set on a card table, and a large desk and office chair in the living room. A small wooden dining table and two chairs in the dining area. An unmade, horribly rumpled bed in the single bedroom. The man obviously had sleep issues.

"I haven't actually seen the coin," I said to Ranger, handing him the computer printout. "Benji gave this to me. He took it off an article about the game, The Treasure of Gowa. He didn't have a photo of the coin we're trying to find."

Ranger studied it for a beat and handed it back to me. "Do you know how many coins were made?"

"I looked it up. Every game came with one coin and there were thirteen million games produced. That doesn't put it in the top twenty games of all time, but it had a good run before the company decided to close up shop."

Ranger pulled the shades and went to the wall of cabinets.

"Start searching at the far end," he said to me, "and I'll start here."

After an hour we met in the middle.

"I found lots of coins," I said, "but no Knights Templar."

"There are more of these cabinets in his bedroom. I'll go through the bedroom cabinets, and you can comb through the apartment. It was a new acquisition so he might not have cataloged it yet. It might be lying around somewhere."

I worked my way through the living room and was starting on the dining room when Ranger walked up to me.

"I found a drawer filled with Knights Templar coins," he said. "Twenty-three to be exact. Six were stamped with the game name and 'Made in Hoboken.' "

"Beedle would know the coin."

I FaceTimed Beedle, showing him all six coins. "Which coin is it?" I asked him.

"I don't know," he said. "It's hard to tell over the phone."

"Don't go anywhere. We're coming over."

Twenty minutes later we were at Beedle's house.

"This is tough," Beedle said. "Some are in better shape than others, but I couldn't say which coin I sold. It's not like I'm an expert. I didn't pay that much attention to it. Maybe Benji would know."

"Do you know how to get in touch with Benji?"

"Only at the store. He's just Benji. I don't know his last name."

Ranger called his control room and asked for information on the comic book store. Three minutes later we had Benji's last name, home address, and cell phone number.

"Whoa, that's cool," Beedle said. "You're like the FBI or something."

"It's *or something,*" I told him.

It was close to midnight when we met up with Benji Crup. Ranger had tracked him down at a bar close to his apartment. He was playing darts and chugging beer with two other guys.

"Hey, look who's here," Benji said when he saw me. "Did you come in for some brew? We got a pitcher somewhere."

He spun around, looking for the pitcher. The dart slipped out of his hand and found a home in the thigh of a big guy standing next to him.

The big guy yanked the dart out of his leg and threw it at the dartboard, scoring a bullseye. "Cripes, Benji," the big guy said, "that's the second time tonight you stuck a dart in me. It's getting old."

"It was an accident," Benji said. "I was looking for the beer."

"We drank the beer," the big guy said.

I laid the six coins out on a nearby hightop table. "We need you to identify the coin," I said to Benji.

"These are all the same," he said. "They're all from the game."

"Yes," I said, "but you only sold one of them. Which one did you sell?"

He took a closer look. "I don't know. They all look alike. Even if I was sober, I couldn't tell you which one I sold."

"How do we get in touch with the kidnapper?" Ranger asked when we were back in the Porsche.

"I'm supposed to hang a sign in the office window."

"Babe, that's borderline pathetic."

"Yeah," I said. "He might not be a professional kidnapper. Are we going to give him all seven coins?"

Ranger pulled away from the curb. "Yes."

He drove to the end of the block and turned at the cross street.

"Do you think we'll get Connie back?" I asked him.

"It's possible."

"But not guaranteed."

"Not guaranteed," Ranger said.

Ranger stopped for a light and looked over at me. I knew the look. If it was any hotter it would have set my panties on fire.

"Where do we stand?" he asked.

"I'm in a relationship."

"And?"

"That's it," I said.

"You'll let me know when it's ended?"

"You'll be the first person I tell."

Ranger almost smiled. I amuse him.

The light turned green, and Ranger headed toward downtown. His apartment was in town. Beyond town on the other side of the railway tracks were Hamilton Avenue and the bail bonds office.

"Your call," Ranger said. "Where are we going?"

"We're going to the office to hang a sign."

"And then?"

"And then I'm going to wait for a phone call."

He glanced over at me. "It's only a matter of time, babe."

I suspected he wasn't referring to the kidnapper's phone call.

He crossed the tracks, turned onto Hamilton Avenue, and cruised past the bail bonds office. He hung a left into the alley and parked in the small lot.

The back room in the office was pitch-black when we entered. Ranger has vision like a cat, but I was stumbling, blind in the dark without the aid of my cell phone flashlight. I crashed into a file cabinet and Ranger grabbed me from behind and moved me away from the files.

"Are you okay?" he asked. "Anything broken? Concussion?"

"I'm fine."

"Are you sure?" He was standing very close, and his voice was soft, his words whispered against my ear. "I'm good at kissing things and making them feel better."

There was a flutter of panic in my chest and heat in body parts farther south. I knew without a shadow of a doubt that he was speaking the truth. "It wasn't my fault," I said. "The cabinet jumped out at me."

He reached across me and flipped the light switch. "You don't want to miss too many opportunities. You never know when they might go away forever."

"Do you have plans?"

He brushed a light kiss across my lips. "Yes, but they don't involve going away."

I followed Ranger into the front room. It felt strange being there at this time of night. The overhead lighting was harsh without the addition of sunlight, and Connie's desk was a stark reminder that she was being held hostage somewhere. The windows were black glass. Never a good look. A single set of headlights slid past the windows. The headlights disappeared and the blackness returned.

I swiped a piece of paper from the printer and wrote on it with black marker, I'VE GOT IT. I taped the paper up on the front window and transferred the office phone to my cell phone, and I was ready to leave.

Ranger drove me home and walked me to my door. We stepped inside and he pulled me close and kissed me. The kiss deepened and when we came up for air, I realized I had two fistfuls of his shirt in my tightly curled hands. I think my toes were also curled in my shoes, but that was my secret. I released the shirt and smoothed out the wrinkles.

"You'll be the first to know," I said, repeating my earlier promise. I hadn't actually meant it when I'd originally said it, but I was closer to meaning it at the moment.

"Babe," Ranger said.
And he left.

CHAPTER SEVEN

It was another early morning for me. My first thought was of Connie when I awoke, and there was no going back to sleep after that. I took a fast shower and made coffee while I gave my super hamster and best bud, Rex, fresh water and filled his food dish. I put the coffee in a to-go mug and headed to the office. I hadn't received any calls overnight, and I was anxious to make sure that the sign was still taped to the window.

The sky was light, approaching sunrise, and the roads were mostly empty. I cruised past the office and saw that the sign was still in place. I made a U-turn and stopped at Tasty Pastry Bakery.

Walking into the bakery at this time of the morning is like returning to the womb. It's warm. It's cozy. It's welcoming. I don't know what the womb smells like but at dawn the bakery wraps you in a scent blanket of powdered sugar and dough rising. Jenny Wisnowski was bringing out fresh baked bread and transferring the warm loaves to the shelves. I went to school with Jenny. She was married now and had four kids. Her husband worked at the button factory.

"Hey," Jenny said when she saw me. "What brings you here at this hour of the morning?"

"I thought I'd get an early start on my day. Lots to do."

"I hear you," Jenny said. "It must be hard without Connie. From what I hear she hasn't shown up yet. I'm thinking she went on vacation without telling anybody. Lord knows, she deserves it after all those years with Vinnie."

"Have you heard anything else interesting about Connie?"

"No. People have sort of moved off Connie disappearing. Mostly the big topic of conversation is Paul Mori getting shot."

"Who do you think did it?"

"I'm going with a random drugged-up nut job. Trenton has a lot of them," Jenny said.

I got eleven Boston creams and one jelly doughnut with powdered sugar and raspberry filling. The jelly doughnut was for Connie in case she showed up. She wasn't a Boston cream girl.

I parked at the curb in front of the bail bonds office and did a fast assessment of the area. No suspicious-looking individuals skulking around. No cars stopping to read the sign in the window. I didn't need the key under the rock by the dumpster. I had my own now. I unlocked the office and walked in. It wasn't nearly so creepy this morning. Light streamed in and traffic hummed on the other side of the plate-glass window.

I sat at Connie's desk, helped myself to a doughnut, and scrolled through her email. No new FTAs. That was bad news for me. I only made money when I captured someone. As it was right now, the only outstanding FTA was Morelli's grandmother. The thought of approaching her caused a chunk of doughnut to stick in my throat.

I checked my personal email, surfed a couple news sites, tried my hand at a crossword puzzle book I found in Connie's top drawer. Time dragged on. No phone call about Connie. I took two calls from men who needed a bail bondsman and I referred them to an office downtown. Without Vinnie or Connie, I was unable to help them. I looked at my watch for the zillionth time. It was still too early to call Vinnie.

Lula swung through the front door at

eight o'clock.

"What's with the sign?" she asked. "Is that for the kidnappers?"

"Yes. I found the coin. I made the twenty-four-hour time limit. I'm waiting to get a call about Connie."

"Thank the Lord. I couldn't hardly sleep last night." She looked at the bakery box on my desk. "Is that doughnuts?"

I flipped the lid and Lula took a Boston cream.

"How'd you get the coin?" Lula asked.

"Ranger got me into Sparks's apartment last night."

"Hold the phone. I forgot about the Ranger-helping-you part. That's the best part. I gotta know about that part. What happened with the man of mystery?"

"Nothing happened."

"I know that's not true. It's Ranger. Something always happens. He's Mr. Dangerous. He's Mr. Tall, Dark, and Freakin' Sexy. Let's start with the basics. Did he kiss you?"

"Yes."

"I knew it! I knew it!"

"It was no big deal."

"Girlfriend, it's always a big deal with Ranger. If he touches you with his fingertip, it's a big deal. Was there tongue?"

"What?"

"Tongue," Lula said. "Was there tongue?"

"Maybe a little."

"Just a little? I bet there was a lot. Not that it matters. Tongue is tongue. What else?"

"Nothing else."

"He didn't cop a feel?"

"No."

"Not even a little brush with his thumb?"

"No. At least I don't think so. I don't remember feeling anything."

"That's 'cause you were concentrating on the tongue. That happens sometimes. I bet he snuck a feel in. It would be disappointing if he didn't at least sneak a feel."

"He understands that I'm in a relationship with Morelli."

"I'm pretty sure Ranger don't care about details like that. He gave you the tongue. That's cheating right there. Tongue counts as a cheat. Especially if it's Ranger's tongue. That's definitely a cheat."

"Okay, but I didn't start it."

"Did you finish it?"

It took me a couple beats to review the kiss. "No. He finished it."

"See, if you had been the one to finish it, the cheat might have been erased, but as is, you might as well have continued the cheat until you at least got to see him naked. No one in their right mind would pass up the chance to see that man naked."

She was right. I'd seen him naked. He was awesome.

I got up and surrendered Connie's desk chair to Lula. "I checked the email and there were no new FTAs, but it might have been too early."

I called Vinnie and was shocked when he picked up.

"What?" Vinnie said.

"Connie is still missing and there's no one here who can write a bond."

"Don't get your panties in a bunch. I'm on my way."

"He's on his way," I said to Lula.

"I like it just fine without him," Lula said. "He's a inconvenience."

Twenty minutes later, Vinnie swaggered into the office. Vinnie is five feet nine inches, is slim, and appears boneless. His complexion is naturally swarthy, his eyes are narrow and feral, his brown hair is slicked back. His shoes are pointy toed, his pants are tight across his ass and narrow legged. He's the human equivalent of a lizard. And he's my cousin.

"Oh jeez," he said when he saw Lula sitting at Connie's desk. "Can life get any worse?"

"You bet your ass it can get worse," Lula said. "The day's just starting. And you better be nice to me and appreciate that I'm here running this crap-ass office because I'm all you got. And you're lucky to have me here."

"Yeah," Vinnie said. "Lucky me. What's happening with Connie?"

"She's being held for ransom," I said. "The kidnapper wants the coin you got from Paul Mori."

"That's weird," Vinnie said. "Did you call the police? The FBI?"

"No," I said. "I called Ranger."

"Even better," Vinnie said.

He disappeared into his inner office, slamming the door shut.

Lula gave the closed door the finger.

"I saw that," Vinnie yelled from the other side of the door.

Lula and I looked around for a hidden camera, but we didn't see any.

"This here's gonna be a good day," Lula said, turning back to her computer, taking another doughnut. "I can tell. I got a feeling."

My phone rang with an unknown-caller number. Not unusual for a bail bonds office but my heart skipped a beat all the same.

"I saw the sign," the caller said. "Do you have it?"

"Yes," I said. "In fact, I have six. I found them in a collection. I'm not sure which coin is yours. You can have all six. Where do you want to make the exchange?"

"Downtown. There's a coffee shop on the corner of Greely and Broad. There are a few outdoor tables. At ten o'clock you need to be seated at the red table. Alone. Stay there and wait for my phone call."

He disconnected.

I redialed. No one picked up.

"I'm dying here," Lula said. "Talk to me. Is Connie okay?"

"I don't know. I didn't get a chance to ask. He gave me a meeting spot and told me to wait for another phone call when I got there."

"I'm going with you," Lula said.

"No. He said I had to be alone."

"Yeah, but I could be somewhere nearby in case we need to do a takedown."

"I'm sure Ranger will be there," I said. "He's probably tapped into my phone, planted a bug in my messenger bag, and equipped my car with a GPS tracker."

"That's an important thing to know," Lula said. "A man who takes that many precautions to keep you safe is gonna have a good supply of quality condoms."

Ranger called. "Come to Rangeman and I'll outfit you with better equipment."

"Gotta go," I said to Lula. "I'm getting equipped."

"Be careful."

I gave her a thumbs-up, took a second doughnut, and left the office.

Rangeman is on a quiet side street in the center of the downtown district. It's a perfectly maintained, unremarkable building. I used my passkey to get into the secure underground garage and parked next to one of Ranger's personal cars. I waved at the security camera, stepped into the elevator, and pressed the button for the fifth floor. That's where the Rangeman nerve center, a small cafeteria, and Ranger's offices were located.

The elevator doors opened, and Ranger stepped in and tapped the button for the seventh floor. His apartment. He was dressed in the Rangeman uniform of black fatigues with the Rangeman logo on the sleeve. This was his usual work uniform. It was the same uniform every other man in the building wore. The only woman in the building was his housekeeper, Ella. Ella kept everyone perfectly pressed and organically fed. Her husband maintained the building. Every part of the building, with the exception of Ranger's apartment and office, was under constant video and audio surveillance. The result was a very quiet building where people moved about with measured efficiency. I'd learned not to talk in the elevator with Ranger. Even innocent small talk was enjoyed by the men in the control room. I don't mind, but Ranger is a privacy and control freak.

The elevator opens to a small foyer with one door. The door leads to a short hallway with crisp white walls and subdued lighting. A narrow, exotic wood console table sits pressed against the wall in the middle of the hallway. A silver tray designed to hold Ranger's personal mail and keys is the only object on the table.

Beyond the hall is a small, sleek kitchen equipped with high-end appliances that Ranger rarely uses. There's a dining area off the kitchen with seating for six. Beyond the dining area are a designer-furnished living room, small office, and master bedroom and bath. The walls and window treatments are white, the upholstered pieces are man-sized and comfortable, the fabrics are warm browns and creams with black accents.

The first time I saw the apartment I decided that Ranger must have slept with the designer, because she got everything exactly right for him.

Today there was a black tote bag on the floor by the entry table. Ranger picked it up and carried it into the kitchen.

"The kidnapper has chosen a busy intersection for this meeting," Ranger said. "There are midrise buildings on all sides. The windows and balconies look down on the red table. Several businesses with front and back doors open into the area. Bottom line is that the kidnapper has good visibility and good access. So do we. I have men on the street and men on rooftops. I'll be on the street." He took a small box out of the tote bag. "You need to take your hair out of the ponytail, so it covers the earbud I'm going to give you. It looks like an Apple Air-Pod but it's a state-of-the-art sending and receiving device. I'll be able to talk to you through it and I'll also hear everything you say."

He handed the earbud over to me and we gave it a test run.

He took a second device out of the bag. "This is a backup to the earbud. It's a little larger and has a little more power. You need to slip it onto your bra. I'd personally insert it, but it might make us late for the kidnapper."

I smiled and raised an eyebrow. "So, you think it would take that long?"

"Not for me, but past experience tells me you require more time."

Okay, now I'm officially embarrassed. "You're talking about inserting the listening device, right?"

Ranger took a step closer and raised the bottom of my T-shirt, exposing my Victoria's Secret lavender lace demi. "Pretty," he said, his fingertips brushing across my breast as he slipped the flesh-colored piece of plastic into the demi.

He leaned in to kiss me and I thumped him on the chest. "Stop it," I said, tugging my shirt down.

He stepped back and smiled. "You'll come around."

I looked in the bag. "Do you have anything else in there?"

He handed me a Glock 42 handgun. "Small but deadly," he said. "And it's loaded, unlike that Smith & Wesson you sometimes carry."

I dropped the Glock into my messenger bag and looked at the time. "I need to get on the road."

"I'll be right behind you. I want to stop in

the control room before I leave."

I found a parking place on the street a block away from the coffee shop. I was fifteen minutes early so I went into the shop and ordered a caramel frappe. I took my drink outside and sat at the red table. There were three other little round tables, and they were all empty. To say I was nervous would be a vast understatement. I had my cell phone on the table and the six coins in a plastic baggie in my messenger bag. I looked up and down the street and at all the buildings. The car traffic was heavy. The foot traffic was light. I wasn't sure what a kidnapper looked like, but I didn't see anyone who stood out as suspicious. I'd spotted one of Ranger's men at a high-top table inside the coffee shop. He had a coffee, and he was working on a laptop.

Ranger came on in my earbud. "I'm in a van across the street. I'm here with my technician, who will be monitoring your devices. You can relax. We've got your back."

"Good to know," I said.

At precisely ten o'clock my phone buzzed, and I answered.

"Do you have the coin?" he asked.

"I do. Where are you?"

"I'm around. It's not important where I am. I want to see the coins."

"I want to see Connie."

"Reasonable request," he said. "I'm changing to FaceTime."

A video of Connie came into view on my phone. She was tied to a chair. She was gagged and had a sleep mask over her eyes. Her head was down. Her hair was a mess.

"Go ahead," the kidnapper said to Connie. "Say something to your friend."

He kicked the chair and Connie grunted.

I felt physically sick. I went light-headed and swallowed back nausea. I got a grip on myself, sucked in some air, and said, "That's enough. Where do we go from here?"

Connie disappeared and the kidnapper came back on the phone. "I want to see the coins. I have to make sure you have the one I'm looking for. Put them all out on the table with the knight side up."

I laid the coins on the table knight side up and looked around. "Where are you?" I asked. "How are you going to see the coins?"

"I have ways," he said. "Be patient. Drink your coffee."

I sat back and focused on the van across the street.

"Don't stare," Ranger said in my earbud.

"He's checking the coins out with a drone."

I looked up and saw the drone. Heard the telltale buzzing.

"You don't have the coin," the kidnapper said.

"Of course I have the coin," I told him. "I personally stole these from the man who bought it."

Ranger laughed out loud into my earbud, and I did a mental eye-roll.

"My coin had a small notch on the edge. It's visible from the knight side. None of these coins have a notch. This exchange is aborted," the kidnapper said. "We'll keep her alive and intact for another twenty-four hours. Beyond that I can't make promises."

The line went dead, and I scooped the coins back into the bag. "This is horrible," I said to Ranger. "Connie looked terrible. Was anyone able to see where the drone landed?"

"We know the general direction," Ranger said. "No one was able to track it fast enough to see it land. Meet me back at Rangeman."

I finished my frappe and walked back to my car. I drove around a little, concentrating on the area where the drone might have originated. I didn't see anything remarkable. No one dragging a bound and gagged woman down the street. And I had another twenty-four-hour deadline.

CHAPTER EIGHT

I parked in the Rangeman garage, took the elevator to the fifth floor, and found Ranger in his office. I removed the listening device from my bra and handed it over to him.

"Keep the earbud and the gun," Ranger said. "This isn't over. We replayed the phone conversation. The kidnapper said '*We'll* keep her alive.'"

"That sounds like there's more than one of them."

"Has he indicated this to you before?"

"No. He implied that he wanted the coin for personal reasons. Could he really see a small detail like a notch on a coin from a drone?"

"Depends on the drone. Sanchez was on a rooftop next to the coffee shop and was able to get a photo. The kidnapper's drone was equipped with a decent camera, so the answer to your question is 'probably yes.'"

"Then where's the coin with the notch?" I asked.

"Three people handled the coin. It could be with any of them," Ranger said. "It would make life good if the coin is still with Sparks. We could have missed it in the search, or he could be carrying it on him."

"I agree. It makes no sense that Carpenter Beedle or Comic Book Benji would have it. They passed it on. They obviously didn't want to keep it."

Ranger stood at his desk. "Let's talk to Sparks."

Twenty minutes later we were in the lobby of the Ivy. We took the elevator to the fifth floor and Ranger rang the bell of 5B. No answer. Ranger knocked on the door. No answer. Ranger did his magical door-opening thing and we walked into Sparks's apartment.

Melvin Sparks was in his kitchen making a ham and cheese sandwich, and he was all dressed up like Sir Lancelot.

"What the — ?" he said when he saw us.

"Hi," I said. "Remember me?" I pointed to his costume. "Nice. Very authentic looking. Sir Lancelot, right?"

"Yeah. How do you know that?"

"*Monty Python and the Holy Grail.* It's one of my boyfriend's favorite movies."

Sparks looked at Ranger. "Is this your boyfriend?"

"No," I said. "Not my boyfriend."

Boyfriend was not a description anyone would ever assign to Ranger. Maybe when he was twelve.

"We're looking for the coin you purchased from Benji at the comic book store," I said to Sparks.

"I don't have it," he said. "I went to get it today to carry with Sir Lancelot and it's missing. My whole collection of *Gowa* Knights Templar is missing."

I placed the plastic bag with the six coins on his kitchen counter. "Don't ask how we got these," I said.

Sparks looked at Ranger. "Okay."

"The coin isn't in this collection," I told him.

"Sure it is," he said. "I had five and now there are six." He opened the plastic bag and spread the coins out on his counter. "Six," he said.

"Which one did you get from Benji?" I asked him.

"I don't know, exactly," he said. "They all sort of look the same."

I looked at Ranger.

"Do you have any other Knights Templar coins?" Ranger asked Sparks.

"Yes, but these are the only ones from the game. This is my whole collection."

"Thanks for clearing this up for us," I said. "Sorry to disturb your lunch, Sir Lancelot."

Sparks grinned. "I'm not really Sir Lancelot."

We left the Ivy. Ranger put the Porsche in gear and pulled away from the curb. "Do you believe him?"

"I don't know. He sounded like he was telling the truth but he's the logical person to have the coin."

"Let's talk to Benji."

Benji was organizing the manga section when we walked in. He smiled and nodded to me and then he acknowledged Ranger. The acknowledgment had a tinge of panic.

Morelli and Ranger are very different people. They have different body types and different personalities. They dress differently, walk differently, talk differently. The one thing they have in common is instant recognition that they're the alpha dog.

"Are you shopping?" Benji asked.

"No," I said. "Not today. I'm still looking for the Knights Templar coin."

"Did you talk to Melvin Sparks?"

"Yes. I looked at his coin collection. He

had six coins but none of them were the one I'm looking for."

Benji put a stack of manga down on a round table. "That's a bummer. I guess the coin I got from Carpenter wasn't the one you want."

"Do you know where Carpenter got his coin?"

"No," Benji said. "He didn't say."

"Is he a regular customer?"

"Not really. He panhandles on the corner sometimes and comes in to pass the time between rush hours. He's more a D&D gamer. He bought some rad dice from me a while back."

"He knew the coin had some value to it," I said.

Benji shrugged. "Every thirty-year-old geek played that game in middle school and knows about the coin. It's not worth serious money, but a collector like Sparks would be willing to put out twenty or thirty bucks for it, depending on the condition."

"What was the condition of the coin he bought from you?"

"It was good. It had some signs of wear but nothing serious."

"Did it have a notch in the edge?"

"Not that I can remember."

Five minutes later we were back in Ranger's Porsche.

"Next up," Ranger said.

"Carpenter Beedle. He lives with his parents on Maymount Street."

"This is the guy who shot himself in the foot?"

"Yep."

"And he's a professional panhandler."

"Yep. And apparently a halfway-decent pickpocket."

Ranger cut over to Chambers and turned onto Maymount.

"It's the yellow house with the red door," I said.

And it's the house with the empty driveway, I thought. No rusted Sentra. I hoped that wasn't a bad sign. The rest of the neighborhood was business as usual. In other words, no business at all. No activity.

I rang the bell and Mrs. Beedle answered.

"Oh dear," she said when she saw me.

This wasn't the greeting I wanted to hear. "I'd like to speak with Carpenter," I said to her.

"He isn't here," she said. "He was gone when I got up this morning."

"He wasn't supposed to leave the house."

"He never listens. He does what he wants. He's probably panhandling somewhere. He's a bum but he's got a work ethic. He gets that from his father, God rest his soul."

"Mr. Beedle has passed?" I asked.

"Ten years ago. Mowing the lawn and had a heart attack. I told him to get a power lawn mower, but he wouldn't listen. Used a push mower. Can you imagine? Like father, like son. Don't listen."

I looked sidewise at Ranger and saw a smile beginning to twitch at the corner of his mouth. He was liking Mrs. Beedle.

"Does Carpenter have a car?" Ranger asked her.

"Yes," she said. "He drives a Sentra."

We returned to the Porsche, and Ranger called the control room and got the plate number on the Sentra.

"Do you know where he usually hangs?" Ranger asked me.

"He tried to rob the armored car on State Street. There's a bank on the corner of State and Third. That's probably a good place to start."

Ranger put the car in gear, drove two blocks, and got a call from his control room. One of his clients had been shot and robbed during a home invasion. A Rangeman car was on the scene with police and medical.

Ranger made a U-turn. "Change in plans. This is a new account in Yardley. We installed security cameras two weeks ago."

We crossed the Delaware River into Pennsylvania and minutes later Ranger turned off the main road into a neighborhood of million-dollar houses and hundred-year-old trees.

"It's really pretty here," I said.

"Until recently it had zero crime. I have several clients here, and I've had to increase patrol car presence. This is the fourth armed home invasion in this neighborhood in the past two months. It's the first time it's my account."

"Always the same MO?"

"Yes. The victim is an older woman driving an expensive car. They follow her home to an empty house and force her to let them in. Then they rob it. Something obviously went wrong this time because someone got shot."

We saw the lights flashing a block away. A fire truck, a couple cop cars, an EMT transport, two Rangeman cars. The house was a large, rambling two-story white clapboard with black shutters and lots of professional landscaping. A woman was on a stretcher. The back of the stretcher was elevated to allow her to sit. Two med techs were with her.

Ranger parked by the Rangeman SUVs, and we joined the cluster of responders. Two

Rangemen were at the open front door to the house. Two more Rangemen, Hal and Jose, were with the woman on the stretcher.

Ranger approached Hal.

"She was carrying groceries into the house when four men came up behind her with guns drawn," Hal said. "They told her to get on the floor facedown and stay there, and she told them to go fuck themselves. And then she swung a six-pack of beer she was carrying at one of them and smashed him in the face. Then she got shot."

Ranger looked over at the woman. "How bad is it?"

"Could be worse," Hal said. "She got shot in the arm. Looks like they panicked when they shot her and took off. She was able to hit the alarm by the door. We were the first on the scene."

"I'm going to be here for a while," Ranger said to me. "I know you want to look for Beedle, so take my car. I'll catch up with you later."

I glanced at the gleaming black Porsche turbo. "Are you sure you want me to take your car? I have a history of accidents with your cars."

Ranger handed me the keys. "Keep it interesting."

■ ■ ■ ■

I crossed the bridge to New Jersey and went straight to the office. "Anything new?" I asked Lula.

"Vinnie is at the courthouse bonding out some moron. And we got a notice that the charges were dropped on Brad Winter. I guess the ladies got enough satisfaction out of tattooing him. That's about it. What's with you? Where's Connie?"

"She's still with the kidnapper. He said I didn't have the right coin."

"How'd he know? Did you get to see him?"

"He looked at them with a drone camera. I didn't get to see him."

"This is a freaking downer. I was sure you'd come back with Connie. What are you going to do now? How do you get the right coin?"

"For starters, I need to find Carpenter Beedle."

"I thought he was supposed to stay in his house," Lula said.

"Turns out he's not good at following directions."

"Well, I'm going with you to look for him. Now that Vinnie's in town I don't need to

135

stay here. Especially since you're driving Ranger's Batmobile."

"The first stop is my parents' house. I need lunch and I need information."

"I'm all about that," Lula said.

Grandma was in the living room doing Zumba with a woman on television. "You should try this," Grandma said to Lula and me. "It gives you endorphins and tight butt cheeks."

"And heck, who doesn't want endorphins and tight butt cheeks," Lula said.

"I'm going to have butt cheeks so tight I could crack a walnut," Grandma said.

"Sign me up," Lula said.

"I'm going to pass," I said.

"It's over anyway," Grandma said. "There's another one coming on but it's for seniors and there's no walnut-cracking expectations."

"What's the point then," Lula said. "My philosophy is aim high and fail big."

"I like the way you think," Grandma said. "Have you had lunch? We already ate but there's cold cuts and leftovers."

Grandma shut the television off, and we all went to the kitchen. My mom was sitting at the table with a cup of tea and a basket of yarn, and she was knitting what looked like a twenty-seven-foot scarf.

"Hey, Mrs. P," Lula said. "That's a nice thing you got going there. I like the pink sparkly yarn you're using. Adds some glam. What are you making?"

"I'm not making anything," she said. "I'm just knitting. It's relaxing as long as you don't have to worry about making a perfect sweater."

I found some leftover chicken parm in the fridge. I shared it with Lula, and we finished it off with ice-cream bars.

"What's the latest on Paul Mori, the dead dry cleaner?" I asked Grandma. "Any suspects?"

"I haven't heard about any. People are saying he might have made an enemy in jail. The timing is strange. And he wasn't robbed. He still had his watch and his wallet. I imagine there'll be talk about him at the Leoni viewing tonight. We should scout around before we make a move on Bella."

My mother sucked in some air and stopped knitting. "You will *not* make a move on Bella at the viewing," she said. "It would be disrespectful."

"I guess we could wait to snatch Bella at the Mori viewing," Grandma said. "His viewing is tomorrow. It's going to draw even better than Len Leoni tonight. A shooting always tops an aneurism."

My mother looked at Lula. "This is why I knit."

"I hear you," Lula said. "There's rules about polite society. All you gotta do is watch *Bridgerton* and you can see people with lots of rules. Of course, that was England, and this is Jersey. Our rules in Jersey are more commonsense. Like you don't double-dip the chip in sauce if someone's looking. And if someone's got a gun rack or a big dog in his truck you don't cut him off in traffic."

"News at the bakery this morning is that Connie isn't back yet," Grandma said. "I didn't say anything about you-know-what. So far as I can see, we're the only ones who know what's going on."

My mom looked from Grandma to me. "What's going on? What's you-know-what?"

"Connie's been kidnapped," I said. "We're keeping it quiet while we work to get her released."

"Oh my God!" my mom said. "*Kidnapped*. Why would someone kidnap Connie?"

"It's complicated," I said. "A special coin passed through the bail bonds office. The kidnapper is holding Connie hostage until the coin is found and returned to him."

"What if it's not found?"

"It'll be found," I said. "In the meantime, we're keeping the details quiet."

"Poor Connie," my mother said. "This must be terrible for her. Is she okay? Has anyone talked to her?"

"She's okay," I said.

"That's why we're going to snoop around at the viewing tonight," Grandma said. "Viewings are always good for picking up information. People have a couple drinks to fortify themselves, and then they get loose lips."

I grabbed my messenger bag. "We have to get back to work now," I said to my mom. "Things to do."

"I don't see where we got any useful information out of this visit," Lula said when we buckled ourselves into Ranger's Porsche.

"We know there isn't any information being passed on the Burg gossip line. That tells us something. Whoever has Connie is being very careful and is probably not keeping Connie in the Burg or surrounding neighborhoods."

"So, we know where she isn't, but we don't know where she is," Lula said. "I have to tell you I'm feeling a lot of anxiety about this."

I was trying to stay focused and ignore

the anxiety. Ranger was at the home invasion, but I knew someone in his control room was working to find the kidnapper. They were attempting to trace the call the kidnapper had made to my phone, and they were looking at downtown security and traffic cameras, following the path of the drone. Ranger has ways of tapping into systems that aren't supposed to be available to him.

I drove to State Street and turned toward Third. "Keep your eyes open for Carpenter Beedle," I said to Lula. "He used to hang here. And look for his car. Rusted Sentra. The license number is written on the top of his file."

I concentrated on State Street, but I also hit some other hot spots for vagrants and panhandlers. After two hours I gave up and took Lula back to the office.

"Call me if you need help or if anything good happens," Lula said.

I gave her two thumbs up and went home. Rex was asleep in his soup can den, but I said hello to him anyway. I got a bottle of water from the fridge and took a seat at my dining room table. I never have company, and I eat most of my meals standing at the kitchen sink. If Morelli is over, we usually eat in front of the television. So, the dining room table has become my desk, and the only time I eat at it is when I'm working.

I opened my laptop and checked my email and socials. Nothing exciting there. I called Morelli.

"Connie is still missing," I said. "Have you heard anything?"

"A notice went out to look for her. Almost everyone knows her. That makes the alert more personal, but nothing's turned up so far," Morelli said. "Anything on your end?"

"No. I've got Ranger looking, too. I thought I had a lead, but it hasn't worked out."

"Anything you want to share?" he asked.

"No." A part of me wanted to join forces with him. He was smart and he was a good cop. Problem was that a kidnapping would bring feds into the equation, and I worried that the investigation would get big and messy. Plus, I'd already tarnished the case by committing a felony while gathering evidence. "How about you?"

"Nope."

There was a long silence.

He's holding something back, I thought. And he knows I've got something.

"Okey dokey then," I finally said. "I have to get back to work."

"Are you free tonight?"

"Sadly, no. I promised I'd take Grandma

Mazur to the Leoni viewing."

"Lucky you," Morelli said.

Morelli was possibly the only person I knew who hated going to a viewing more than me.

I said goodbye to Morelli and called Mrs. Beedle.

"Have you heard from Carpenter?" I asked her. "Is he at home?"

"No," she said, "but that's not unusual. He often comes and goes at odd hours."

I cleaned the hamster cage and gave Rex fresh food and water. This involved giving him a new soup can, so I multitasked and had Campbell's Tomato Soup for dinner. I supplemented the soup with a peanut butter and olive sandwich and washed it down with a Stella. I was pretty sure this combination gave me all the necessary food groups, with the exception of chocolate.

CHAPTER NINE

At six o'clock I changed into a sleeveless black knit dress with a short fitted white jacket with black trim. I added an extra swipe of mascara to my lashes, freshened my lipstick, and neatened my ponytail. I was wearing black flats in case I had to chase down a bad guy, and I had Ranger's gun in my purse. I hadn't heard from him since this afternoon. I assumed this meant there was no news about Connie.

I had a decision to make when I got to the parking lot. I could drive my Honda or I could drive Ranger's Porsche. I justified taking the Porsche by telling myself Grandma would be disappointed if I picked her up in the Honda.

Doors opened at the funeral home at seven o'clock. I got us there with ten minutes to spare and already there was a crowd on the front porch.

"Ordinarily I'd muscle my way through

all those people, so I could get a seat up front," Grandma said. "I don't care about that tonight on account of we've got a job to do."

"We aren't capturing Bella," I said.

"I know. I'm not talking about that. I'm talking about listening for word about Connie. We need to have a plan. One of us should take the cookie table and one of us should float around the room. Which do you want?"

"I'll float," I said.

The doors opened and we all rushed inside. The funeral home had several slumber rooms and a large lobby. On peak days, like today, the packed lobby became a sweltering torture chamber. The cloying smell of funeral flowers, sweat, and whiskey breath permeated every part of the room and clung to every mourner and cookie moocher. Voices rose and blended into a sound that was something between the roar of Niagara Falls and extreme tinnitus.

I worked the perimeter of the room, half-heartedly eavesdropping on conversations about hernias, bloat, gas prices, toilet paper preferences, Mrs. Moyers's cat, kidney stones, Harry Wortle's erectile dysfunction, and Loretta Kulicki's yeast infection. I didn't catch anyone talking about Connie or known kidnappers.

I spotted crazy Bella in line to take a last look at the deceased and give condolences to Len Leoni's widow. I made sure there was distance between us.

The crowd was beginning to thin out at eight thirty, and I was able to make my way to Grandma at the cookie table. She was talking to Ethel Scheck and some other woman. Another clump of ladies was on the far side of the round table. I helped myself to an Oreo and realized that the cookie table conversation had suddenly stopped, and everyone was staring at something behind me. I turned and was face-to-face with Bella.

"You!" she said to me. "Slut girl. Get out of my way."

I stepped aside, effectively blocking Grandma from grabbing Bella by the throat.

"Nice to see you, Mrs. Morelli," I said.

"I bet," she said. "Maybe you've been looking for me, eh?" Bella stared at the selection of cookies. "Where's the pignoli? There's no pignoli here."

I cut my eyes to Grandma and saw her smile. She had the pignoli in her purse.

"Someone ate my pignoli," Bella said. "I give the eye to them when I find them."

The women on the other side of the table

scurried away.

Bella spied Grandma Mazur. "I see you hiding behind your worthless granddaughter. You big coward. You the one who took my pignoli."

"Excuse me?" Grandma said to Bella, pushing me aside. "Are you calling me a coward, you miserable old crone?"

"You Hungarian washerwoman," Bella said. "Don't have the cojones like Italian."

"Oh yeah?" Grandma said. "You want a piece of me? I could kick your ass any day of the week."

"I give you the eye," Bella said.

"And I give you the finger," Grandma said. "You don't scare me. You're just a big bag of wind."

Bella turned on me. "What you think, slut? Am I big bag of wind? You want a piece of me too? You got cojones? Put the cuffs on me. We see what you got."

"It would be disrespectful to the Leoni family," I said. "Grandma and I were just leaving."

"You don't care about the Leoni," Bella said. "You care about the eye. What you want? Boils? Hair fall out? Maybe I make you talk like chicken." She stuck her arms out. "Go ahead. Cuff me. I dare you. I give you double whammy."

There was a collective, simultaneous gasp from everyone in the room. It was as if all the air had gotten sucked out of the building and no one could move. No one could turn away from the spectacle. People were creeping out of the slumber room to cautiously join the crowd in the lobby.

The good Stephanie and the bad Stephanie were at war in my head. The bad Stephanie wanted to punch the hag in the face and drag her off to jail. The good Stephanie argued that she was a crazy old lady, and if I punched her in front of all these people my mother would cut me off from her famous pineapple upside-down cake. So, what it came down to was, did I really want to live the rest of my life without the cake?

I narrowed my eyes at Bella. "I'm not going to cuff you," I said.

I sensed the crowd relax a little. People resumed breathing.

Bella pulled herself together, marshaling her forces for another attack. "Do it," Bella said, holding her arms out. "Put me in cuffs. See how my grandson like you then."

There was another communal gasp.

The funeral director was behind me, restraining Grandma. "For God's sake, do it," he whispered. "Put her in cuffs and get her out of here. I'm begging you."

I reached into my purse, found my cuffs, and clamped them on Bella. The click of them locking in place was like a thunderclap in the still room. I imagined everyone's eyes bulging out of their sockets, mouths agape. Probably a television crew was on its way. News at eleven. I wouldn't be able to give an interview because I would be talking like a chicken.

"What's this?" Bella shrieked. "You do this to a defenseless, sick old woman? What person are you that you do a thing like this. Your family be ashamed. Someone get a doctor. My heart. I can't see. Someone get oxygen."

"Where's her daughter?" I asked the funeral director. "Who brought her here?"

"She usually comes alone," he said.

"Now what?" I asked him. "Do we call for an ambulance?"

"They won't touch her," he said. "Last time she did this she gave one of the EMTs the eye and he ended up passing a kidney stone the size of a golf ball."

I looked around the room. People were smashed together, cowering in corners and hiding behind potted plants.

I grabbed Bella by the arm and tugged her toward the side door that led to the parking lot.

"Help," she yelled. "Help this sick old lady. I'm being kidnapped."

Grandma was behind us. "Put a sock in it, Bella," she said. "For two cents I'd give you a good kick in your keister."

"I'd get a bruise and you'd be in big trouble," Bella said. "Old lady brutality."

We got to my car and I realized that it was Ranger's car and realistically it only had room for two people.

"Some hotshot car you got," Bella said. "Slut car."

I stuffed her in, buckled her seat belt, and went around to the driver's side.

"I'll only be ten minutes," I said to Grandma. "Wait here and I'll be right back."

"It'll take longer than that to check her in downtown," Grandma said.

"I'm not taking her downtown. I'm taking her home."

"That's not satisfying but I guess it's smart," Grandma said. "You don't have to come back for me. I can get a ride with Ethel Scheck. After viewings she likes to go to Pino's for nachos and a drink."

It was a short silent ride to the Morelli house. I parked at the curb and went to the passenger side to help Bella out. I unbuckled her seat belt and Bella hunkered down.

"You arrested me," she said. "I'm in

handcuffs. This is the way you want it. Take me to the police."

"If I take you in now, you'll have to spend the night in jail. I'll come back for you in the morning. You can get immediately bonded out and you can go home."

"I'm not getting out of this car until the police make me get out. We'll see what they think of you doing this to a poor sick old lady."

"You aren't poor. You aren't sick. And you aren't that old."

"A lot you know," Bella said. "Slut gold digger."

"Get out."

"No."

"Get out!"

"Make me. Give me bruises so everybody can see. Then I give you the eye and you pee yourself."

I turned on my heel and went to the front door. I rang the bell several times. No one answered. I banged on the door. Still no answer. Okay, go to plan B. Drop Bella off at Joe's house. She was his grandmother. He could deal with her.

I stepped off the front porch and Bella drove away in the Porsche. She chirped the tires when she took off, raced down two blocks, and squealed around the corner.

I was gobsmacked. For a bunch of beats there was nothing in my head beyond mind-boggling, stupefying disbelief.

Bang!

My brain kicked in. Bella had hit something.

Bang! Bang! Bang!

Crap. What the hell?

I sprinted down the street and turned the corner. There was enough ambient light from houses and the moon that I could see Bella had sideswiped three parked cars and finally jumped the curb and smashed head-on into a small tree. The tree had broken in half and the car was partially impaled on it.

Bella was struggling with the airbag when I reached her. The driver's-side door was bashed in, and the car was hanging from the splintered tree at a forty-five-degree angle. Tiny flames were licking along the undercarriage. I wrenched the door open. My purse tumbled out and Bella followed. I dragged her away from the car and helped her get to her feet.

"Are you okay?" I asked.

"I'm tough Sicilian," she said. "This car no good. I give this car the eye."

She touched her finger to her eye and the car burst into flames. "Whoa," she said.

"Good one."

I was tempted to point out that the car had been on fire before she gave it the eye, but I decided it was pointless.

A cop car angle-parked at the curb. It was followed by a fire truck and a second cop car. My phone rang and I knew it was Ranger without looking at the caller ID.

"I'm okay," I said. "Your car, not so much."

"Babe," he said. And he hung up.

I unlocked Bella's cuffs and returned them to my purse. A couple firemen rolled out a hose and made sure the fire didn't spread to the houses. Locals were standing in small groups, watching the circus. An EMT truck arrived and left when they saw Bella. A uniformed cop approached us. The tag on his uniform read CHUCK KRIZAK.

"Who was driving the vehicle?" he asked.

"Me," Bella said.

"I'll need to see your license," Chuck said to Bella.

"I don't have a license," she said. "I'm old. I don't need one. I only drive sometimes."

"Did you hit any cars other than the three on this street?"

"I hit a tree. I didn't hit cars."

"I'm pretty sure you hit some cars,"

Chuck said.

"I might put the eye on you if you don't watch out," Bella said.

"Have you been drinking?" he asked her. "Maybe a glass of wine with dinner?"

"Everyone has wine with dinner," Bella said.

"I'd like you to step over to the squad car," Chuck said.

"Good," Bella said. "You can drive me home."

This wasn't going to end well, I thought. He wasn't going to drive her home. He was going to test her alcohol level. And she was going to flunk the test.

I called Morelli. No answer. I left a message. "I have a situation here with your grandmother. She's about to be arrested for driving without a license, driving under the influence, and destruction of private property. Call me when you get this message."

I tried calling Morelli's mom. No answer. There were now four cops arguing with Bella. I didn't know any of them. They didn't look angry. They looked like they were trying hard to calm Bella down and get her into a squad car. I walked over to see if I could help.

"What's going on?" I asked Chuck.

"She blew a point eighteen. I don't know

153

how she's still standing. And she's talking crazy talk."

"That's normal," I said.

"We need to bring her in for evaluation, but she's not cooperating."

"You!" Bella said, turning to me. "This all your fault. You give me bad car." She stuck her arms out at Chuck. "Here. Put me in handcuffs, too. Put the sick old lady in handcuffs. See where that get you. Take me away to jail."

Chuck looked at me.

"Been here, done this," I said. "Don't leave her alone in the car or she'll drive off with it."

I answered a few more questions for Chuck and waved goodbye to Bella. She looked at me from the backseat of the squad car and stuck her tongue out at me.

I loved Joe Morelli, but did I really want to marry into this family? Honestly? Not that it was a current issue because Morelli wasn't showing signs of desiring marriage. So as long as I didn't get pregnant I figured it was all good.

I saw a Rangeman SUV and a black Porsche Cayenne arrive on the scene and park a short distance from the first-responder vehicles. Ranger got out of the Cayenne and walked over to me. He put an arm around me and kissed me on the top of my head.

"You smell like cooked Porsche," he said. "I assume that's my car smoldering, skewered on what used to be someone's maple tree."

I could feel myself choking up. It had really been an awful day. "Yep," I said.

"I'm always amazed at how you never destroy my cars the same way twice. This one is especially clever the way it's impaled on the tree."

"I can't take credit for it. I wasn't driving."

"Anyone hurt?"

"No."

"Ready to go home?"

"Yes."

Frequently Ranger comes to my rescue. It doesn't usually feel like a rescue, because I almost always know that I could rescue myself. Ranger knows this as well. It's kind of like killing a spider. I could kill a spider if I had to, but I'm perfectly happy to have a big, strong, sexy guy do it for me. Especially if he gets off on killing the spider. And of course, I'd be happy to rescue Ranger if he ever needed rescuing. In this case giving me a ride home wasn't much of a rescue. It was more of a chance to talk business.

He drove out of the Burg and paused at Hamilton Avenue. If he turned right, the road would take us to my house. If he turned left, it would lead to Rangeman. I wanted to go to Carpenter Beedle's house on Maymount Street.

"I haven't been able to question Beedle about the coin," I said. "Lula and I covered all his known haunts, and we didn't see him. Let's drive past his house to see if his car is there."

Ranger turned right on Hamilton, toward Chambers.

"Did you have any luck tracking the drone?" I asked him.

"Whoever you were talking to used a throwaway burner phone bought at a Walmart in Oklahoma. We were able to trace it through the carrier. All the information they gave to the carrier was bogus. The drone returned to a location a half mile away from where you were sitting. We have its landing narrowed down to one block but haven't been able to pinpoint the building yet."

"I'm running out of time. I need the coin tomorrow morning. I don't see that happening."

"Put up another sign that tells them you're still working on it. We have cameras set up to monitor all street and sidewalk traffic passing in front of the bail bonds office. If they read the sign with a drone, it makes life more complicated."

My phone buzzed. It was Morelli.

"Was that a serious message about Bella?" he asked.

"Yes. They said they were taking her away for evaluation. Not sure what that means. I drove her home from the viewing and when I went to get your mother to get her out of the car, she jumped into the driver's seat and drove off. She hit three parked cars and a tree. When the police showed up, she blew a point eighteen percent and threatened to give them the eye. Then she insisted they arrest her. So, they did."

"Was she hurt?"

"No."

"Is there more to the story?" Morelli asked.

"Yes, but you don't want to hear it now. I imagine you want to see what's going on with Bella. Chuck Krizak was the arresting officer."

"I know him. He's new. He's a good guy."

"He tried to be helpful, but Bella wasn't cooperating."

"No surprise there. What about your car?"

"It wasn't my car. It was Ranger's 911. It got impaled on the tree, caught fire, and melted down to a glob of black goo. If you don't want Bella spending the night in jail, you're going to have to call Vinnie. For a price he can get Judge Luca out of his La-Z-Boy chair to set bail for her. I didn't have any luck reaching your mother."

Ranger looked over at me when I disconnected. "Bella drove off in the Porsche?"

"Yes, and I didn't tell Morelli the best part. She was handcuffed. She was making a scene at the viewing, and I was asked to remove her. The woman is a maniac. Although, you have to give credit to someone her age who could climb over that console wearing a granny dress and handcuffs."

"Just as well the car caught fire," Ranger said. "I would have had to destroy it after that anyway."

Ranger humor. Or maybe not.

My thoughts moved from Bella to Connie. I was finding it hard to muster optimism. I was bottomed out on positive energy.

"I'm screwing up," I said to Ranger. "I haven't made any progress at getting Connie released."

"It's a process," Ranger said. "Have faith."

"If I had faith, I'd be a better Catholic."

Ranger reached over and wrapped his hand around mine. Okay, so maybe he did rescue me sometimes. Anyway, I liked it. There are times when you just don't want to be alone, and you need someone to hold your hand. And when it's Ranger holding your hand, you get all warm inside and fear goes away. You could probably get sucked up in a tornado and if you were with Ranger, you wouldn't give a fig.

He cruised down Maymount Street and idled in front of the Beedle house.

"No Sentra," I said.

"Babe."

Ranger parked the Cayenne next to my Honda CR-V. He walked me to my apartment and stepped inside with me.

Rex was awake and running on his wheel. He stopped running and blinked his shiny black eyes when the light went on. I took a shelled walnut from the jar on the kitchen counter and dropped it into Rex's cage. Rex scurried over to the walnut, stuffed it into his cheek, and disappeared into his soup can. It's easy to make a hamster happy.

Ranger went to my brown bear cookie jar, lifted the lid, and removed my S&W .38. He spun the barrel. Empty. No bullets. He looked at me. "Babe. It's hard to shoot people when your gun isn't loaded."

"I don't want to shoot people."

"In that case, you're in good shape."

He stepped closer and kissed me. His lips were soft against mine, his hands found my waist, and desire curled in my stomach.

"Do you want me to stay?" he asked.

"Yes," I said. "No."

"Want me to decide?"

"No! And Lula says kissing is cheating."

"What do you think?" he asked, his lips brushing against my ear, his hands moving up my rib cage.

"I think I'm going to rot in hell."

"That's encouraging," he said.

I put some distance between us. "Do you really believe that we'll get Connie back?"

Ranger's phone buzzed and he looked at a text message. "Ramon has a visual of two men. One of them is carrying what looks like a drone case. He has them entering and exiting a building in the right time frame."

"How did Ramon get this?"

"There are cameras everywhere. Some are DOT. Some are owned by individual property owners. Some are city of Trenton. We thought we knew the block where the drone touched down, so it made the camera scan easier."

This is why I went to Ranger for help. Ranger isn't hamstrung by rules and regulations and privacy issues. Ranger just hacks into whatever system he thinks will be helpful.

"I'm going back to Rangeman," he said. "I want to see what we've got. Do you want to come with me?"

I hesitated. I wanted to see the men with the drone kit, but I knew if I went to Rangeman I'd spend the night.

"You're already going straight to hell," Ranger said. "You might as well make the most of it."

"Tempting," I said, "but I'm going to stay here. Keep me in the loop."

Morelli called at midnight. "Bella's home," he said. "I had to pay off a judge, and I made a bunch of promises I don't ever want to keep."

"Bella made a scene at the viewing and the funeral director begged me to take her away."

"She said you put her in handcuffs."

"She insisted. She said she wanted to go to jail. It was the only way I could get her out of the funeral home."

"She got her wish," Morelli said. "I was tempted to leave her there."

"She would put the eye on you if you did that."

"I'm her favorite grandson. She would

never put the eye on me. She'd put the eye on you in a heartbeat. She said she put the eye on Ranger's car, and it caught fire."

"It had a head start."

I said good night to Morelli, and I went to bed with my laptop. I pulled up a map of Trenton and zeroed in on the area where the drone supposedly landed. I switched to satellite view and examined the buildings. This was all commercial real estate, packed together. No yards or parking lots. None of the buildings appeared to have balconies, so the drone probably landed on a rooftop. Several rooftops looked like they could hold a couple guys and a drone.

Ranger would have pinpointed a building by now. He would be tapping into internal security cameras on the building and checking out cars parked on the street. He had pictures of suspects. I gave myself a mental head slap. I should have gone back to Rangeman with him. Stupid, stupid, stupid. On the other hand, I was virtuous. Mostly. I hadn't done the *big thing.* And it's not as if I would have been any help. I would have been a bystander. Okay, so it was a wash.

CHAPTER TEN

When my phone rang at seven in the morning my first thought was that someone had died. My second thought was that I was turning into my mother.

"Babe," Ranger said. "I want you to take a look at the videos we have."

"I'm on my way."

I took a fast shower, got dressed, and went out of the house with wet hair. I rolled all the windows down on the Honda and by the time I got to Rangeman my hair was frizz and tangles, but at least it wasn't wet. I ran a brush through it in the garage and put it into a ponytail.

I found Ranger in a small conference room next to his office on the fifth floor. He was at the conference table with his laptop. A large monitor was on the wall across from the table.

"Babe," he said. "You look like you need coffee."

"You got me out of bed. I didn't take time for breakfast."

He made a phone call and asked that coffee and breakfast be brought to the conference room. "We have a high-res monitor here. I thought it would be better than trying to look at images on my laptop. I'll start at the beginning. I have two angles of the same thing. Two men walking into a building. The quality of one isn't good. DOT inferior equipment."

The first video was black and white and grainy and lasted about thirty seconds. Two men came into focus. They were wearing hooded sweatshirts. Dark pants. Running shoes. Hard to see their faces. One was carrying a case that presumably held the drone. The second video was in better focus and shot from a slightly different angle.

"Do you recognize either of the men?" Ranger asked.

"No. I couldn't see their faces. If I had to make a guess, I'd say they were in their forties or early fifties based on their build and the way they walked. Caucasian. It looked like the one carrying the case might have had a tattoo on his hand."

Ranger isolated a frame that showed the hand and the tattoo. "It's an anchor," Ranger said. "Not especially unique, but not everyone has an anchor tattooed on their hand."

There was a knock on the door and Ella came in with a tray. A pot of coffee, breakfast pastries, fruit, a slice of bacon, and a cheese quiche.

"I knew this was for you," Ella said to me. "So, I brought pastries."

"It's perfect," I said. "Thank you."

I drank coffee and ate quiche and pastries while Ranger played two more videos.

"We have them leaving the building," he said. "They're walking with their heads down, but you can catch a partial glimpse of one of their faces. It looks like he has a two-day beard. Maybe some gray in it when I enlarge the frame. That would fit your age assessment." He played the videos a couple times and moved on to a street view. "Another DOT camera picked them up on the corner of the block. They took the cross street and got into a Camry. We were only able to get a partial plate number. Jersey plate JZ and the rest is obscured. The DOT needs to improve their equipment."

"Did anyone here recognize them?"

"No."

I topped off my coffee and took an almond croissant. "Anything else?"

"That's all we have right now. We've been

able to determine the building from the façade and the front door. I have someone inside, checking occupants and roof access. Ramon is scanning interior cameras. Put your sign in the window. Tell them you need more time. We'll see where that gets us. I have someone on Hamilton, watching for the Camry."

I left Rangeman and drove to the bail bonds office. Lula was already at Connie's desk, working on the day's box of doughnuts. Vinnie was somewhere else.

"Hey, girl," Lula said. "You didn't call me so I'm guessing nothing good happened."

"Ranger is making some progress. He has video of two men carrying a drone case. Their faces are hidden in hoodies, but it looks like they're in their late forties and one has an anchor tattooed on his hand. They were driving a Camry with Jersey plates."

"Ranger's the shit. He's Mr. Magic. He's the Mailman. What are we going to do now? Are we going out to look for the tattooed guy?"

"I need to make a sign for the window and then I'm looking for Beedle."

The sign said MAKING PROGRESS BUT NEED MORE TIME. I stuck it in the window and went back to Lula. She was scrolling through email and text messages.

"I'm heading out," I said.

"I'm going with you. Nothing happening here. No new FTAs."

I made sure the office phone was forwarded to my cell, Lula took the box of doughnuts, and we went out the front door and locked the office. I took a moment to look up and down the street for Ranger's man. I didn't see anyone loitering in doorways or hiding behind shrubbery. There was a panel van parked in front of a house across the street. It was a possibility.

I drove to Beedle's house and parked at the curb. No Sentra in the driveway. We went to the door and knocked, and Mrs. Beedle answered.

"Is Carpenter here?" I asked her.

"No," she said. "But I did hear from him. He said he was thinking he needed a change in scenery, and he would let me know when he settled somewhere."

"When did you talk to him?" I asked.

"This morning. He called about an hour ago and said he didn't want me to worry. And that he was fine. He's very resourceful."

I drove to the Trenton Transit Center and parked in a no-parking zone. Lula jumped out and looked around the bus stop area.

She returned to the car and said there was no sign of Beedle. I drove into the downtown area and came up empty after an hour of cruising.

"This is disturbing," Lula said. "I bonded that man out and this is the thanks. Vinnie's surety company isn't going to be happy about this."

No kidding. Vinnie could be out of business, and we could all be unemployed. Comic Book Benji was next on my list. He was the middleman. I didn't think he would have much to contribute but I was going to talk to him anyway.

I took Maymount to Chambers and cut across town to Benji's store. Lights were off and a sign in the window said it was closed.

"It should be open," Lula said. "This is regular business hours."

I hadn't been paying attention when Ranger drove to Benji's apartment, so I typed "Benji Crup" into an app on my phone and got his address. His apartment was on the second floor of a neglected three-floor row house. One of his roommates answered my knock.

"Yuh," he said.

I looked past him into the room. There were boxes of comic books stacked against the wall, a mattress on the floor, a sad couch that had a tan slipcover on it, a large flat-screen TV on the wall in front of the couch. That was as far as I could see.

"I'm looking for Benji," I said.

"Dude's not here."

"I went to the store and there's a Closed sign in the window."

"Dude's off on a wander."

"What's a wander?" Lula asked.

"It's when you wander," the roommate said.

"Like a drugged-out trip?"

"No, like a vacation."

"Do you know where he went?" I asked.

"Not exactly. He said something about buying a car, or maybe he was going to Hawaii. And he was gonna hang out with Aquaman. He's like total Justice League."

"When did he leave?"

"About an hour ago. What are you, preggers or something?"

"Looking to buy a comic," I said.

"Or an action figure," Lula said.

"We got comics here if you want to look through," he said. "Discount price."

"Some other time," I told him.

We went back to my Honda, and I pulled into traffic.

"He must do okay selling comics if he's going to Hawaii," Lula said.

I was getting a bad vibe. I thought it was a strange coincidence that Beedle and Benji both gave notice an hour ago that they were setting off on a wander.

"Where are we heading now?" Lula asked.

"We're visiting Melvin Sparks."

"Do you think he'll let you in?"

My fear wasn't that I wouldn't get in. My fear was that he wouldn't be home.

I parked in front of the Ivy, and we went to the fifth floor. No one answered at Sparks's apartment.

"Maybe he's sleeping," Lula said. "He works nights."

"Maybe he's off on a wander," I said.

"I got my equipment with me today," Lula said. "You want me to get us in?"

"Sure."

Lula took a screwdriver and a small hammer out of her massive purse and bumped the lock. We slipped into the apartment and closed the door behind us.

"Hello," I yelled. "Melvin Sparks?"

Nothing.

"Looks like he had company," Lula said from the kitchen. "There's three coffee mugs in the sink and three dishes with crumbs. And there's an empty Sara Lee coffee cake box on the counter."

I went to the wall of collection cabinets

where Ranger had found the coins. The coins were still there. Nothing seemed out of place. I went to the area Sparks used as an office. There was a monitor but no computer. No laptop.

My phone rang. It was the office number. No caller ID.

"Now what?" he said.

"This isn't easy," I told him. "I'm running down leads. I need more time."

"I had an unpleasant experience this morning. Someone shot at my drone when it flew past your office. You wouldn't know anything about that, would you?"

"This is Jersey. We shoot at everything."

"I'm losing patience," he said.

And he hung up.

"So, how'd that go?" Lula asked.

"Someone shot at his drone."

"Was it us?"

I shrugged. It could have been Ranger's man. Or it could have been Mr. Ruffles in the house across the street. He has anger issues.

"Here's what I think," I said to Lula. "I think Beedle, Benji, and Sparks have the coin."

"And they ran away with it, right? On account of it's valuable, and we're not talking sentimental valuable. Personally, I always thought that was a lot of bull pucky."

I called Ranger. "I heard from the kidnapper," I said. "He wasn't happy. Someone shot at his drone."

"I had Sanchez parked in a van across from your office. He said the drone was hovering in the middle of the street and an old bald guy ran out of his house and took a potshot at it."

"Did he down it?"

"No, but he put a round through the bonds office's front window. Vinnie should replace it with impact glass."

"That's Mr. Ruffles," I said. "Last month he shot at a bird and took out the satellite dish. Was Sanchez able to follow the drone?"

"No. And he didn't spot any foot or vehicle traffic that looked suspicious."

"Beedle, Comic Book Benji, and Sparks have disappeared. Beedle's mother said he needed a change in scenery. Benji's roommate said Benji's gone wandering. And I'm in Sparks's apartment right now. Lula bumped the lock. There's no Sparks. It looks like he had company this morning. Everything seems to be in place but there's no computer or laptop. Just the monitor."

"And?" Ranger asked.

"And I think they have the coin."

"Do you need help?"

"No. I've got it."

"Babe," Ranger said.

Lula and I did the best we could to secure Sparks's apartment. I drove to the office and parked at the curb behind a Trenton PD car. Vinnie was on the sidewalk talking to a uniform.

"Look at this," Vinnie said when he saw me. "Some asshole shot up my window."

"Good thing no one was in the office," I said.

"Who would do this?" Vinnie asked.

I shrugged. Lula shrugged.

"Last month someone took out the satellite dish," Vinnie said.

I shrugged. Lula shrugged.

"Someone's out to get me," Vinnie said.

"That would be everyone," Lula said.

Lula and I went into the office. Lula took the couch and checked her mail, and I went to Connie's desk and ran Beedle, Benji Crup, and Sparks through a bunch of search engines.

Beedle didn't show any surprises. He was a smart guy. Got a BA from Rutgers and a master's from Wharton. Worked as a CPA for a respectable firm until his divorce. His credit rating sucked. Lots of expenses while he was married. After the divorce there were crickets. Nothing. It was like he no longer existed. He had an apartment for a while but just recently moved in with his mother. He drives a rusted Nissan Sentra.

Benji Crup lasted through two years at the University of Pennsylvania and dropped out. Worked at GameStop for a year and transitioned to the comic book store. He was the only employee. He made minimum wage. He roomed with a bunch of guys and drove a 2009 Kawasaki Ninja 250.

Melvin Sparks had a high school education. He was in the drama club and the Dungeons & Dragons club. After high school he worked at a Camelot-themed restaurant as a waiter. He spent a year at Disney World as Goofy. After Disney he moved to LA and worked as a waiter at Olive Garden. The next year he landed in Trenton and got a job stacking shelves at a discount box store on the night shift. He didn't have a car.

I got phone numbers for all of them. No one answered at any of the numbers.

"You look like you got nothing," Lula said.

"It's interesting. They're all three very different people, but in a strange way they have a similar history. It's like they had early aspirations that didn't turn out and eventually they settled into a comfortable undemanding existence."

"That's not me," Lula said. "I always shoot for big stuff. Like I said before, I'm an overachiever who isn't discouraged by underachieving."

"One of your best qualities," I said.

"Fuckin' A. Where we taking this?"

"I don't know. I thought I'd check in with Grandma."

"I like that idea," Lula said. "There's an added advantage of getting lunch."

CHAPTER ELEVEN

"Just the person I want to see," Grandma said when I walked into the kitchen. "Are you going to the Mori viewing tonight? I could use a ride."

"Is it really necessary to go to a viewing tonight?" my mother said. "Can't you let things calm down a little after last night's scandal?"

"What scandal?" I asked.

My mother laid down two more place settings at the little table. "Everyone's talking about how you took Bella out in handcuffs."

"She insisted," I said. "And the funeral director begged me to remove her from the building."

"It's true," Grandma said. "I was there. I saw it all. Bella needs to have her head examined." She looked at Lula. "What about you? Are you going to the viewing tonight?"

"No way," Lula said. "Dead people give

me the creeps."

"Dead people are okay," Grandma said. "They always look their best at a viewing. It's a good way to remember them . . . all dressed up with their hair done. It's like they're big dolls that are still in their box. It's the live people that give me the creeps. What's new in your world?" Grandma asked me.

"The three men involved with Paul Mori's Knights Templar coin, Beedle, Benji Crup, and Melvin Sparks, have disappeared."

"Like snatched?"

"I don't think they've been snatched," I said. "I think they're hiding out somewhere. I ran them through some search engines but didn't turn up anything useful."

"I don't know any of them," Grandma said. "Do they have family in the area?"

"Beedle lives with his mom on Maymount," I said. "She hasn't been helpful. The other two have family scattered around the country. None of them are married."

"Maybe they'll show up at the viewing tonight," Grandma said.

I didn't think Beedle, Benji, or Sparks would show up at the viewing. I thought it was possible the kidnappers might be there. They really wanted the coin, and my efforts weren't getting results. They might be reaching the point of going proactive on their own. And Paul Mori was the last person they knew who had the coin before Vinnie lost it.

We had egg salad sandwiches for lunch, and Grandma brought out a plate of pignoli cookies for dessert. I cut my eyes to her, and she smiled at me. They were the cookies she'd swiped from the viewing. Bella's cookies.

"I met Shirley Weingarten at the bakery this morning," Grandma said. "She lives next door to Manny Tortolli, and she was in the backyard when the Tortolli garage caught fire. She said it wasn't kerosene in the can Bella was holding. It used to be a kerosene can, but Bella used it to get hooch from Tortolli. He had a still in his garage. Shirley said they had a big argument because Tortolli raised his price and Bella wasn't having any of it. Shirley said there was a lot of arm waving and yelling and there was a crash and that something got knocked over and next thing the garage was on fire."

"So, it wasn't arson?" I asked.

"Not exactly," Grandma said. "Nobody wants to say anything because they all get hooch from Tortolli. They figure nothing's going to happen to Bella on account of everyone knows she's a crazy old lady."

"She gets a lot of mileage out of being crazy," my mother said.

"Yeah," Grandma said. "I gotta admit, it works for her."

I pushed back in my chair and grabbed my messenger bag. "Things to do," I said.

"What kind of things?" Lula asked.

I took my plate and put it in the dishwasher. "Things!"

We got into my Honda and Lula buckled herself in. "What things are you talking about?"

"I don't know," I said. "There has to be something. I can't just sit around in my mom's kitchen while Connie is held hostage somewhere."

"Well, I haven't got any ideas. Do you have ideas?"

"No."

"Maybe if I went home and took a nap," Lula said. "To tell you the truth, I could hardly get that egg salad sandwich down, and that's saying something, because your mom makes kick-ass egg salad."

"I'm checking on Beedle, Benji, and Sparks again. I don't know what else to do."

"I hear you. I'll ride along. Maybe we could stop at the bakery and get some cannoli to settle my stomach. Those cookies Grandma put out didn't do it for me."

I drove to Hamilton and stopped at Tasty Pastry Bakery. Lula ran in and got a dozen cannoli and hopped back in the car.

"There were two women in there, and they were talking about the Mori viewing tonight. They were all excited to see if Bella was going to be there. I guess there's a rumor that she's on house arrest."

I hoped that was true because I really didn't want to have to handcuff her again. I swung by the Beedle house first. Still no Sentra in the driveway. I left Lula in the car with the cannoli, and I went to the door and knocked. Mrs. Beedle answered.

"Stephanie," she said, "I have good news! Carpenter stopped in about an hour ago. He looked wonderful. He was shaved and he was wearing nice clothes and he had a new car. He said things have really turned around for him."

"What kind of car?"

"A Mercedes," she said. "It was black, and it looked brand-new."

New clothes and an expensive car. That required a fast infusion of cash. Like selling something very valuable. Something like a Knights Templar coin. And not just any Knights Templar coin. One in particular.

What the heck was so special about that one coin?

"Wow, he must have won the lottery," I said to Mrs. Beedle, fishing for information.

"I didn't think about that," she said. "It sounded more like he was back in finance somehow. It was a short visit. He stopped in to pick up a few of his things."

"So, he's in the area. Did he say where he was staying?"

"No, not exactly, just that he had to get back on the road."

"That's great," I said. "I'm glad he's doing well. Next time you talk to him, remind him that he has a court date coming up. Even better, you could put me in touch with him and I'll make sure he gets to court."

"That would be wonderful," she said. "I'll give him the message."

"So, how'd that go?" Lula asked.

"I don't know. I can't tell if Carpenter's mom is naïve or devious. She said Carpenter stopped by to pick up a few things and he was driving a new Mercedes."

"He must have picked a good pocket," Lula said.

"You can't buy a new Mercedes with someone else's credit card. And it's difficult to believe someone was carrying that much cash."

"Drugs?" Lula said. "Maybe he's dealing."

"I don't see him dealing drugs. This has something to do with the coin."

"You got a feeling, right?" Lula said. "It's like when I get nipple radar if there's rabid rats or man-eating spiders coming at me. How are your nipples doing? Are they feeling all shriveled up and tingly?"

I looked down at myself. I didn't see any evidence of shrivel, so I continued driving to the comic book store. It was still closed. No new Mercedes in sight. I cut across town and parked in front of the Ivy. Lula had worked her way through half of the cannoli and felt like she could take a break, so she came up to the fifth floor with me. I knocked and there was no answer. The door wasn't locked since Lula had damaged the lock when she bumped it with her screwdriver on the earlier visit. I stepped inside and yelled for Sparks. No answer. We walked through the apartment, looking for signs that Sparks had returned. We didn't see any signs. I checked his closet and pawed through his costumes.

"Sir Lancelot is missing," I said to Lula.

"Say what?"

"It's his favorite costume. And it's missing."

"Maybe he wore it when he rode out of

town on his big white horse," Lula said. "Those guys always had big white horses."

"So far as I know, Sparks didn't even have a bicycle."

"Just as well," Lula said. "Sir Lancelot would look like an idiot on a bicycle."

I dropped Lula off at the bail bonds office, and I drove to my apartment. I said hello to Rex, gave him a cracker, and took a Diet Pepsi out of the fridge for myself. I went to my dining room table and opened my laptop. I wanted to know more about *Gowa* Knights Templar coins.

After a couple hours of searching, I knew that the game was created by a man named Randy Gowa. He'd owned a factory that produced a bunch of board games, but his big-ticket item was the Treasure of Gowa. He had two sons and a daughter. None of them wanted anything to do with running a factory. When Randy turned eighty, he sold the factory but kept the rights to the Treasure of Gowa game. He died a year later. None of my research showed that there was one special coin, and I couldn't find any evidence that a coin could bring more than $30 on today's market.

I had a peanut butter and banana sandwich for dinner, changed into my viewing clothes, and headed for my parents' house.

Morelli called. "Are you going to the viewing tonight?" he asked.

"Yes. I'm on my way to get Grandma. Are you going?"

"No. It's poker night at Mooch's house. Schmidt is going to the viewing. He's the primary on the Mori case. Bella is supposed to be confined to the house but that doesn't mean much with Bella. Give me a call if she shows up and I'll come get her."

"Are you having any luck finding Connie?"

"Nothing worth mentioning, but I wouldn't mind knowing about the signs in the bonds office window."

I'd known this was coming and I'd decided to partially confide in Morelli.

"Connie's been kidnapped and the kidnapper has been in touch with the office," I said. "We're working with him."

"Without police involvement?"

"I decided to go with Ranger."

Silence for a beat. "Good decision," Morelli said. "That would have been my choice. He has all the technology, and he can operate outside the law. Let me know if you change your mind and you need my help."

"I assume we never had this conversation."

"What conversation?" Morelli said. "I don't remember a conversation."

"Good luck with the poker game."

"Luck has nothing to do with it. By the end of the night, I'll be the only one who's halfway sober and I'll cash in. Works every time."

"And the other guys haven't figured this out?"

"I'm playing with Mooch, Anthony, Little Dick, Big Dick, and Bugsy. They're good guys, but collectively they couldn't figure out how to unscrew a lightbulb."

This was a real dilemma for me. I was withholding information on a murder. Schmidt was the primary on the Mori case and as far as I knew, he had no clue that the murder was attached to a mysterious coin and a kidnapping. It was one thing for Morelli to close his eyes to the kidnapping. It would be impossible for him to walk away from information on the Mori murder. So, I was hanging out alone because I didn't want to do anything to jeopardize Connie's rescue.

Grandma was standing at the curb waiting for me. That meant she'd slipped out of the house early, before my mom had a chance to confiscate her .45.

"This is going to be a good viewing," Grandma said, getting into the car. "I hear they filled in all the bullet holes and Mori looks real lifelike, considering he's dead. It's even an open casket. He didn't have a lot of relatives but supposedly a sister is here from Detroit."

This was way too much information for me. I was already counting the minutes to the end of the viewing. I dropped Grandma off and went in search of parking. All the on-street parking was already taken and there was one spot left in the lot. It was at the back and almost swallowed up by bushes, but I was happy to have it. This was going to be a monster viewing.

By the time I parked and made my way to the funeral home the doors were open, and the mourners had already rushed in. I assumed Grandma was in line to pass in front of the deceased. I had no desire to do this. I stayed in the lobby and scanned the crowd.

I saw Schmidt at parade rest on the other side of the room. Ranger and Tank were also there. They were all in casual black. Black jeans, black blazers, black collared shirts, black track shoes. Ranger looked like a bad-ass movie star. Tank looked like the Hulk in a blazer, minus the green.

We knew the drill. We'd all attended viewings and funerals before with the hope that the murderer would be drawn to the drama of the event. This was different because this time we didn't know what the murderer looked like beyond a shadowy figure in a hoodie.

I wandered around the room, looking for a stocky, middle-aged man who might have killed Mori. I found a lot of men who fit that description. Some were probably sorry they hadn't gotten to Mori first.

I went to Ranger and stood beside him for a moment. He was the only person in the room who smelled wonderful. Ella, his housekeeper, stocked his shower with Bulgari Green shower gel and the scent stayed with him like magic.

"You look bored," I said. "Would you like me to bring you a cookie?"

"Babe," Ranger said with enough of a sexual threat to have me moving along.

An hour into the viewing I caught sight of a black-frocked woman scuttling toward the cookie table. Bella. I instantly called Morelli.

"Are you kidding me?" he said. "She's really there?"

"Yep. She's making her way to the cookie table and she's going to be really pissed off again because Grandma already scarfed up all the pignoli."

"Your grandma is almost as evil as my grandma."

"True, but my grandma knows enough to get to the cookie table early."

"I'm on my way."

I hung back, not wanting to get involved. Mooch lived in the Burg so Morelli was about seven minutes away. Three minutes if he put the Kojak light on. Grandma had returned to the viewing room, so she wasn't in Bella's sights. Thank you, God.

After a couple minutes I saw Ranger cut his eyes to the front door and I knew Morelli was here. He walked straight to the cookie table and seconds later he was escorting Bella out of the funeral home. We all have our crosses to bear, and Morelli had a bunch of them. It was impressive that he'd been able to deal with it all and achieve a level of maturity that I hadn't been able to find for myself.

At nine o'clock there were the usual chimes and the announcement that visitation hours were over. The viewing had been sedate. No drunken brawls. No grieving hysteria. Mori's sister had been stoic. Most people left early with a sense of mild disappointment. Ranger and Tank disappeared just before the chimes. Schmidt stayed to the end. Grandma and I were among the last stragglers to leave the building. I saw that Ranger and Tank had positioned themselves across the street and were watching the cars that were exiting the lot.

The night air was cool, and the sky was dark and moonless. I used my cell phone flashlight to guide us to my Honda.

We were approaching my car when a stocky man stepped out of the shadows and blocked my way. He was wearing a hoodie and a surgical mask. There was a second man behind him, also in a hoodie and surgical mask. My heart gave a couple hard thumps in my chest, and I went breathless for a beat. The second man lunged at me with a stun gun, and I instinctively jumped away.

Grandma was quicker on the draw. "Son of a peach basket," Grandma said, and she fired off a shot at the man with the stun gun. She missed the man and took out my driver's-side window. She got off another round that whistled past my ear, and I hit the ground. The two men bolted out of the lot and disappeared into the night.

I felt my ear to make sure it was still there, and I looked up at Grandma. "Are you done shooting?"

"I guess so," she said. "Are you okay?"

I stood and dusted myself off. "You almost removed my ear."

"My gun got stuck in my pocketbook, so I just started shooting. It's hard to take aim when your gun's in your pocketbook." She turned her purse upside down and examined it. "I'm going to need a new bag," she said. "This one got all torn up."

Ranger ran over to us. "We heard gunshots," he said.

"Two guys jumped us," I said. "Grandma took a couple shots at them, and they ran away."

"Anyone injured?"

"Not that I could tell," I said, "but she took out my window."

"They were big brutes, and they were armed," Grandma said.

"I saw a stun gun, but I didn't see any weapons beyond that," I said.

"Well, I shot at them so they must have shot at me first," Grandma said.

It was very dark, but Ranger's teeth are very white, and I could see that he was smiling. "That sounds logical," Ranger said.

I nodded. "My mistake. Now that I think about it, I do remember seeing guns."

Tank joined us. "Everything okay?"

"What did these guys look like?" Ranger asked me.

"Average height. Stocky. Wearing dark hoodies and surgical masks. Caucasian. Couldn't see much more than that," I said. "It's dark and it went down fast. No one said anything."

"That's not true," Grandma said. "One of them said the word for poop when I started shooting."

"Caca?" Tank asked.

"No," Grandma said. "The S-word."

"Since when aren't you saying the S-word?" I asked Grandma.

"It's left over from Lent. God told me to keep going with it."

Tank looked impressed. "Did God really talk to you?"

"I'm pretty sure it was God," Grandma said. "It happened at Mass when I couldn't find my phone. I said you-know-what and this voice told me not to ever say that word again. It was either God or Morgan Freeman."

I thought it was unlikely that either of them would be talking to Grandma, but hell, I've been wrong before.

Tank opened the passenger-side door for Grandma, who settled herself and put her purse on her lap.

Ranger opened my car door and brushed chunks of window glass off my seat. "Do you want me to send someone over to fix this?"

"Thanks," I said, sliding behind the wheel. "I can handle it."

"Babe," Ranger said.

He closed the door and waited while I backed up and left the lot.

Grandma took another look at her purse. "We have to figure out what we're going to tell your mother. And I'm going to need a new black pocketbook."

"Take your phone but leave your bag and gun with me. I'll get you a replacement tomorrow. Are you going to a viewing tomorrow?"

"No," Grandma said. "Tomorrow I'm going to bingo. I like to mix it up a little. You don't want to go to a viewing every night. After a while the lilies get to me."

I dropped Grandma off and headed for home. I turned onto Hamilton and noticed I'd picked up a tail. I called Ranger.

"Are you following me?" I asked him.

"Yes," he said. "I want to make sure I'm the only one attacking you in your parking lot."

Fifteen minutes later I parked in my building's lot and Ranger parked next to me. He walked me to my door and unlocked it for me.

"No one attacked me," I said.

"Disappointed?"

"No. I've already been attacked once tonight. Once is already too much."

We stepped into my apartment and Ranger flipped the light switch. "Did you see enough of the two men tonight to recognize them as the kidnappers?"

"I saw enough to say that they *might* be the kidnappers. I'm struggling with the motive. Why would they come after me?"

"Intimidation. Interrogation. They're losing patience. They thought this would be easy and it's going south on them. There's something valuable about the coin. They might be worried that you've discovered the value and are trying to cash in."

"And sacrifice Connie?"

"We're dealing with men who kidnapped a woman and maybe murdered a man. It wouldn't be a stretch for them to think you'd sacrifice Connie." His phone buzzed and he answered it. He listened for a moment and nodded. "Where is he?" he asked. He nodded again and disconnected.

"Bad news?" I asked.

"One of my men has been injured. Not life-threatening but I have to check on him." He gave me a quick kiss. "I'd feel better if you didn't look so relieved to see me go."

"I'm not *entirely* relieved," I said.

I locked and bolted the door, went into my kitchen, and stared into Rex's cage. He was running on his wheel.

"I'm a mess," I said to Rex.

Rex stopped running for a beat and looked at me with his shiny black eyes. He twitched his whiskers and resumed running.

"Exactly," I said. "We have a lot in common. We keep running in place."

CHAPTER TWELVE

I had a frozen strawberry Pop-Tart for breakfast and told myself it was healthy because it was strawberry. Strawberry is a fruit, right? Check that food group off the list of today's requirements. I washed the Pop-Tart down with black coffee, said goodbye to Rex, and told him I loved him. I was extra vigilant leaving my apartment, keeping watch for chunky guys in hoodies. I felt more relaxed once I was in my car. True, my window was mostly missing, but at least the doors were locked. I drove to the office and parked at the curb.

"Hey, sunshine," Lula said when I walked in. "How'd the viewing go?"

"The viewing was uneventful, but after the viewing Grandma and I were attacked in the parking lot. Two guys in hoodies. One of them tried to stun gun me."

"Shut up!"

"Grandma took a shot at him and scared

them away."

"Did she hit him?"

"No, but she took out my driver's-side window."

"You want me to call the Glass Guy?"

"Yeah, thanks."

A half hour later the mobile glass repair truck parked behind my Honda, and the guy got out and stood staring at my window. Lula and I joined him.

"I'm guessing someone shot at you," he said.

"Occupational hazard," I told him. "Can you fix it?"

"Of course I can fix it," he said. "I'm the Glass Guy."

I got the new window put in and Grandma called.

"I think I'm onto something," she said.

Grandma was at the front door when I pulled into my parents' driveway. Lula and I followed her into the kitchen, where my mother was knitting.

"I see you got the mental health knitting thing going," Lula said to my mom. "Can't blame you what with the stress of life and all."

"It's too early to drink," my mom said. "I've got six hours and ten minutes to go."

"You could probably add about a quarter

mile to that scarf by then," Lula said. "You're going along at a good clip."

"What have you got for me?" I asked Grandma.

"It just occurred to me that one of the men you're looking for is Benji, the comic book guy, right?"

"Right."

"Maybe he's at GoComic."

"What's GoComic?"

"It's a big deal," Grandma said. "It's almost as big as ComicCon. It's at the convention center in Atlantic City this week. I was thinking of going with Carol Lumbardi, but she punked out on me."

"Are you a comic book fan?" Lula asked Grandma.

"No. I heard Jason Momoa is going to be there. I thought he might be worth seeing."

"He's hot," Lula said. "Not as hot as Ranger, but still pretty darn hot."

"Local news did a story on it this morning and I thought about Benji," Grandma said.

"Good thinking," Lula said. "When's this comic thingy start?"

"It's going on now," Grandma said. "Yesterday was the first day and it runs through the weekend."

"There will be hundreds, maybe thousands of people attending," I said. "What are the chances of finding Benji?"

"Here's Miss Rain-on-the-Parade," Lula said. "You gotta think positive. And if we can't find Benji, we might be able to find Jason Momoa." Lula looked over at my mom. "How about you, Mrs. P? Are you up for GoComic? We got room in the car."

"I'm going to stay home and knit, but thank you for asking," she said. "There's a crafts show coming up next month and I thought I might enter my scarf if I can get enough length."

"If it gets much bigger, you're gonna have to rent a truck to get it to the show," Lula said.

Atlantic City is a little less than an hour and a half from Trenton. Considering it's Jersey, it's a fairly pleasant ride. I took Hamilton Avenue to Route 129, drove south, and got onto I-295. The rest was a straight shot down 295 and the Atlantic City Expressway.

"I'm on the GoComic website," Lula said. "It looks like you gotta pay to get into this."

"I get a break because I'm a senior citizen," Grandma said.

"How much does it cost for us?" I asked Lula.

"It's fifty dollars. Good thing this is official business. I brought petty cash from the office, and I got a new credit card that I gave myself as temporary office manager."

"Do you see anything about Jason Momoa?" Grandma asked.

"There's an Aquaman panel discussion but it doesn't say who's on it."

Here's something promising, I thought. Benji's wasted roommate said Benji was going to hang out with Aquaman. I was about to get lucky.

"When is the Aquaman panel?" I asked Lula.

"Three o'clock."

"That makes things tight for us," Grandma said to me. "Your mother isn't going to be happy if we're late for dinner."

"You can't be thinking about dinner at a time when we're about to crack this case wide open," Lula said to Grandma. "One of our prime suspects could be in the audience for that Aquaman panel. Aquaman himself might even help us make an apprehension."

"I guess when you put it that way it would make sense to miss dinner," Grandma said.

"We want to *talk* to Benji, not apprehend him," I said. "He hasn't committed a crime. At least none that we know about."

■ ■ ■ ■

The Atlantic City Convention Center is a massive structure at the end of the Atlantic City Expressway. It isn't directly on the ocean but it isn't far away either. I parked in the center's garage, and we all hustled over to the main building.

"This is exciting," Grandma said. "I always wanted to go to one of these things. I've seen pictures of people who come dressed up like their favorite characters. If I'd known ahead, I would have dressed up like a Power Ranger. I got all the moves."

"I'd be Sexy Loki," Lula said. She looked at me. "Who would you want to be?"

"Iron Man."

"That's a serious superhero," Grandma said.

Lula bought our tickets and got a map and a schedule of events.

"This is bigger than I expected," Grandma said. "It's like you don't know where to go and there's people smashed in everywhere."

She was right about the people. They were packed in the cavernous building like sardines in a can. They were taking selfies, buying franchise junk, and rushing off to panel discussions and autograph sessions.

"I see Thor," Grandma said, "but I don't think he's the real one."

"Now that we're here, I want to get horns like Loki," Lula said.

"We're supposed to be looking for Benji," I said.

"Yeah, but I'm one of those multitaskers," Lula said. "I can shop with one eye and look out with the other. The map they gave us makes it easy to find the Loki stuff."

"I want a cape like Doctor Strange," Grandma said. "How much do you think one of them would cost?"

"It wouldn't cost anything," Lula said. "We got an expense account. We're on official business relating to Carpenter Beedle."

"You're a good office manager," Grandma said. "You know how to take charge."

"You bet your ass," Lula said. "And you notice I'm even willing to do fieldwork like going on this trip."

"According to the map, the Avengers section is next to the food court," Grandma said. "I wouldn't mind grabbing something for lunch."

We joined the tide of conventioneers moving toward food, swept along cheek by jowl with Darth Vader, Bart Simpson, some hobbits, and a bunch of lowly Muggles.

By three o'clock Grandma had a red cape,

and Lula was wearing Loki horns. We'd managed to get into the room that was hosting the Aquaman panel, and we were all on the lookout for Benji. I was in the very back of the room because I wanted to see everyone leaving. Grandma and Lula were in the second row. They wanted to see Aquaman. As it turned out it was an Aquaman stand-in, but they wanted to see him all the same.

After forty minutes of Aquaman lore I still hadn't caught sight of Benji. The event came to a close. We all applauded. Everyone stampeded to the door. And there he was. Benji. Wearing a T-shirt and jeans. No horns. No cape. Not carrying an Aquaman trident. Part of the horde trying to get to the next event. I stood on my seat and waved at Lula and Grandma, pointing to the door, mouthing, *Benji!*

Lula waved back and lowered her horns to get through the crush of people. I jumped off my seat and shoved my way to the door.

"So sorry," I said. "Excuse me. Emergency."

I made it out of the room, and I saw Benji turn toward the food court. There were a lot of people between us, and I was doing my best to weave my way through them. I lost visual on Benji and my fear was that he'd turned into one of the side aisles without my realizing it. The food court was just ahead. It was a wide-open space filled with tables and I would have a better shot at finding him there.

I finally broke out of the crowd and was able to scan the area. I saw Benji a good distance in front of me, making his way to an exit that led to more exhibits. There was a commotion going on behind me. Raised voices, a couple shrieks, and a woman yelled, "Crazy horned bitch."

Benji turned to see what was going on and spotted me. For a beat he froze, deer in headlights, and then he was off and running. I ran after him, dodging people carrying drinks and burgers, skirting tables. I reached the exit and heard more noise behind me. I took a quick glance back and cringed when I saw Lula on the floor with another woman. In an instant Lula was on her feet and running.

"I'm coming," Lula yelled. "I got your back."

Grandma was a short distance behind Lula. "Me too," she yelled. "Don't let the little bugger get away!"

I left the food court and lost Benji. He'd been swallowed up by the crowd. I stopped to catch my breath and Lula and Grandma caught up to me. Lula had what looked like a chocolate milkshake down the front of her and some French fries stuck in her cleavage.

"These people don't know enough to get out of the way," Lula said. "Anybody could see I was on the chase. There's a bunch of dumb people here."

"She might have gored someone," Grandma said. "We should watch the news tonight."

I hurried Grandma and Lula through the main hall, to the building's entrance. "We can hang here and watch the doors," I said. "Maybe we can catch him leaving."

"Is this the only way out?" Lula asked.

"I'm sure there are lots of other ways out," I said. "Vendors and employees would use other doors, but this is the one available to fans. You watch for Benji. I'm going to canvass hotels to see if he's staying around here."

I called my mom and told her we were still in Atlantic City and wouldn't be home for dinner. I called Morelli next. We have a standing date for Friday night. Usually, he eats dinner with me at my parents' house and then we spend the night together.

"I'm in Atlantic City," I said. "I'm going to miss dinner, but I'll see you later."

"That's the best part anyway," he said. "If

you're not here by eleven o'clock I'm going to start without you."

"I'll keep that in mind."

I tried the Sheraton first since it was the convention center hotel. No luck there. I tried some other budget hotels. Nothing. I sat down on a bench, looked at a map, and called some of the classics. Caesars, Showboat, Bally's, Tropicana, Harrah's. I tried Hard Rock last. No Benjamin Crup.

I left my bench and walked over to Lula and Grandma, standing watch a short distance away. "I've tried the most obvious hotels, and no one has Benji registered," I said.

"Maybe he's not using his real name," Grandma said.

"Yeah, or maybe he's with somebody," Lula said. "Maybe Sparks is here parading around like Sir Lancelot and the room is under his name. You said the Sir Lancelot costume was missing from his closet, right? We didn't see him but maybe that's on account of we weren't looking for him. Maybe the Sir Lancelot people were hanging out in a different part of the building."

I went back to my bench and started calling my way through the hotels asking for Sparks. Halfway through I stopped to think about the three men. If they were working together, who would most likely be in charge? Carpenter Beedle. He had the most education, and more important, he was an accountant before becoming a panhandler. He was a detail guy. I continued calling hotels but now I was asking for Beedle. I got a positive hit on the Hard Rock. Mental head slap. I should have gone to the Hard Rock first. It was the right fit for a guy who'd just reinvented himself with new clothes and an expensive car.

"They're staying at the Hard Rock," I said to Grandma and Lula.

"Good choice of hotel," Lula said. "What's the plan?"

"Benji ran when he saw me," I said. "He had no reason to do that. It's not as if he's one of Vinnie's skips. He ran because he didn't want to talk to me. I'm sure he knows we're onto him about the coin."

"He thinks we know something," Grandma said, "but what he *doesn't* know is that we really don't know anything. So we have the advantage."

"All true," I said.

"We gotta be sneaky about this," Lula said. "You can't go busting down the door at the Hard Rock. And ordinarily we could be pizza delivery people or offer our services as erectile engineers, but since Benji saw

Stephanie, they're going to be suspicious."

"I can legally apprehend Beedle," I said. "We can wait in the lobby and get him on the way to the elevators. It will be easier to catch him in the more confined space."

"I like that idea," Lula said. "It'll be comfy in the Hard Rock lobby. And the café is right there."

I drove out of the parking garage and got onto Virginia Avenue, and it took us straight to the Hard Rock. I parked in a nearby lot, and we marched into the hotel lobby. We stopped after a couple feet and looked around.

"I haven't been here in a while," Grandma said. "I'd forgotten how big it is."

I was having the same thought. The lobby was larger than I'd remembered, and at this time of the day there were a lot of people passing through. And a lot of them were from GoComic. They were carrying Go-Comic bags, and they were in various stages of GoComic dress. If Benji, Beedle, and Sparks came through the lobby as stormtroopers or Wookiees, I wouldn't recognize them.

"We'd be better off waiting for them in their room," Lula said. "We could easily miss them here."

"Two problems with that," I said. "We need to get their room number and we need to get into the room."

"I can get us into the room if you can get the number," Lula said. "I got to be real good at getting into men's hotel rooms when I was a ho."

I called Ranger and asked if he could hack into the hotel system to get Carpenter Beedle's room number. Ten minutes later I got a text with the number.

"You all wait here," Lula said. "I'll text you when I'm in and you come up and do the secret knock."

"What's the secret knock?" Grandma asked.

"Knock, knock, knock. And then you wait a beat and do another knock."

Grandma and I hung out in the lobby, scanning the crowd. She was still wearing her red cape, and oddly enough, it made us less conspicuous. We fit right in with the geeks and freaks and uberfans who were filing in after a long day at the convention center.

"This is just like being on another planet," Grandma said. "It's like in the *Star Wars* movies when Han Solo goes into a cantina and all the people have two heads or it looks like their faces got melted. Maybe we want to blow off finding Benji and go to the casino."

"That would be fun, but we're supposed to be rescuing Connie."

"I forgot about that for a minute."

Lula called and said she was in Beedle's room.

"It's a long elevator ride," she said, "but the view is good. When you get up here don't let anybody see you."

We took the south tower elevator to the thirty-eighth floor and Grandma gave the secret knock on Beedle's door. Lula opened the door and hurried us in. "I told one of the housekeeping ladies I was here with Sir Lancelot and when I stepped out to get some horns, I forgot to take my key."

"That worked?" Grandma asked.

"I can be real believable when I want to be," Lula said. "And then I gave her a generous tip from petty cash."

Beedle had taken one of the nicer suites. It had an ocean view, a small kitchen area with a dining table and six chairs, a separate bedroom, and a living room with a large flat-screen TV. There was a day pack that I thought belonged to Benji, a cheap, dented suitcase that I assigned to Sparks, and a small Tumi suitcase that I was guessing belonged to Beedle. A bunch of plastic bags from GoComic were stashed in a corner. I bolted the door, and we went to work searching for the coin.

"It's not here," Lula said. "Someone must have it on him. Or maybe they sold it."

"We need a plan," Grandma said. "What are we going to do when the three guys come back?"

"You two hide in the bedroom, and I'll hide behind the door," I said. "When they get inside, I'll slam the door shut and tell them we want some answers."

"What if they don't want to give us answers?"

"I guess we'll threaten them."

"With what? We had to leave our guns in the car."

"We'll threaten to expose them. We'll tell the kidnappers that Beedle, Benji, and Sparks have the coin. And we'll remind them that Paul Mori is dead."

"That's good," Grandma said. "That would scare me."

We heard men talking in the hall and I ran to the door and flattened myself against the wall. Grandma and Lula ran into the bedroom. The door opened. Sir Lancelot, Beedle, and Benji walked in, and I slammed the door shut behind them.

"What the heck?" Benji said. "How did

you get in here?"

"I have ways," I said.

Grandma and Lula came out of the bed-room.

"Damn right she got ways," Lula said. "We all got ways."

"What do you want?" Beedle asked. "I haven't skipped on my new court date."

"I want the coin," I told him.

"I gave it to Benji," Beedle said.

"I gave it to Sparks," Benji said.

"You had my six coins," Sparks said. "You had all of them."

"I want the seventh coin," I said.

Sparks fidgeted with his fake sword. "There's no seventh coin."

"Liar liar pants on fire," Lula said.

"Where did you get the money for the car and the clothes and this suite?" I asked Beedle.

"I got lucky panhandling."

"I thought you liked the simple life," I said to Beedle. "Remember how you were happy not having any encumbrances? What about all that?"

"I still don't have any encumbrances," he said. "I paid cash for the car and this suite. My life is still simple. It's just simple in an expanded universe of luxury."

"How about you?" I asked Benji. "Has

211

your universe of luxury expanded?"

"I got a cool bike," he said. "And I'm going to Hawaii to live in a yurt next to a waterfall."

"Do you got a bathroom in that yurt?" Lula asked. "I wouldn't want to live in a yurt without a bathroom."

I looked at Sir Lancelot.

"I bought a Saxon helmet yesterday," he said. "And I got a lap dance from a wench."

"This is all terrific," I said, "but I'm pretty sure this fun stuff has been bought with money you made off the Knights Templar coin. And here's the problem. There are some very bad guys who want that coin. They kidnapped our office manager and they're holding her for ransom. I'm ninety-nine percent sure that they killed Paul Mori. All this for the coin. So, what I'm going to do is tell them that you three guys have what they want. I'm taking myself out of it. You're on your own. You can deal with the kidnappers."

"And don't forget they're killers, too," Grandma said.

"For real?" Benji asked.

"Yes," I said.

Benji looked at Beedle. "This isn't good."

"I hadn't planned on this development," Beedle said.

212

"You've got an impulsive nature," Grandma said to him. "This is like when you decided to rob the armored truck."

"Not true," Beedle said. "I'm really very methodical. I think things through. I make decisions based on logical thought. The armored truck was a fluke. My sudden windfall is the result of my knowledge of finance. And I admit that luck played a part. I was in the right place at the right time. My stars were all in alignment."

"And now?" I asked. "How are your stars now?"

"They'd still be in alignment if you weren't such a meanie," Beedle said. "You're ruining our good time."

"Do you understand that there's a woman being held hostage somewhere?" I said. "That we have no idea what sort of condition she's in? That she's got to be terrified?"

"I didn't know that," Beedle said.

"Me either," Sparks said.

"Me either," Benji said.

"Does it make a difference?" I asked them.

"Sure," Beedle said. "You can have the coin, but we already spent the money."

Oh boy. "What money?" I asked him.

"When Melvin got the coin he examined it under magnification," Beedle said.

"It's standard procedure for us collectors,"

Sparks said. "It helps to determine the value of the coin. In this case there was a small visible smudge on the knight side. When I looked at it magnified, I could see that it was numbers and alphabet letters. I figured it meant something, so I asked Benji where he got the coin."

"And Benji came to me," Beedle said. "I knew right away that the letters and numbers were a cryptocurrency password. It took me a while to finagle my way into the right account but eventually I got in."

"And?" I asked.

"And there was money in the account. We figured it was finders keepers and that we'd divide it up between us."

"How much money?" I asked.

"When it got changed to dollars it came to eleven million," Beedle said.

"Damn," Lula said. "Losers weepers."

"It's stealing," I said.

"We didn't see it that way," Beedle said. "It's one of those chances you take with cryptocurrency. People lose their passwords all the time. Especially if it's an older account without backup systems. Once you lose your password the money is gone. You can't access it and it stays in the account forever. Not doing anybody any good. So, we figured the way everything progressed from me relieving Vinnie of what was assumed to be a nearly worthless coin, to it eventually going to a collector who was smart enough to examine it — it was like providence. Divine intervention. Like God wanted us to have the money. And we didn't see anybody getting hurt by it."

"Somebody lost eleven million dollars," I said. "You didn't see that as being painful?"

"It was an old account, started back when mostly criminals were using crypto," Beedle said. "Besides, we didn't see how it could get traced back to us, and we didn't know about the kidnapping."

"Makes sense to me," Grandma said. "I'd have kept the money."

"Me too," Lula said. "I'm not in favor of rewarding killers with good deeds."

"Okay, so where's the money now?" I asked Beedle. "How much is left?"

"Nothing's left. I cleaned out the account," Beedle said. "Usually, you have to remove your currency in relatively small increments, but I knew how to move it into other investments that I could trade and sell. Everything we took out of the account has been washed and dispersed."

Oh boy, again.

"That's a wonderful story," Grandma said. "It's like you got a second chance at having a life."

"Yeah," Lula said. "You were three losers and now you're rich. It's one of them life-affirming stories you hear about on the news. Makes me believe in the American dream all over again." She dabbed at her eye. "Gets me all choked up."

Beedle took the coin out of his pocket and gave it to me.

"I was carrying it for luck, but you can have it," he said. "Are you going to rat us out?"

"No," I said. "I can't see any good coming from that."

"Dilly dilly," Sir Lancelot said.

"Dilly dilly," we all repeated.

"You didn't sound like you had your heart in the *dilly dilly,*" Lula said to me when we were back in the lobby.

"I'm getting worn down," I said. "It's like I'm always taking one step forward and two steps backward. I finally have the coin but I'm not sure it's going to get Connie released. And even if she does get released, they're going to come after me when they realize their money is gone."

"You're in deep doody," Lula said. "I'm glad I'm not you."

■ ■ ■ ■

We had dinner at the Hard Rock Cafe and by the time we got home it was nine o'clock. I dropped Grandma off and called Morelli.

"Where are you?" I asked him.

"I'm in your apartment. Rex was lonely."

"I'll be there in ten minutes. Do you want me to pick anything up? Did you have dinner?"

"I already ate. My mom brought me meatballs in red sauce. I have enough for two weeks."

Morelli's mom is a good cook. It's a requirement for living in the Burg. Every woman in the Burg is a good cook. Except me. If I hadn't moved out of the Burg I would have been kicked out. I have a pot, a fry pan, and a glass casserole dish. I buy food magazines and I watch the food channel. I eat food all the time. That's as far as it goes.

I pulled into my parking lot and found a place close to the back door. I had Ranger's gun in my messenger bag. I didn't see anyone hanging out. I had Morelli in my apartment, and he'd hear me screaming unless he had the TV too loud. I left my car, hurried into the building, and took the stairs two at a time.

Morelli met me at my door.

"I was watching you from the window," he said. "You sat in your car for a while and then you ran into the building. The cop part of me is curious."

"Two men attempted to stun gun me after the viewing last night. Grandma fired off a couple shots and scared them away."

"Was this a random attack?"

"Might have been," I said, "but more likely it was the kidnappers getting impatient."

I hung my messenger bag on a hook in what served as a foyer and went into the kitchen. I said hello to Rex and looked in the fridge. Jackpot. Morelli'd brought me a six-pack of beer and saved me some of his mom's meatballs in sauce.

"If I'd known this was in my fridge I would have run faster," I said.

I got a fork and ate a meatball. No need to get fancy and heat it up and sprinkle it with grated cheese. A cold meatball is still a treasure. I forked a second meatball and brought it into the living room.

"Catch me up," Morelli said, sitting next to me.

"Do you want the short version or the long version?"

"The long version."

An hour later I was at the end of my story and Morelli was leaning forward, taking it all in.

"So that's why I was being careful in the parking lot just now," I said.

"They cleaned out the crypto account."

"Yup."

"And you have the coin?"

I pulled it out of my jeans pocket and handed it over to Morelli.

"I'm a cop," Morelli said. "I'm supposed to be the one with the dangerous job, but you keep one-upping me."

"You're just being modest. What about the women who beat you up on the bridge?"

"You're right. That was scary."

"So where do I go from here? Do you have any suggestions?"

"If it was me, I'd throw Benji, Beedle, and Sparks under the bus."

"I don't want to do that."

"They've probably broken at least a dozen laws."

"I know, but they aren't bad people and putting them in prison would ruin their lives."

"You're a bounty hunter. It's what you do."

"It feels different."

Morelli froze for a beat, no doubt trying to adjust to the logic of female reasoning.

"You're limiting your options," he said. "You can't bring the feds in without implicating Benji, Beedle, and Sparks."

"I'm not ready to bring the feds in anyway. Now that we know all this . . . what should I do?"

"Go proactive. Give them the coin and let them find out for themselves that they've been robbed. You were right in assuming they're going to come after you. Ranger will have to be ready to take them out."

"How do you feel about that?"

"I hate it."

"Yeah, me too," I said. "You have any other ideas?"

"Aside from putting you on a plane to Costa Rica, no."

I was relieved that I'd spewed out the big secret to Morelli. A nice warm glow swirled through my stomach.

"How about ideas not related to Benji, Beedle, and Sparks," I said to Morelli. "You have any ideas on other subjects?"

Morelli grinned. "I have lots of ideas." He slid his hand under my T-shirt. "I've waited all week to demonstrate my ideas."

"New stuff?"

"Some new stuff and some old favorites."

"And you're going to cram all this into one night?"

"I have a plan."

You gotta love a man with a plan.

CHAPTER THIRTEEN

Morelli finished up the last part of his plan at the crack of dawn. He told me he loved me, gave me one last kiss, and rolled out of my bed.

I was disoriented from lack of sleep and the final fireworks display. "Are you going to work?" I asked him. "What day is it? Isn't it Saturday?"

"I'm not working today," he said. "I have to get home to Bob. He's used to going out first thing in the morning. I should have brought him with me, but I wasn't thinking ahead. Come home with me and I'll make you breakfast."

"I'm not up for breakfast yet. Aren't you tired?"

"No, but I'm a little sore. I think I pulled a muscle on one of my new ideas."

No kidding. I had a pretty good idea which muscle.

An hour later I was still awake. I had a lot

on my mind. Kidnapping, torture, death, Costa Rica. I dragged myself out of bed, took a shower, and called Ranger.

"I have the coin," I said, "but there's a problem. We need to talk."

"Babe," Ranger said.

I took that to mean *anytime,* so I grabbed my messenger bag and drove to Rangeman. I got a breakfast sandwich and coffee from the fifth-floor dining area and took it to Ranger's office.

"Do you want the long version or the short version?" I asked him.

"I want the bottom line."

"I have the coin to trade for Connie, but the kidnappers aren't going to be happy with it and will probably want to torture and maybe kill me."

"Give me the long version," Ranger said.

"So here are the choices," I said at the end of the long version. "I can give up Benji, Beedle, and Sparks to the FBI. The FBI come up with a plan and if it works, we get Connie back and the bad guys will go to jail. There's also the chance that Benji, Beedle, and Sparks will go to jail. Second choice is that we swap the coin for Connie and when the bad guys realize they've been robbed, I give them Benji, Beedle, and Sparks. This would be ugly for Benji,

Beedle, and Sparks. Third choice is I give the bad guys the coin, they give us Connie, and when they discover they've been robbed they come after me."

"And you chose door number three," Ranger said.

"Yes."

"I would have to eliminate the bad guys."

"Yes. Would that damage your karma?"

"Probably, but I've been storing karma credits."

"So, it's not a problem."

"No, it's not a problem. Put the sign in the window."

The office was dark when I parked at the curb. Lula usually showed up halfway through the morning on Saturday. Vinnie showed up never. I unlocked the door, switched the lights on, and made coffee. I didn't want to drink it. I wanted to smell it. It humanized the office. It made things feel a little more normal.

I got the I HAVE IT sign from the storeroom and taped it on the window. I texted Lula and told her to bring doughnuts. Doughnuts made everything better. I sat in Connie's chair and opened her computer. I waded through the junk mail, the invoices, and the threatening letters to Vinnie. There were two new FTAs. Grand theft auto and armed robbery. Both carried a high bail bond. Ordinarily I'd have been all about them, but right now I just wanted a doughnut. Actually, I wanted a miracle. I wanted Connie to walk in and tell me that the kidnappers had decided the coin wasn't worth the effort and they were getting on with their lives.

I printed the information on the two FTAs and shoved the papers into my messenger bag. I looked out the front window and saw Lula park the red Firebird behind my Honda. Seconds later she swung into the office and set the box of doughnuts on Connie's desk.

"You're early," I said. "You usually sleep in on Saturday."

"I couldn't sleep. I kept wondering if you put the sign in the window. And then when you texted about the doughnuts, I figured you were sitting here cracking your knuckles, waiting to get the phone call."

I looked in the box. "You got an assortment. What happened to all the Boston creams?"

"I felt like we needed some color today. I got a pink glazed, one with rainbow sprinkles, a butterscotch, a couple chocolate, and some with powdered sugar."

I chose the butterscotch. "I imagine Ranger is doing surveillance," I said to Lula. "Did you notice any vans when you parked?"

"No, but I wasn't looking for any either. I was keeping my eyes open for a drone."

"They might not be using a drone after the shooting incident," I said.

"Did you do the emails?" Lula asked.

"Yes. There was grand theft auto. Some guy borrowed a fire truck and drove it into Garden of Life Flowers on Comstock Street."

"Good one," Lula said.

"And an armed robbery."

"Anybody we know?"

"Sylvester Brown. Held up a convenience store on Stark Street."

Lula took another doughnut. "This is boring, sitting here waiting for some fool to call. It's going on six days. It goes on this long and there's things that come into consideration. Like, who's doing Connie's laundry? And what happens if it's her time of the month? Some kidnapper's gonna have to go out and get tampons and Midol."

I looked around the office, wondering if Ranger was listening in and cracking up. You never knew where he had equipment.

The call came in at eleven o'clock.

"Talk to me," the man said.

"What do you want to hear?" I asked him.

"I want to hear that you have the right coin."

"I have the right coin. It has a small notch in the edge."

"Text me a photo," he said.

He gave me a cell number and hung up.

I took a photo of both sides of the coin and sent it to him.

I'll call back with instructions, he texted back.

"Smart," Lula said. "He never stays on long enough to get traced."

My phone rang again, and it was a different voice. "You'll find her in the cemetery on Third Street. She'll be at the gate."

"What about the coin?"

The connection was broken. They didn't want the coin. They'd gotten the number off the photo.

I grabbed my messenger bag. "Let's go. She's at the cemetery gate on Third."

My phone buzzed with a text message from Ranger. *Got your back.*

The cemetery was ten minutes away. After three minutes on the road, I got another text from Ranger. *We have her sighted. Holding back for you to pick up. We can move in if necessary.*

Tears were rolling down my face and my nose was running.

"Are you okay to drive?" Lula asked.

I wiped my nose on the sleeve of my sweatshirt. "Yeah, I'm fine. Just relieved." I checked my rearview mirror. I was being followed by a shiny black SUV. "Is that a Rangeman car behind us?" I asked Lula. "Or is it the bad guys?"

Lula turned and looked. "It's Rangeman. Tank's driving."

I made an effort to relax my grip on the wheel. I took a couple deep breaths. I turned onto Third and I saw Connie at the cemetery gate. She was holding on, leaning into it. She was disheveled and looked disoriented. I stopped at the gate, bolted out of the car, and ran to her with my heart beating in my throat. Lula was right behind me.

I wrapped an arm around Connie and hugged her close to me. "Are you okay?"

"I don't know," she said. "I can't think."

My emotions ranged from knee-buckling relief that I had my arm around Connie to blind rage that someone had done this to her.

I moved her forward, toward the car. "We need to get out of here."

I didn't know if the kidnappers were still

in the area, and I didn't know how much time I had before they accessed their crypto account and realized their money was gone. Ranger was running security for us, and I had total confidence in him. Still, I didn't want to waste time putting distance between us and the pickup point. And I wanted to get Connie medical help.

I maneuvered her into the backseat, and Lula slid in next to her.

I got behind the wheel and headed for St. Francis Medical Center. I was driving fast and sneaking through red lights when possible. Lula was pressed against Connie like a big mama hen with a chick, talking to her, telling her it was okay now, she was safe.

I was monitoring Connie's response to Lula, and I could hear that she was coming around. By the time I pulled into the emergency room driveway, Connie was fully coherent. I got out and ran around to help her out of the car.

Connie waved me away. "The drug's wearing off," she said. "I don't need the hospital. I need coffee."

"Are you sure?" I asked her. "It wouldn't hurt to get checked out."

"No. I'm feeling much better. I don't want to get poked and prodded in the ER. I want a shower and some clean clothes and a decent cup of coffee with real half-and-half. Just take me home."

"Taking her home might not be a good idea," Lula said. "Her mother's gonna freak out when she sees her like this."

I was thinking the same thing. Plus, I wanted to talk to her. I could take her to my apartment, but I didn't have real half-and-half. I could take her to Rangeman, but it might be an uncomfortable environment after being held captive. That left my parents' house.

I parked in their driveway, and our Rangeman escort parked down the street. Lula and I walked Connie across the small front yard and into the house. The living room was empty because my father spent Saturday morning playing bocci ball with his lodge buddies. Grandma was at the dining room table with her computer. She looked up when we entered the room and instantly stood with her hand over her heart.

"Omigod," Grandma said. "Omigod, omigod!"

My mother came in from the kitchen and had the same reaction.

"Omigod," my mother said, and she instantly took over. "Come sit in the kitchen," she said to Connie, taking her by the hand, leading her to the little table. "What can I get you?" she asked Connie. "Tea?"

"Coffee," Connie said.

"Have you eaten? It's almost lunchtime. Would you like a sandwich? Some soup? Entenmann's coffee cake?"

In minutes Connie had fresh-brewed coffee laced with half-and-half and Jack Daniel's. The table was filled with bakery bread, deli meat and cheese, mugs of minestrone soup, pickles, chips, and a whole Entenmann's cherry cheese Danish. Connie was wrapped in one of my mom's robes and her clothes were in the washer.

I called Connie's mom and told her Connie was okay and with me and she'd be home soon. Connie got on the phone and gave the same message to her mom.

"What did your mom say when she heard your voice?" Grandma asked Connie.

"She yelled at me for giving her a fright," Connie said. "And then she said we're having ricotta shells for dinner."

"We haven't had ricotta shells for an age," my mom said. "I'll have to put them on the menu next week."

We all sat around the table with Connie. She drank half a cup of coffee and ate two slices of the cheese Danish before taking a mug of soup. No one else ate anything. We were too intent on watching Connie, looking for signs that she might need help, thankful that she was at the table with us.

"What can you tell me?" I asked Connie when she finished the soup.

"It was bad," Connie said. "I was stun gunned and drugged. When I came around, I was in a small dark room. There was a cot with a single blanket and a chemical toilet. No window. One door that was locked. They took my watch and my purse, so I had no way to tell time. I tried to keep track of the days by counting the meals. Three times a day I'd get a bag of fast food and a soda."

"Could you see their faces?"

"No. They were always masked. After the first day they never talked to me. Toward the end I could tell they were angry. Sometimes I'd hear them shouting, but it was muffled, and I couldn't tell what they were saying. Honestly, I was afraid they'd kill me or maybe abandon me to die from starvation."

"Just terrible," Grandma said. "Did they do anything to hurt you?"

"Only the first day, and it could have been worse. They burned my arm with one of those click-and-flame things you use to light candles." She pulled the bathrobe sleeve up to show us the scars. Four spots on her arm about the size of a dime.

"We should put something on them," my mother said. "I'll give you some ointment."

"They were trying to get me to talk," Connie said, "but I didn't know anything. After that they left me alone."

"Do you have any idea where they kept you captive?"

"No clue," Connie said. "I was stun gunned from behind when I was opening the back door to the office. They dragged me inside, and when I was able to talk, they quizzed me about the coin. I'd never seen the coin so I couldn't tell them anything. They found the fire starter in the junk drawer. That was the first time they burned me, but I couldn't tell them anything. They searched the storeroom and the office and when they couldn't find the coin, they decided to take me as a hostage. I was stun gunned again, handcuffed, and they wrapped a towel around my head and duct-taped it. I could barely breathe. I know I was in a car. The ride was smooth, but I don't know anything beyond that."

"Was it a long ride?"

"Maybe a half hour but I wasn't thinking clearly."

"And what about when they dropped you off at the cemetery?" I asked her.

"I was stun gunned and drugged. I don't

remember anything from the ride. I was really out of it when I started to come around. I thought I was dead."

"That makes sense since you were in a cemetery," Lula said.

"We need to come up with a good story before we take you home," Grandma said to Connie. "Your mom is going to tell Mabel Shigatelli right off. And Mabel is going to tell Jean Frick and in an hour everyone in the Burg is going to know."

"Is that a problem?" Connie asked.

"I didn't go to the police," I told her. "I went to Ranger for help. There were complications with the coin."

"I was wondering why it was taking so long," Connie said.

"It's a long story," I said. "Do you want to hear it now?"

"Freakin' A," she said. "I want to know every detail. And then I want to track them down and kick their ugly asses all the way to hell."

We all relaxed in our chairs and smiled. I was smiling so wide my cheeks hurt. Connie was back.

I took Connie home, and Lula and I went to the office. We walked in and my phone rang.

"Where's the money?" he said.

I got a chill and had to take a beat to steady my voice. I'd anticipated this call and I'd decided to play it dumb and straight.

"You must have the wrong number," I said.

"I have the right number. I want the money. Where is it?"

"Are you talking about the coin? You didn't want it. If you changed your mind, I can leave it at the cemetery gate."

"We're coming for you, and you better have the money ready to turn over to us. Is that clear?"

"Yes, but —" I looked over at Lula. "He hung up."

"Rude," Lula said. "No manners."

I called Morelli and told him Connie was back home.

"And?" Morelli said.

"And the kidnappers are unhappy with me."

"How unhappy?"

"Very unhappy. They want their money. The money I don't have."

"Are you reconsidering Costa Rica?"

"No, but I'm considering putting bullets in my gun."

"That's serious."

"I suppose it is, but right now I'm just

happy Connie is in one piece and has all her fingernails. I feel like celebrating."

"I'm good at celebrating," Morelli said. "Do you have plans for tonight?"

"I don't know. Do you have any ideas that didn't get road tested last night?"

"No. Tonight will have to be oldies-but-goodies night."

"Works for me. Your place at six o'clock. I'll bring pizza."

I hung up and wondered if Ranger was listening in. Probably not. He had software that looked for certain numbers and blocked others. He was picking up calls that had been transferred to my phone from the office number.

"Now what?" Lula asked. "Are you going home to rest up for tonight?"

"No. I need an activity to get my mind off Connie and her burn scars."

"And we should be thinking about how we're gonna keep you safe," Lula said.

"I'm going to be careful," I said.

"Maybe you should lay low for a while. Make it hard for the bad guys to find you."

"You can't win a war by hiding in the castle," I said.

"Wow, that's profound," Lula said. "Who said that? Yoda? Galadriel? Tom Cruise? I bet it was Thor!"

"I think I read it in a fortune cookie. Who are we going to find today?"

"We could go after the moron who stole the fire truck. That could be fun."

I pulled his file out of my messenger bag. "Steven Plover. Caucasian. Twenty years old. Student. Lives with his parents."

"I hate to lock a kid up over the weekend," Lula said. "What about the armed robbery guy?"

"Sylvester Brown. Lots of tattoos and piercings. Nasty-looking dreads. Lives on Sally Street."

"He wouldn't be expecting us on a Saturday afternoon," Lula said. "Probably sitting around in his shorts and wifebeater shirt getting high and drinking warm beer out of a plastic glass."

"Did you get that from the course you took on criminal profiling?"

"No. I just know a lot of guys who do that every Saturday," Lula said.

We locked the office and looked across the street at a faded gray Ford Escort.

"Ranger's version of plainclothes stealth surveillance," I said.

"They going to follow you around?"

"Probably."

"It's kind of comforting being that you got a big target on your back now."

I didn't want to think about the target. I glanced at our cars. "Do you want to drive?"

"Hell no. I'm not putting some smelly beer-drinking idiot in my Firebird. I just had it detailed."

I never had my car detailed and I needed the money from the capture, so driving was okay with me. Lula was on salary, but I only made money when I delivered an FTA.

"Sally Street is a couple blocks away from Stark Street," Lula said. "It's not as bad as Stark Street, but it's not Rodeo Drive, either. There's a bunch of little bungalows in not such good condition all packed in together. One of my friends from a previous life used to live there. It was okay during the day, but it could get dicey at night."

"Where is she now?"

"I don't know. She just disappeared and never came back. Somebody said they saw her get on a bus to Tucson."

I drove through the city center and took Grove Street to Sally Street. Brown's house was on the third block. It was a tiny bungalow with stucco siding and a shingle roof. Small hardscrabble front yard. No sidewalk. A driveway but no garage. A backyard that was enclosed with chain-link fence.

"Probably got a big dog in the backyard," Lula said. "There's always a big dog with these houses. And bars on the windows."

"What do we know about Mr. Brown?" I asked Lula.

"It says here on his bond application that he's in the music business. He's twenty-eight years old. Has some priors for petty theft. Did a couple months on destruction of personal property. No details on that. Looks like his girlfriend turned him in on the armed robbery charge."

I parked and unbuckled my seat belt. "Let's do it."

I got out, nodded to the Rangeman guy who was parked two houses down, and walked to the front door. Lula was standing beside me.

"There's no doorbell," she said. "We'll have to do it the old-fashioned way."

Bang, bang, bang. Lula hammered on the door.

A scrawny guy opened the door and looked out at us.

"Sylvester Brown?" I asked.

"Yeah, that's me," he said.

I introduced myself and told him we were there to help him reschedule his court date.

"Hah," he said. "That's a good one." He looked over his shoulder and yelled, "Francine, come here. You gotta see this."

Francine shuffled over and squinted at us.

"So what?" she said.

"These two chicks came to haul my ass back to jail. Someone sent two chicks out to take down big, bad old me."

Brown was about Lula's height, but she easily had fifty pounds on him. Plus, Lula was wearing FMPs that added five inches to her height.

"You don't look so big to me," Lula said.

Brown leaned in a little. "Big enough to kick your fat ass."

"Excuse me?" Lula said. "Did you just do a derogatory comment on my ass?"

"It's fat," he said.

"Well, you haven't got no ass at all," Lula said. "You're a stick with a little dick."

"You want to see my dick?" he said. "I got a dick that could choke a horse."

I couldn't believe this was happening. This was turning into a dumpster fire. "No!" I said. "We don't want to see your dick. I'm sure it's perfectly frightening."

"What then? How about my ass? You want to see my ass?" he said.

"I don't want to see that either," I said. "I just want to take you downtown so you can reschedule your court date."

"It's Saturday, bitch," he said. "I won't get rescheduled until Monday."

"Yeah, but they give you a double cheeseburger and fries for lunch and dinner," Lula said. "And you get one of them greasy breakfast sandwiches for breakfast."

"I'm a vegan," he said. "I don't eat that shit."

"Get the heck out," Lula said. "Everybody knows vegans don't do armed robbery. You're a fibber."

I had cuffs tucked into the back of my jeans. I grabbed them and got one on Brown's wrist, but he jumped away before I could get the second one on him.

"Francine," he said, "get my gun and shoot them."

"Hold on," Lula said. "We got guns, too. I got one in my purse. Stephanie, show them your gun while I try to find mine."

"This is ridiculous," I said. "Nobody is doing any shooting. I just want —"

"Screw this," Brown said, and he bolted out the door.

"I got him," Lula yelled, taking off after Brown. "I'm on it."

I ran out the door after her. Brown was running barefoot, and Lula was running flat-out in her heels and a skintight red spandex dress that barely covered her hooha. I was close behind Lula. She took a flying leap and tackled Brown, taking him to the ground. Brown gave a shrill whistle and I turned to see a huge German shepherd clear the chain-link fence, cross the driveway, and go after Lula. He clamped on to the hem of her dress and tore half the skirt off.

"What the bejeezus," Lula said, rolling off Brown and scrambling to her feet. "Bad dog!" she yelled at the shepherd. "Do you see what you did? This here's one of my favorite outfits. Who's gonna pay for this? Do you think this idiot laying on the ground is gonna pay for it? He'd have to rob another store."

The dog was holding its ground and growling.

"And that's another thing," Lula said. "You want to stop the growling. You need to sit there and be quiet while we sort this out. *Sit!*"

"Crazy fat bitch," Brown said. "I sprained my ankle. Maybe I broke it."

I got the other cuff on Brown and Francine joined us.

"Good tackle," she said to Lula. "I like your red thong."

Lula had a cheek exposed and the dog still had the chunk of dress in his teeth.

"I'll take Sweetie Pie back to the house," Francine said. "Sorry about your dress."

"Sweetie Pie?" Lula said.

Francine bent over and made a smooshie face at Sweetie Pie. "He's Mommy's dumpy lumpkin."

We helped Brown hobble to my car, and we stuffed him into the backseat. The gray Rangeman car was idling behind me. The driver gave me a smile and a thumbs-up, and the guy next to him looked like he was about to explode from trying not to laugh.

It was a short ride to the police station. I turned Brown over to the cop at the desk, got my receipt, and took Lula back to the office so she could get her car.

"I'll see you Monday," Lula said. "Or sooner if you need me."

I wasn't planning on needing anyone. Okay, maybe Morelli. I was going to head home and take a shower. At six o'clock I'd bring a couple pizzas to Morelli's house, and I'd spend the weekend there. If the weather was nice, I'd talk him into going to the shore. With any luck the kidnappers would realize the money was a lost cause and get on with their lives.

CHAPTER FOURTEEN

It was Monday morning, and I woke up in Morelli's bed thinking life was good. It had been days since anyone tried to stun gun me. Connie was back home. And so far, none of Bella's threats about boils and incontinence had come true. Morelli had left for work a couple hours ago, but his big goofy dog Bob had taken Morelli's place next to me.

"This is going to be a perfect day," I said to Bob. "It feels like all my stars are finally in alignment."

I didn't want to say it out loud to Bob, but I was having serious thoughts about Morelli. It had been a really good weekend. Comfortably intimate. Pleasantly relaxing. Especially nice not to have a lot of drama after the chaos of last week. I thought I would like to have more weekends like this. Maybe I wanted it full-time. Maybe I wanted to get married.

"That's sort of a scary thought," I said to Bob. "What do you think?"

Bob didn't look like he thought much about marriage. Bob was chill this morning. If Bob thought about anything it would be breakfast.

Connie was at her desk when I got to the office. The box of doughnuts was on the desk, and the office smelled like fresh brewed coffee. Never underestimate the joy of normal, I thought. And never take normal for granted.

A single Boston cream was still in the box, but I was in a magnanimous mood, so I left it for Lula. An hour later, Lula bustled in.

"I wanted to get here early but I over-slept," Lula said. "Did I miss anything? What's going on?"

"Nothing's going on," I said.

"I didn't see the Rangeman car out front," Lula said.

"It was a quiet weekend, so Ranger switched to electronic surveillance."

Morelli called. "I have a problem," he said. "Bella is supposed to be confined to the house, but a neighbor called and said Bella just got picked up by an airport limo service. I called the service and Bella told them she was going to Italy."

"Can she do that?"

"Maybe. She has a credit card. I don't know about a passport."

"Didn't your mom stop her?"

"My mom isn't home. She's at the hospital with my Aunt Bitsy."

"What's wrong with Bitsy?"

"I don't know. There's always something wrong with Bitsy. I can't keep up with it. My sister-in-law was supposed to be keeping an eye on Bella, but I can't reach her. She's not picking up when I call her."

"Which sister-in-law?"

"Marylou."

I was getting a queasy feeling in my stomach. "Why are you calling me?"

"I was hoping you'd go to the airport and get Bella."

"No. No, no, no, no."

"I can't go. I'm in the middle of a double murder."

"What about Anthony?"

"I've called everybody I know. Every relative. No one will go," Morelli said.

"Why don't you just let her go to Italy?"

"Yeah, that would be tempting, but I don't think we have any relatives left in Italy, and I'd be the one who would have to go find her and bring her back."

"Why don't you tell the car company to

turn around and drive her home?"

"They've already dropped her off at Newark."

"She's going to make a scene. She's not going to want to come home with me."

"Yes, but you have a legitimate reason for wrangling her out of the airport. You have a bail bond agreement and she's a flight risk."

So much for the perfect day. "Text me the flight information. I assume you know where she is in the airport."

"I don't know exactly. I think she might be flying American."

I hung up and grabbed my messenger bag. "Come on," I said to Lula. "We're going to Newark airport."

"I was only hearing half of that conversation," Lula said, "but it didn't sound good."

"Bella is at the airport, and we're going to get her and bring her home."

"There's no *we.* I'm not doing that. She'll put the eye on me, and my hair will all fall out. I don't want that to happen. I like my hair."

Her hair was currently pulled back into a massive puffball of pink frizz.

"There's no such thing as the eye," I told her.

"Are you sure?"

"Mostly," I said. "Anyway, I'm going. You

don't have to go with me. I totally understand."

"Well, I can't let you go by yourself," Lula said. "Especially after you left me the Boston cream. Not many people would do a thing like that."

I took I-95 to the Jersey Turnpike and didn't hit traffic until the exit to the airport. That was disappointing. If I'd hit traffic sooner Bella might already have boarded by the time I got to the gate.

I parked and Lula and I walked into Departures. There was a line of people in front of the American ticketing counter, and a clump of uniformed police and airline employees at the desk.

"The nightmare has begun," I said to Lula.

"It don't look good," she said. "That's a Bella cluster if I ever saw one."

I waded into the uniforms and came in behind Bella.

"You know nothing," Bella said to one of the cops. "If you don't watch your step, I fix you good."

"What's the problem?" I asked the ticket agent.

Bella turned and narrowed her already narrow eyes at me. "Slut! What you doing here."

"Your grandson sent me to bring you home."

"I'm not going home. I'm going to Italy."

"She doesn't have a passport," the ticket agent said to me.

"I don't need passport," Bella said. "I'm old lady. I'm American citizen. We go where we want. I have credit card and money. Money talks, eh?"

"Let's go home and look for your passport," I said to Bella. "You can come back tomorrow."

"You big liar," Bella said. "God will strike you down."

"Hey," Lula said. "You can't talk to Stephanie like that."

"That's it for you," Bella said to Lula. "I'm giving you the eye."

"For Pete's sake," I said to Bella. "That's enough with the eye."

"I give you one too," Bella said.

"Okay," I said, "how about if I put you in handcuffs."

Bella held her arms out. "Look at this. This is how sick old ladies are treated. Handcuffed. Somebody take a picture."

"You can't handcuff her," one of the cops said.

I pulled Bella's papers out of my messenger bag. "I can handcuff her and forcibly remove her. She has an active bail bond and she's obviously a flight risk."

"Thank goodness," the desk clerk said.

One of the cops scanned the papers and looked over at me. "Are you Stephanie Plum?"

"Yes," I said.

He looked at the two cops behind him. "It's Stephanie Plum!" he said.

Everyone was smiling.

"You're the one who burned the funeral home down," he said. "And last year you jumped out of the window of that hooker hotel. I saw your picture in the paper."

I put the cuffs on Bella. "The funeral home wasn't my fault," I said. "It was an accident. And only part of it burned down."

"Can I get a selfie?" the cop asked.

"Sure," I said.

Everyone crowded in, several pictures were taken, and Lula and I escorted Bella out of the building.

"I don't want to go to Italy anyway," Bella said when we got to the car. "Everybody is dead there. Italy isn't what it used to be."

I got Bella secured in the backseat and I texted Morelli that I was bringing her home.

"You!" Bella said. "The fat one. Why your hair is big bushy pink."

"First off, I'm not fat," Lula said. "I've

got an abundance of voluptuousness."

"You look fat to me," Bella said. "What about the hair?"

"I regard hair as a fashion accessory. I think hair should be fun."

"So, you make it pink? I think you don't know how to have fun."

"How do you have fun?" Lula asked her.

"I drink and I smoke. I like weed," Bella said.

"Fuckin' A," Lula said.

"You got dirty mouth," Bella said. "I give you the eye."

"I think giving people the eye is how you have fun," Lula said.

"It my job," Bella said.

I parked in the Morelli driveway and got Bella out of the car. I took the cuffs off her and walked her to the door.

"This is good," Bella said. "Go away."

I tried the door. Not locked. A red RAV4 was parked at the curb. Probably the sister-in-law was here. I opened the door and followed Bella inside.

"Go away or I give you the eye," Bella said.

Lula was behind me. "There's something wrong in this house," Lula said. "I hear something thumping."

"Water heater," Bella said. "No good."

251

I stopped and listened. "I hear it too," I said.

"I get it fixed tomorrow," Bella said.

I followed the thumping to the kitchen. "It's louder here. It's coming from the door next to the refrigerator. What's behind the door?" I asked Bella.

"Nothing," Bella said. "Closet with mop."

"Help!" someone yelled behind the door. *Thump, thump, thump.* "Let me out!"

An old-fashioned skeleton key was stuck in the lock. I unlocked the door and Marylou crashed the door open and lunged out into the kitchen. She was red-faced and sweating.

"Thank God you showed up," she said to me. "This crazy old hag locked me in the cellar. She said there was something wrong with the water heater and when I went down to look, she locked me in. It's just a crawl space down there with about a million spiders."

"We heard you banging on the door," Lula said.

Marylou shoved some hair off her face and turned to me wild-eyed. "Do *not* marry into this family. They're all nuts." She whirled around and jabbed her finger at Bella. "You are a horrible, evil person. You aren't even a person. You're a . . . fruitcake!"

Marylou snatched her purse off the kitchen counter and stomped off to the front door. "I'm out of here. I'm done. I don't care if she burns the house down."

"Good riddance," Bella said. "She knows nothing."

I called Morelli. "I brought Bella home," I said.

"Is Marylou there?"

"No. Bella locked her in the cellar. We heard her banging on the door, and when we let her out, she left."

"If you could just stay with her until four o'clock, I can take over. And then my mom will be home."

"Have you tried taking her to a doctor?"

"We did that. Bella gave him the eye and he got shingles. I have to go. I'm treading water here."

Maybe Marylou was right. Marriage to Morelli might not be a good idea.

"I'm supposed to stay with you until Joe gets off work," I said to Bella."

"Good," Bella said. "You can make me lunch and wash the floor."

Connie called. "We just got an alert on Zane Walburg. He didn't show for court this morning and Vinnie is freaked out. It's a super-high bond."

"The name sounds familiar."

"He got a lot of publicity when he was arrested. He makes bombs on demand. His big seller is the retro pressure cooker bomb. Vinnie wants you to drop everything and find this guy before he seriously disappears. I have the paperwork ready for you to pick up."

"I'm hung up until four o'clock."

"That's okay," Connie said. "I'll see you at four."

I could hear Vinnie ranting in the background. "Four o'clock isn't okay. What the hell is she doing? She's supposed to be working. This guy is going to run."

"I have to go to the office," I said to Lula. "Can you stay with Bella?"

"Not now. Not ever," Lula said.

"Then we're all going to the office. Everybody out to the car."

"What about my lunch," Bella said.

"I might be getting a migraine," Lula said.

I locked the door to the house and went to the car. Lula and Bella were arguing about who should get the front seat.

"Your head is too big," Bella said to Lula. "I can't see anything from the backseat."

"You're supposed to look out the side window," Lula said.

"You sat in front last time," Bella said.

"That's because you were a prisoner,"

Lula said. "Handcuffed prisoners always sit in the backseat. Everybody knows that."

"I'm not handcuffed now," Bella said. "I'm senior citizen. I deserve front seat."

"Let her have the front seat," I said to Lula. "You can have the front seat next time."

"It's because of my pink hair, isn't it?" Lula said to me. "You don't want me in the front because of my pink hair."

"That's ridiculous. You sat in the front this morning, didn't you? Was your hair pink?"

"Nobody cares your hair is pink," Bella said, getting into the front passenger seat. "It's your head is too big. Now you take your big head and sit in the back."

I drove to the office and parked, being sure to take the key with me. I dashed inside, grabbed the papers, and went back to the car. I handed the papers to Lula.

"Where are we going?" I said to Lula.

"Hamilton Township. Curly Tree Gardens. Looks like an apartment complex."

"I've been there," I said. "It's by the pet cemetery."

"What is this?" Bella asked. "What we doing?"

"I'm doing my job," I said. "A man failed to appear for his court appearance, and I need to find him and bring him back to the court to get rescheduled."

"Why? What he do?"

"He builds and sells bombs."

"What's wrong with that?" Bella asked.

"It's illegal," I said.

"This country have too many rules," Bella said.

"Remember when Salvatore Perroni's Cadillac got bombed and Sal lost four fingers on his hand? That's why bombs are illegal," I said.

"I didn't like that," Bella said. "That was bad bomb. Sal couldn't hold cards to play poker. Only had a thumb."

Curly Tree Gardens was a large complex of three-story cinderblock and stucco buildings that looked like they were built by the Russian army. Number 126 was a garden-level apartment without the benefit of a garden.

It had two parking spaces allotted to it. One space was occupied by a Hyundai. I took the remaining space.

"You stay here," I said to Bella.

"Take the key and crack the window for her," Lula said.

"Hunh," Bella said. "Fat head."

Lula and I walked to the door, and I rang the bell. In my peripheral vision I caught a dark shadow scuttling toward us. Bella.

The door opened and a guy who looked like a twenty-six-year-old, chubby Harry Potter peered out at us.

"Zane Walburg?" I asked.

"Yeah," he said. "What's up?"

"I represent Vincent Plum. You missed your court date this morning."

"No biggie," he said. "I'll go some other time."

"Absolutely," I said. "I came to take you downtown to reschedule."

"Okay, but not now. I got a rush order last night." He looked past me at Lula and Bella. "Did they miss a court date, too?"

"No," I said. "They're with me. It's a long story. You don't want to hear it."

"Do you build bombs?" Bella asked him.

"Yep," he said. "Bombs R Me. That's my website."

"I want to see one," Bella said.

"Do you want to buy one?"

"Maybe," Bella said.

"I don't have a lot of inventory," he said. "Mostly I build on demand, but I have a classic pressure cooker bomb that was never picked up. I could give you a good price on it."

"We aren't buying bombs today," I said to him. "And I know you're busy but you're going to have to take a half hour out to go to the courthouse with me to reschedule."

"No," he said. "Not now. I have work to do."

"You became a felon when you missed your court date," I said, taking cuffs out of my back pocket. "I'm going to have to insist that you come with me."

"I'll cut a deal with you," he said. "I'll give you the pressure cooker bomb in exchange for you going away and never coming back."

"I don't need a pressure cooker bomb."

"How about a firebomb? Everyone should have a firebomb. I could put one together for you in a couple minutes."

"You aren't paying attention," Lula said to Walburg. "You need to get your chubby behind out to our car. It happens that I don't have a lot of patience and I'm getting cranky."

Walburg adjusted his round Harry Potter lenses. "It happens that you don't know who you're dealing with," he said. "I'm the bomb maker. I could blow you to smithereens at the touch of a button."

Bella shoved Lula aside. "Too much talk," she said. "You do what the slut say, or I put the eye on you."

"What's the eye?" Walburg asked.

"It's a curse," Lula said. "She does this thing with her eye and bad things happen to you."

Walburg looked at me. "Are you people serious?"

I shrugged.

"Go ahead," Walburg said to Bella. "Put the eye on me. Give it your best shot."

"I go easy on you first time," Bella said. "I make you poop your pants."

Walburg burst out laughing and then . . . *BRRRUP.* He stopped laughing.

"Holy crap," Lula said, stepping farther away from Walburg.

Bella gave a soft chuckle. "Heh, heh, heh. Good one, eh?" She looked at Walburg. "You coming to car now?"

"That was coincidence," he said. "I get irritable bowel sometimes."

"Okay, here goes," Bella said. "This time I make your pee-pee swell up like watermelon. Maybe I give it big boils. I have good luck with boils curse."

"No!" he said. "No boils. Look, I'm going to the door. This won't take long, right?"

"Right," I said.

"Is this your car?" he said. "I'm getting in. You want me in the back, right? Let's go."

Bella started to get in the front and Lula stopped her.

"My turn to sit up front," Lula said. "We made a deal."

"Deal is off," Bella said.

"No way," Lula said.

"I give you the eye," Bella said.

"I'll squash you like a bug," Lula said.

"I don't want to sit up front anyway," Bella said.

We all got in and I backed out of the driveway.

"It don't smell good back here," Bella said.

"It don't smell all that good up front either," Lula said. "It's coming from Walburg. We should have put him in the shower before putting him in the car. Maybe we should go back to his apartment."

"Ignore it," I said. "I'm not turning around."

"Stop the car," Bella said. "I'm getting out."

I hit the child lock button and opened all the windows. "No one's getting out until we're at the municipal building."

"It's all your fault anyway," Lula said to Bella. "You made him poop his pants."

"Seemed like good idea," Bella said. "I was tired of standing there. I wanted lunch. I didn't think ahead to sitting in backseat."

Twenty minutes later, I pulled into the parking lot for the municipal building, and everyone jumped out of the car. I cuffed Walburg, walked him across the street to the police station, and apologized to the desk cop.

"Sorry about the smell," I said. "Not my bad."

Lula and Bella were standing at a distance from my car when I got back to the parking lot.

"Anyone still want lunch?" I asked.

"We should go to Cluck-in-a-Bucket and get takeout," Lula said. "That way we can replace the Walburg smell with fried-chicken-and-onion-rings smell."

I cut through town to Hamilton Avenue and got buckets of fried chicken, onion rings, fries, and coleslaw. We took it to the office and set it all on Connie's desk.

Vinnie popped out of his office, spied Bella, and instantly retreated, slamming his door shut and locking it.

"Va fancul," Bella said to the closed door, hand gesture included.

"Amen to that," Lula said.

We pulled chairs up to Connie's desk and dug into the food.

"I got good stuff," Bella said, taking a flask out of her pocketbook. "Who want some?"

"I'll take a hit," Lula said, pouring out a shot glass of hooch. She threw it back and gasped. "Fire," she said. "I'm on fire. That's one hundred percent grain alcohol."

"Amateur," Bella said to Lula, chugging some down.

Connie and I passed.

"Why was Walburg considered a flight risk?" I asked Connie.

"He has clients who value his expertise and would prefer not to see him come to trial," Connie said. "They have the ability to relocate him."

"Or terminate him?" Lula said.

"It's possible but not likely. I hear he's very clever. A bomb savant," Connie said.

Bella ate two pieces of chicken and drained her flask. "I'm done," Bella said. "What now? You got any more job to do?"

"Not today," I said.

"Okay. Take me home."

I was half a block away from the Morelli house when I saw Joe's mom pull into her driveway. Hooray! I turned Bella over to Joe's mom and drove the short distance to my parents' house. I'd promised to take Grandma shopping for a new pocketbook.

"This is just in time," Grandma said, getting into my car. "I'm going to bingo tonight and I want to look nice. Mort Blankowski is calling numbers. He's a cutie and his wife just died so he's up for grabs."

I cruised out of the Burg and headed for Route 1.

"This car smells bad," Grandma said. "It smells like fried chicken and doody."

I opened the windows. "It's been a hard day."

"You should take some probiotic pills," Grandma said. "They say yogurt is good too."

"I'm not the one who had a problem. I brought an FTA in today and he had an accident."

"Must have been a beauty."

"I don't know the details. I have air freshener in the glove compartment."

Grandma sprayed the air freshener around and stuck her head out the window. When we rolled into the mall parking lot and she pulled her head back in, her hair looked like it had been spray varnished in a wind tunnel. She looked at herself in the visor mirror.

"I could be in one of those punk rock bands," she said. "I might leave it like this for bingo. Morty is ten years younger than me. He might appreciate this look. There's going to be a lot of competition for him. I'm going to have to up my game."

An hour later we returned to the car with Grandma's new pocketbook and the car smelled worse than ever.

"Now it smells like fried chicken, doody, and lavender air freshener," Grandma said. "I'm grateful for the ride, but when I get home, I'm going to have to throw my clothes away and take a shower."

I didn't throw my clothes away when I got home but I took a shower and washed my hair twice. I had a meatball sandwich on white bread for dinner and washed it down with a bottle of beer.

I shut the television off at ten o'clock and I went into the kitchen to say good night to Rex.

"It wasn't such a bad day," I said. "It ended pretty good except for the smell in my car."

I gave him a peanut, turned to go, and my apartment was rattled by an explosion in the parking lot. I ran to a living room window and looked down at smoke and mangled car parts where my Honda used to be parked. It didn't take a lot of thought to come up with an explanation. Somebody put up the bail bond for Walburg. I returned to the kitchen and ate a celebratory Tastykake Butterscotch Krimpet. The odor issue was solved.

I lowered the lights and watched the action outside. Police, fire trucks, gawkers.

The Rangeman SUV arrived seconds after the first fire truck. Ranger called minutes later.

"I'm okay," I said. "I captured an FTA bomber today and obviously someone immediately bailed him out."

"And he bombed your car."

"I'm guessing."

"Zane Walburg?"

"Yep."

"He makes a decent bomb, but he has some delusions-of-grandeur issues," Ranger said. "Do you need a car?"

"No, but thanks for the offer."

"Babe," he said. And he was gone.

I strolled downstairs to the parking lot. I got there just as Morelli rolled in. He parked behind a fire truck and walked over to me. We were standing near a shredded tire.

"Your car?" he asked.

"Of course," I said.

"Good thing you weren't in it."

"He was making a point. He didn't want to kill me."

"He?" Morelli asked.

"Zane Walburg was FTA and I brought him in for rescheduling today. I'm guessing someone bonded him out."

"He's good," Morelli said. "For instance, notice the way your car is completely destroyed, but very little damage has occurred to the cars surrounding it. That takes talent."

"It sounds like you've had previous dealings with him."

"Not personally," Morelli said. "Walburg is a local celebrity in the law-enforcement community. He's been building bombs for several years and has always been able to avoid prosecution."

"Until now," I said.

"Last month he shipped a bomb using his own name and got caught."

"Ranger said Walburg has delusions of grandeur."

"From what I hear, he's on the spectrum."

The crowd dispersed. The fire trucks left. I answered all necessary questions. A flatbed tow truck arrived and started to scoop up what remained of my Honda.

Morelli wrapped an arm around me and steered me toward my building's back door. "I have to be on the road early tomorrow," he said.

"Does that imply that you're staying over?"

"I thought you would need comforting after this traumatic experience."

It was a win-win. I got rid of the smelly

car and now I was going to get comforted.
Lucky me.

CHAPTER FIFTEEN

At nine o'clock in the morning life wasn't such a win-win. I didn't have a car. Lula was supposed to pick me up, but she was a half hour late. I was about to give up and call my dad for a ride when the red Firebird rumbled into my parking lot and stopped in front of me.

"Sorry I'm late," Lula said. "I had a fashion dilemma. Tuesday is always boho day, but my ankle boots didn't look right with my boho fringe bag. Both of them go with my paisley dress, so you see the problem." She looked around the lot. "Where's your car? Why do you need a ride?"

"My car no longer exists."

"Say what?"

"It got blown up last night. Bombed."

"Get the heck out."

"I'm thinking it was Zane Walburg, but I don't know for sure."

Lula left the lot and connected with

Hamilton Avenue. "Do you want to visit him?"

"No. I want to go to the office and get a doughnut. Then I want to get the kid who drove the fire truck into the Garden of Life. I need the capture money to get a new car."

"Doesn't sound like you're worried about the kidnappers."

"I haven't heard from them. I think they wrote it off."

"I don't know about that," Lula said. "I'm still creeped out. If it was me, I'd have a hard time walking away from eleven million. I think Connie's creeped out too. I noticed yesterday she was parked in front of the office and when I went by today, she was parked there again. She always used to park in the alley spaces and use the storeroom door. She could have PTSD."

I thought back to all of the scary things that had happened to me since I started working for Vinnie. The fear and horror didn't immediately go away. There were night sweats and sick stomachs and a reluctance to go out in the dark. And there was always the temptation to quit and stay home and hide. So far, I haven't quit. The interesting question is, why not?

Ranger and Morelli stick with it because they believe in the job. I used to think I stuck with it because I was too lazy and uninspired to find something else. I'm coming to realize that's no longer true. Maybe it was never true. If I'm honest with myself, I have to admit that I like the chase. And I like when I succeed. Truth is, I might be a bit of an adrenaline junkie. And while I'll never have the skills of Ranger or Morelli, I'm actually halfway decent at retrieving felons. Go figure.

"When you have a bad experience like Connie had, you become more careful," I said to Lula. "At least for a while."

"I always park in the front," Lula said. "I don't want my car getting dinged by people throwing things in the dry cleaner dumpster that's next to us."

I checked the street when we got close to the office. I was looking for two stocky guys in hoodies. They could be walking on the sidewalk or slowly cruising past the office in a Camry with JZ on the license plate. I was telling myself that they'd given up, but I was still looking.

Connie stood at her desk when we walked in. "I need someone to babysit the office for an hour," she said. "One of my burns doesn't look good. I'm going to the walk-in clinic."

"No problem," Lula said. "I'm good at

being the temporary office manager. I got a talent for it."

"Vinnie won't be in until later, and I've done the mail. There was a notice for a delivery this morning. No details. Just keep an eye out for it. It's coming by truck. Probably something weird that Vinnie got in Atlantic City."

"Remember I brought Walburg in yesterday?" I said to Connie. "Do you know if he's already gotten bonded out?"

"Not my bad," Connie said. "I wouldn't have bonded him, but Vinnie likes him."

I took a doughnut and sat in one of the uncomfortable plastic chairs. Lula took her position behind the desk. Ten minutes later a large truck pulled up in front of the office. A guy got out and came to the door.

"I got a delivery for the office manager," he said. "The only name I got is Lula."

"That's me," Lula said.

"Where do you want it? You want me to bring it all in here?"

"What have you got?" Lula asked.

"Furniture. It's from Mel's One Stop Shopping."

Lula jumped up. "It's the stuff I ordered online. I forgot all about it. Bring it in!"

"Did you tell Vinnie about this?" I asked Lula.

"Hell no. Even if I remembered about it, I wouldn't have told him."

The men were unpacking on the street. A couch, a couple armchairs, a desk chair, a rug, a coffee table, end tables. An hour later, the old office furniture was in a heap next to the dumpster and the new furniture was in place.

"What do you think?" Lula asked.

I was speechless. It was nice. Shockingly nice. A big comfortable dark brown couch that was genuine leather. Two cream, brown, and pumpkin striped armchairs in front of the desk. A couple side tables with lamps. A coffee table that matched the side tables. A new ergonomic desk chair for Connie. And a low-pile tweed rug.

"Wow!" I said. "It's fantastic. I love it."

"That's 'cause I got taste," Lula said. "I got vision for this stuff. Mel's One Stop Shopping got rooms already arranged for you, and soon as I saw this room, I knew it was the one. It's casual but sophisticated for a comfortable business or home environment."

Lula arranged some past copies of *Star* magazine on the coffee table.

"Now it's perfect," she said.

Connie walked in and stopped in the middle of the room. "Am I in the wrong place?" she asked. "That looks like my desk."

"I made some purchases while I was temporary office manager," Lula said. "And then I forgot about them until the truck got here, what with all the drama going on."

"Does Vinnie know about this?"

"Hell no," Lula said. "How's your burn?"

"It's okay," she said. "They gave me some antibiotic salve to put on it. They said it looked like I work the fry basket at Cluck-in-a-Bucket."

Vinnie's Cadillac screeched to a stop in front of the office and Vinnie rushed in. "I need forms," he said. "I got a guy locked up downtown. Harry's cousin. Not someone I want to keep waiting."

Connie pulled a packet out of her desk drawer and handed it to Vinnie.

Vinnie took the packet and the last remaining doughnut and he left.

"He didn't notice," I said.

"Sort of disappointing," Lula said. "I was looking forward to him going on a rant. I like when his eyes bulge out and his face gets purple."

Connie answered the office phone and immediately put it on speaker.

"Time is running out," a man said. "We're taking another hostage if we don't get our money immediately."

He instantly disconnected.

"These people are losers," Lula said. "They've got no imagination. All they can think of is taking a hostage."

"It's not going to be me," Connie said. "I'm paying attention and I'm carrying."

"Ditto on that," Lula said. "Not gonna be me either."

I was lacking confidence that it wouldn't be me.

"Business as usual," I said. "Let's collect the guy who drove the fire truck into the flower shop."

"You haven't got a car," Lula said. "And my car isn't suitable for transporting felons."

"What's wrong with your car?" I asked her.

"It's too nice. Why don't we just go get you a car."

"I haven't got enough money. I need the money from the fire truck guy."

"I know a guy who practically gives cars away," Lula said. "We could talk to him."

"Are they legal?"

"Mostly it's that they're refurbished."

"Refurbished would be okay."

Lula drove us down Stark to the end and pulled into the junkyard.

"Hold on," I said, "this is the junkyard."

"Yeah, they have a side business going," Lula said. "Some of the cars get a second chance at life. It's like when you go to the animal shelter, and you adopt one of the dogs or cats and give them their forever home. Only these cars are more like getting a last-gasp home. I know about this because I sort of date one of the guys here. Andy. I called and told him to expect us."

Andy was waiting at the gate. He looked okay. Jeans and T-shirt. Some muscle. Shaved head. Large gold tooth front and center. He motioned for us to park in a cleared area that was next to a line of sad cars.

"So here are the cars," he said to me. "They all run, and the tires have some miles left on them. Just pick one out."

This is what my life has come to, I thought. Last-gasp cars.

"What do you think?" I asked Lula. "Do you see anything you like?"

"If it was for me, no. But your cars never last more than a couple weeks before they get blown up or smashed by a garbage truck. How about the pink one?"

"I don't think I can do pink," I said.

"Truly, the best one here is the little gray Whatever," Andy said. "I think most of it is

Toyota. You can't go wrong with Toyota."

"Does it smell inside?" Lula asked.

Andy walked over and sniffed at it. "It smells like a used car."

"How much is it?" I asked.

"How much do you have?" Andy asked.

"Four hundred and fifty dollars," I said.

"That's a little shy," Andy said. "Lula's gonna have to make up for it in lovin'."

"You wish," Lula said.

Andy grinned at her. "That's the truth."

"What about papers and plates?" I asked.

"They come with the car," Andy said.

Steven Plover lived in a two-story white colonial with blue shutters. The lawn was excellent. There was a new Mercedes in the driveway. The neighborhood was extremely respectable. I did some background and found that his father was a doctor, and his mother was a Realtor.

I parked my gray Whatever in front of the neighbor's house so I wouldn't tarnish the Plover image, and Lula and I went to the front door.

Steven answered the doorbell. I knew him from his photo. Brown hair, cut by someone who knew what they were doing. Five feet ten inches. Medium build. Pleasant looking. Jeans and T-shirt. New and expensive.

I introduced myself and explained that he had to reschedule.

"Sure," he said. "I haven't got anything to do anyway. I guess I forgot about court."

"I'm curious," Lula said. "Why did you take the fire truck and crash it into the flower shop?"

"There's this girl I really like, Jessica. She was in my art appreciation class at Rutgers, and she lives here in the neighborhood. She was home for the weekend, and I wanted to ask her out, but she doesn't know I exist. So, I got this crazy idea that I'd show up at her house in the fire truck and ask her if she'd like to go for a ride. I mean, who could resist a ride in a fire truck."

"You were high, right?" Lula asked.

"Yeah, maybe a little," Steven said. "I'm almost always high. Anyway, it was easy to borrow the truck. They wash it in the morning and then they leave it out all day. They even leave the key in it.

"I took the truck and then I thought I should bring Jessica some flowers, so I drove to the flower shop. Only the truck wouldn't stop fast enough, and I accidentally drove through the big window in the front of the store and took out the case with the orchids. It was pretty funny but sort of embarrassing."

"Did Jessica ever go out with you?" Lula asked.

"No," Steven said. "She thinks I'm an idiot."

"Not much of a surprise there," Lula said.

"Are your parents home?" I asked him.

"Negative. They're never home. It's just me."

"Lock up the house, and I'll drive you to the courthouse so you can reschedule."

"Okay, I'll get the back door," Steven said.

He disappeared into the house and Lula and I exchanged glances.

"He's gonna run," Lula said.

"That would be my guess," I said.

Seconds later we heard the garage door open on the side of the house. Lula and I took off and reached the garage just as Steven rocketed out in a red Tesla.

"That car's got excellent acceleration," Lula said. "And you can't go wrong with red."

"True and true," I said, heading for my gray Whatever. "And red is going to make it easier to spot Steven."

"He turned right when he went out of his driveway," Lula said.

I went straight for three blocks until I got to Mulberry. Mulberry was the first road that wasn't part of Steven's neighborhood.

There was a gas station on one corner and a convenience store next to it. The red Tesla was parked at the convenience store.

"This is too easy," Lula said. "Kinda takes the fun out of it."

Not for me. I liked easy.

I parked behind the Tesla, preventing Steven from backing up. I could see Steven at the cash register, talking to the clerk. I had my cuffs in my back pocket and an illegal stun gun in my sweatshirt pocket. Lula and I walked in and stood on either side of Steven.

"I don't suppose I could borrow some money from you," he said. "I ran out of the house without my wallet, and I have a rad craving for gummy bears."

I paid for the gummy bears and cuffed Steven with his hands in front so he could eat. We got him into the backseat of the Whatever and drove him to the police station on North Clinton. I called Connie after we dropped him off.

"Is Vinnie still in the municipal building?" I asked Connie.

"I don't know," she said. "I haven't been able to reach him."

"I brought Steven Plover in just now. He's going to want to be bailed out before court closes shop for the day."

"I'll take care of it," Connie said. "I'll call his mother."

"Tell her the Tesla is parked at the convenience store on Mulberry. Have you heard any more from the kidnappers?"

"No," Connie said. "There was just that one call."

"Who do you think they're going to take?" Lula asked when I hung up.

"Me," I said. "They tried to get me after the viewing and Grandma scared them away. I'm sure they think I have the money."

I turned onto Hamilton Avenue and saw that I'd picked up a tail. Black SUV. Rangeman. Ranger had no doubt tapped into the call from the kidnappers and reached the same conclusion I'd reached. That I had a big target on my back. Plus, I had a new Whatever that wasn't yet tagged with a tracker.

Lula got out at the office, and I continued on to my parents' house. I parked on the street, got out of the Whatever, and waved at the Rangeman guy.

My mom was knitting, and Grandma was on her iPad when I walked in.

"I'm going to mooch lunch," I said.

"Help yourself," my mom said. "There's leftover pot roast for sandwiches with gravy, or there's deli meat and cheese."

I went with the pot roast, no gravy.

"What's new on Facebook?" I asked Grandma.

"I wasn't on Facebook," she said. "I was on Twitter. I like to watch the rocket launches. What's new with you?"

"I have a new car. Actually it's not new. It's just different."

"What does it smell like?"

"It smells like used car."

"That's a step in the right direction," Grandma said. "How's Connie looking? That was all they were talking about at the bakery. Her disappearance is a big mystery. Even her mother doesn't know where she was. I just about got a rupture trying to keep the secret."

I made myself a pot roast sandwich with mustard, horseradish, and slices of dill pickle. I can't cook but I can make a sandwich.

"Connie's good," I said. "She's back at work."

"Have you heard any more from the kidnappers?" Grandma asked.

"Only that they want their money."

"Can't blame them," Grandma said.

"Are you going to give them their money?" my mother asked me.

"No," I said. "I can't. I don't have it."

"Suppose you did have it," Grandma said. "Would you give it to them?"

"Yes. Would you?"

"Heck no," Grandma said.

"How about you?" I asked my mom. "Would you give the money back?"

"How much was it?" she asked.

"Eleven million."

"That's a lot of money," she said. "A person could do wonderful things with that much money."

"Like what?" I asked. "What would you do with eleven million dollars?"

"I'd go to Paris," my mother said.

"I'd buy a horse," Grandma said. "I always wanted a horse. I'd name him Brownie. What would you do with the money?" Grandma asked me.

"I'd get new towels for my bathroom," I said. "And I'd get a new bathroom." It seemed boring compared to a horse and Paris, but I had a really ugly bathroom.

I finished my sandwich and pushed away from the table. "I have to get back to work," I said. "Stay safe. Be careful."

I went to my Whatever and noted that the Rangeman car was still in place. I suppose it should make me feel safe to have them following me around, but it did the opposite. It increased my anxiety. It was a reminder of the danger. It was like the TSA people at the airport who were there to keep flyers safe, but their presence screamed out that it was perfectly possible for your plane to get exploded at forty thousand feet in the air.

I drove the short distance to the office and sat in my car for a moment, thinking about the eleven million. Suppose it dropped in my lap. What would I really do with it? First thing, I'd buy a condo. Nothing elaborate and not too big, but I'd want it to be new. New paint. New appliances. It should have its own washer and dryer. What else? New furniture. Maybe a fish tank for the living room. And I'd get a pedicure. And a new car. I didn't want to spend time in Paris or get a horse. Probably I should quit my job, but what would I do all day? I could learn to play the piano. No, scratch that. I couldn't see myself playing the piano. I could join a gym and get a trainer and get in really good shape. Ugh. That was a horrible thought. Or I could go to culinary school like Julia Child. She got a husband because she could cook. I have two amazing men in my life but neither of them wants to get married, and I don't think acquiring cooking skills would change that. Maybe if I went to culinary school, I'd meet someone new who appreciated that I could make a soufflé. Something to consider.

A black Mercedes drove past me for the third time. Carpenter Beedle was behind the wheel. I called him and he picked up.

"Why are you driving past the bail bonds office?" I asked him.

"We've been checking to make sure things are okay. I see Connie is back at work. That's a relief. We're sorry we caused so much trouble, but it looks like everything's good now, right?"

"Wrong. The kidnappers want the money."

"Most of it's spent," he said.

"How could you go through eleven million dollars that fast?"

"It got divided up three ways so we each got a little over three and a half million. Half of that I invested in bonds for everyone. They'll have a good yield, but we can't touch them for five years. The rest of the money went to clothes, cars, boats, and entertainment. GoComic wasn't cheap. Benji got his own apartment. Sparks married the hooker who gave him the lap dance."

"What about you?"

"I paid the mortgage off on my mom's house and I bought this car. I got an expensive haircut and some clothes, and I have some money put aside for a defense lawyer. This was found money to us. We didn't know someone was kidnapped over it. We ran out and spent it. Even if we sold off some of the stuff we bought, we couldn't come near to the eleven million."

"Are you going back to panhandling?"

"I don't know. I enjoyed panhandling, but I really liked moving money around and investing it. I might look for a job in finance if I can avoid going to jail."

"Not accounting," I said.

"Not accounting. That ship sailed and sank."

"Good luck," I said. "Don't forget your court date."

"I never forget a date," Beedle said.

I looked across the street at the Rangeman car. Now I had Rangeman, Sir Lancelot, Benji, and Beedle working as security. Why didn't I feel safe?

It was five o'clock when Connie got back to the office.

"Sorry I'm so late. I almost didn't get him out today," she said. "He was last up. The judge wanted to go home, but Steven's mother started crying. Bawling her eyes out. When the judge reconsidered and set bail, Steven's mother turned and winked at me.

I bet she's a hell of a Realtor."

"We didn't mind staying," Lula said. "It's real comfy in here now. It's nicer than my apartment except it doesn't have a bed and TV."

"Anything new?" Connie asked, sitting at her desk, pulling up the email.

"Nope," Lula said. "I checked about an hour ago. There was a threatening email from Vinnie's bookie, but I deleted it."

"I don't see anything that can't wait," Connie said. "I'm closing up. Mom's making an early dinner tonight."

"She going to bingo or a viewing?" Lula asked.

"Viewing," Connie said. "Marion Foscatelli. Pancreatic cancer."

"That's a nasty one," Lula said.

We closed the office and I drove home with Rangeman close behind. I parked in my lot and took a moment to look around. I didn't see anyone hiding behind a car, waiting to jump me. I walked to the building and thought this was the tricky part. The Rangeman guy was in the parking lot. No telling who was in the building. I took Ranger's gun out of my messenger bag and decided the stairs were the safest way to go. I reached the second floor and found Sir Lancelot in full costume standing watch at my door with his new sword at his side.

"Carpenter wanted to make sure you got into your apartment without getting kidnapped," he said.

"Thanks," I said. "I'll be okay now."

"If you want to go out you can call us."

"Good to know. I hear you got married."

He smiled. "Yeah. Who would have thought? And she likes going to Renaissance fairs."

"That's great. Congratulations." I unlocked my door and stepped inside. "Have a nice night and thanks for looking after me."

"No problem. Make sure you lock your door."

When you're in a situation like this a safe haven can feel a little like a prison. Still, it was better than the alternative, which could have been a dark room with a chemical toilet and getting burned with a fire starter.

I was eating cereal out of the box when Morelli called.

"I saw a car parked in front of the bail bonds office today. I'm afraid to ask if it's yours," he said.

"What kind of car was it?"

"I don't know. The front looked like a Toyota, but the back looked like spare parts held together with Bondo."

"Yep. That's mine."

"Aside from the bargain car purchase, how did your day go?"

"It could have been worse. I brought Steven Plover in. That was my highlight."

"He stole the fire truck, right?"

"Borrowed it. He wanted to take a girl for a ride. He said he might have been a little high."

"That's one of the better reasons to borrow a fire truck. Are you locked in for the night?"

"Yes. And I've got a Rangeman car in my parking lot. It follows me everywhere. I need to reinvent my life. I can't keep living like this. Do you think it would help if I got a different job?"

"It would depend on the job. Even then I'm not sure. You're like a magnet for disaster. How many of your cars have gotten blown up?"

"I don't know. I lost count."

"How many of my cars have gotten blown up?"

"Zero?"

"Wrong," Morelli said. "Two. Both of them because of you. Car number one you 'commandeered' and it got blown up in your parking lot. Car number two you parked in my garage, left the garage door open, and Mama Macaroni blew the car and the garage halfway to hell."

"Maybe I need an exorcist."

"Let's assume it's your job and not the Devil. If you quit your job, what would you do?"

"That's the hitch," I said. "I don't know."

"There must be something that's always in the back of your mind that you would like to try. A fantasy job."

"Nope. I've got nothing."

"Do you like kids? Old people? Sick people? Animals? Clothes? Cars?"

"I like all those things, but I don't want a job associated with them. I guess I don't love them on a group level."

"What do you love?"

"Peanut butter."

"That's a little limiting, cupcake."

I could tell he was smiling when he said that.

"It just popped out. I also love olives and wine with screw caps. What do you love?" I asked him.

"I love my job and I love Bob and I love you."

That made me feel warm inside.

"I love you too," I said. "Do you want to give me a job?"

"Maybe. What can you do?"

"You know what I can do."

"I definitely want to give you a job. Are you available tonight?"

"No, I'm in my bunker. I'm under surveillance. I'm going to bed and hide under the covers."

I was in the kitchen eating Ritz crackers and finishing up a bottle of Chianti that I found in the back of my cupboard when Ranger let himself into my apartment. He eased me close into him and kissed me with a touch of tongue.

"Ritz crackers and red wine," he said. "Makes me hungry."

"For Ritz crackers?"

"No."

"For red wine?"

"Wrong again. Unfortunately, I'm going to have to stay hungry because I'm working. I'm taking a shift with a new man. I've got him sitting in the lot with Hal."

"Hal is my night watchman?"

"Until twelve."

"It's really not necessary to have someone out there all night. I'm sure I'm safe here in my apartment."

"The alternative is to have me in your apartment or for you to move in with me."

"I'll consider it," I said.

"Is there anything new that I should know?"

"You heard the phone call."

"I did."

"I haven't had any contact since."

"This is getting tedious," Ranger said. "I'd like to go more proactive but all we've got so far are dead ends."

He took a silver medallion necklace out of his pocket. The medallion was engraved with a cross.

"Don't take this off," he said. "Ever. Wear it in the shower."

"GPS?" I asked.

"Next generation."

He fixed it around my neck, and he gave me a quick kiss. He thought about it for a beat and kissed me with a lot more passion.

"Think about the alternatives," he said.

He left and I did a lot of thinking about the alternatives.

CHAPTER SIXTEEN

There are laundry facilities in the basement of my building, but I've always suspected that a troll lives behind the dryer. A better solution to the laundry problem is to cart my laundry to my parents' house once a week and turn it over to my mom. Since my underwear drawer was empty and I had no clean jeans, this was the day.

I skipped breakfast, hung my messenger bag on my shoulder, and hauled my laundry basket out to the parking lot. The Rangeman SUV was one row away with a clear view of my Whatever. I was certain the occupants were awake and on the job, ever vigilant. No doubt hoping for a hooded guy to jump out from behind a car and try to stun gun me. Then they could pounce on him and this whole nightmare would be over. I was hoping for this too.

I slowly walked to my car, giving the bad guys plenty of time to rush me. The bad guys didn't appear, so I drove to my parents' house with Rangeman following at a discreet distance. I handed my laundry over to my mom, and I sat down to bacon and eggs and crumb coffee cake.

"Anything new from the gossip line?" I asked Grandma.

"Nothing worth repeating from bingo," Grandma said. "And I didn't go to the bakery this morning, so I'm not up on the latest. We had a beauty of a thunderstorm last night, though. Woke me up. And I think I heard fire trucks, but nobody called so far about anything burning down."

"Do you need help with the laundry?" I asked my mom.

"No," she said. "I've already got the darks in the washer."

"Are you going after anybody interesting today?" Grandma asked. "Murderers or rapists? Animal abusers?"

"None of the above," I said. "Business has been slow."

"We're having pork chops tonight," my mother said. "If you want to come to dinner and pick up your laundry."

"I'll see how my day goes," I said. "Thanks. I'll let you know."

Grandma looked at me and rolled her eyes. No one ever wanted to eat my mom's pork chops. She was a good cook, with the exception of pork chops. You couldn't cut her pork chops with a steak knife. You couldn't cut them with a hatchet.

I left the house and drove to the office. I was a block away when I saw the lone fire truck and some random cars. I inched closer and saw that there was no office. There was just rubble where the office used to stand. Connie and Lula were in front of the office remains. I parked and joined them.

"What?" I asked.

"Boom!" Lula said.

I turned to Connie. "Was it hit by lightning?"

"Hard to say for sure at this point," she said. "My best guess is it was hit by Zane Walburg. It didn't catch fire. It just imploded. At least that's what they told me."

I looked around. "Where's Vinnie? Does he know?"

"I talked to Lucille," Connie said. "She said he didn't come home last night. Not that this is unusual for Vinnie."

"Where was he?"

"He bailed out one of his father-in-law's relatives and that was the last anyone heard from him. He's probably passed out in a strip club."

"I can't believe this happened after I did

all that decorating," Lula said.

"What about your records?" I asked Connie.

"Everything is in the cloud," she said. "I can get it all back. The only thing we can't get back is what we had in the storeroom. Items we had in the file cabinets might be intact. I haven't combed through the debris yet. They won't let us any closer than this."

"I suppose we should talk to Walburg," I said to Lula.

"The mad bomber? I don't think so," Lula said. "Let the police piss him off this time."

"I don't want him blowing up any more things. Like my apartment."

"You've got a point," Lula said, "but I'm not going without Bella."

Bella was in the front passenger seat of my Whatever. She was clutching her purse, staring straight ahead with her eagle eyes bright under her fierce eyebrows.

"I want to see what he did," she said. "Before I give him the eye, I want to see damage."

I drove her to the office and idled on the opposite side of the street.

"This is good," she said. "This boy, he do good work."

"He blew up the office," Lula said from

295

the backseat. "I just decorated that office, and I had all my *Star* magazines there."

"I like *Star* magazine," Bella said. "That's a mark against him. Vincent Plum I don't like."

"He put up your bail bond money," I said to Bella. "You would be in jail if it wasn't for Vinnie."

"I want lunch when we're done," she said. "More chicken."

"Absolutely," I said. "Chicken for lunch."

Traffic was light at this time of the morning. People were commuting toward the city, and we were traveling away from it to Hamilton Township. I took the driveway into Curly Tree Gardens and parked in a slot reserved for Walburg's neighbor.

"Now that we're here, what are we going to do?" Lula asked.

"We're going to bring him in for bond violation."

"We going to sneak up on him?"

"There's no good way to sneak up on someone in a garden apartment," I said. "Go around back and make sure he doesn't escape. We'll go in the front door."

Bella and I waited in the car until Lula texted that she was in place.

"This like in the movies," Bella said. "I like this. Maybe instead of the eye, I shoot him, like James Bond."

"No! No shooting. Not ever. James Bond didn't use real bullets."

"I think he did," Bella said.

"Well, we don't shoot people. Stay behind me when we get to the door."

I knocked on the door and Walburg answered. "You again," he said. "Now what?"

"You're in violation of your bond."

"Says who?"

"Says me," I said.

"Me too," Lula said, coming in from the back door.

"And me," Bella said. "Make my day, scumbag."

"Are you kidding me?" Walburg said. "You got the creepy old hag with you again? Big deal. I'm prepared. I googled 'creepy old hags.' "

"What Google say?" Bella asked him.

"Follow me," Walburg said. "I've got it in the kitchen."

We went to the kitchen and Walburg took a bowl off the counter and tossed everything in the bowl at Bella.

"What this is?" Bella said.

"Salt," Walburg said. "It's death to demons."

"I'm not demon," Bella said. "Salt only good for soup and radishes."

"Okay, that didn't work," Walburg said. "How about this?"

He took a pot of water that he had sitting on the counter next to the bowl of salt and he threw the water at Bella. It hit her square in the face and soaked her hair and her black dress.

Bella had her face scrunched up and her hands balled into fists.

"Do *not* shoot him," I said to Bella.

"I don't get it," Walburg said. "It worked in *The Wizard of Oz.*"

"I'm not witch," Bella managed to say through clenched teeth.

"What are you?" Walburg asked.

"I'm Sicilian," Bella said. "I give you the eye."

"No poop!" Lula and I said.

"I make his teeth fall out," she said, putting her finger to her eye.

We all stood perfectly still, staring at Walburg.

"This one takes longer than poop," Bella finally said.

I cuffed Walburg and we walked him out to my car and stuffed him into the backseat. The Rangeman guys were parked next to me. They looked bored.

Cluck-in-a-Bucket was my first stop on my way to the police station. It was early

298

for lunch, but I got lunch for everyone anyway, including the Rangemen.

"I'll take the Rangemen their chicken and biscuits," Lula said. "And I'll hitch a ride with them being that they got a better car than you, and their car don't have the bomber in the backseat." She climbed out of the Whatever and looked back at Walburg. "No offense meant," she said to him.

"No offense taken," he said.

The next stop was the Morelli house.

"Thanks for the help," I said to Bella, handing her buckets of chicken, biscuits, and coleslaw.

"You still slut," she said.

I watched her scuttle away and disappear inside her house.

"Do you think I have to worry about my teeth?" Walburg asked.

"Eventually," I said.

"I don't suppose you'd consider not taking me back to jail?"

"You bombed my car and the bail bonds office."

"Yes, but I didn't bomb your apartment."

"Not yet," I said. "Why are you doing this?"

"It's what I do."

"Yes, but you're going to jail for a long time for it. Doesn't that bother you?"

"I won't go to jail," he said. "The government wants me. I'm a genius. They'll get me off, just like always. At the very worst they'll put an ankle bracelet on me and set me up in a lab in the desert. I have friends in high places. I've done favors for them. They won't want those favors to come to an end. And the military needs my expertise."

"Do you like the desert?"

"I like to make bombs. I don't care where I make them. If I don't want to stay in the desert after a while, I'll cut a deal."

I cut across town, parked in the municipal building lot, and got Walburg out of the Whatever.

The Rangeman SUV parked alongside me.

"Do you need help getting him in?" the driver asked.

"No, but thanks. This shouldn't take long."

Almost an hour later I returned to my car.

"Sorry," I said to the Rangemen, "I had to give a statement about the two bombings." I looked in the SUV. "Where's Lula?"

"She got tired of waiting and called someone to pick her up."

I drove past what used to be the office on my way home. The collapsed building was ringed with crime scene tape, and a CSI truck was parked at the curb. Three men were poking around in the rubble and Connie was standing on the sidewalk, watching the men. I parked across the street and walked over to Connie.

"What's happening?"

"Two of the CSI guys are looking for evidence, and someone from the fire marshal is trying to determine if it's safe for me to access the file cabinets."

"The CSI guys don't need to find a lot of evidence," I said. "I brought Walburg in, and he confessed to both explosions. I hope Vinnie isn't going to bond him out again. My apartment is probably next on Walburg's fun list."

"I haven't heard from Vinnie," Connie said. Her eyes shifted to the street. "Holy mother!"

It was Lula behind the wheel of an ancient, rusted-out yellow school bus. She beeped the horn at us and parked behind the CSI truck. She opened the door and stepped out.

"I got us a mobile office," she said. "It's got a bathroom and everything. What do you think?"

I had no words.

"Um," Connie said.

"I was sitting in the parking lot with the Rangeman guys, waiting for Stephanie, and I remembered seeing this when we went to get Stephanie a car. So, I called Andy and he came and picked me up and made me a real deal. Actually, he gave it to me because no one wanted it. It's perfectly okay as long as you don't drive it too far on account of it gets three miles to a gallon."

"Ingenious," I said to Lula.

"No shit," Lula said. "You gotta go in and see it. Somebody decked it all out to make it a mobile home. They took the seats out and put in a couch and a TV and a teeny kitchen. And the refrigerator has a freezer. It's got a bedroom in the back, only there's no bed so we could put a desk there."

Connie and I went in and looked around. It was sort of horrible but not entirely.

"It needs some cleaning up," Lula said. "It's been sitting in the junkyard."

I opened a cupboard over the kitchen counter and found a dead mouse.

"At least it's dead," I said.

Connie picked it up in a tissue and threw it out the door. "If we park this in the back lot, we can hook it up to electric," she said.

"I can do my decorating magic," Lula said. "I might take it up professionally. I could specialize in old-school buses and crap-ass offices. I could have business cards made up."

Connie's phone rang and she looked at the number. "It's the office number," she said. "Unknown caller." She put it on speakerphone.

"I guess you aren't leaving messages in the window anymore," the caller said.

Connie handed the phone to me.

"Lightning strike," I said.

"Where's our money?"

"No clue," I said.

"Yeah, I almost believe you. Guess who I've got?"

"Who?"

There was some fumbling noise on the phone and the sound of someone growling.

"Vinnie?" I asked.

"Twenty-four hours and we start peeling his skin off."

The phone went dead.

"Omigod," I said. "They snatched Vinnie."

"We should get a bottle of wine and some chips to celebrate our new office," Lula said.

"But they have Vinnie," I said.

"And?" Lula asked.

"He said they were going to torture him."

"Vinnie loves that shit," Lula said. "He pays Madam Zaretsky good money to whip him and do God knows what else."

"That's true," Connie said. "If they pull off his fingernails, he'll get an erection."

"Anyway, what can we do?" Lula asked. "These idiots want money we don't have."

The office number rang again, and Connie put it on speakerphone.

"I forgot to tell you the best part," he said. "After twenty-four hours, when we roast this weasel on a spit like a hot dog, we're coming after you, sweetie pie."

"Which sweetie pie would that be?" I asked him.

"You know which sweetie pie," he said. And he hung up.

"Okay, that's disturbing," I said.

"Yeah, it would give us more incentive to do something if we knew what to do," Lula said.

Morelli appeared in the doorway. "Knock, knock," he said. "Is this the new office?"

"Yep," I said.

"It's leaking something."

"It's motor oil," Lula said. "It's okay, I got a case of it. It came with the bus."

Morelli crooked his finger at me. "Can I see you outside?"

We walked a short distance from the bus and away from the CSI people.

"We found Vinnie's car," he said. "They

just pulled it out of the river. Vinnie wasn't in it."

"That's because the kidnappers have Vinnie," I said. "We got the phone call a couple minutes ago."

"Why did they take Vinnie?"

"I guess they thought we cared if he lived or died or got tortured."

"That's a tough one."

"Yeah, on the surface it doesn't seem like he's worth saving."

"But below the surface?"

"Ditto."

"It's a dilemma," Morelli said.

"On the plus side, I delivered the bomber today."

"I heard. Nice." He looked over at the bus. "That has to be at least twenty years old. It's a dumpster fire on wheels."

"It has a refrigerator with a freezer, and it had a dead mouse, but Connie got rid of it."

"Good to know. Where do you go from here?"

"Do you mean about the office?"

"I mean about the kidnapping and the death and torture threats."

"I don't know. I guess I have to wait for them to make a move. We're at a stalemate. I can't give them what they want, and they refuse to believe that I don't have it."

"Is Ranger making any progress?"

"Nothing significant. Anything on your end?"

"We aren't officially involved," Morelli said.

The CSI guys went to their truck, and the fire marshal walked over to us.

"The site seems to be stable," he said. "The explosion didn't scatter the structure, and it was single-story frame construction so there isn't a lot of the debris that you would see in higher-rise buildings. This basically just collapsed in on itself. There was no fire and all utilities have been disconnected. I see no reason why you can't sort through this. Just be careful where you walk."

"We need to salvage what we can from the storeroom," I said to Morelli. "Connie said all the records are in the cloud, so things could be worse."

"At least Vinnie isn't available to bond out Walburg again."

For a moment I'd forgotten about Vinnie. No matter what was said in the bus, the thought of Vinnie being held hostage wasn't a good one. He was pimple pus, but he was *our* pimple pus.

"I need to get back to work," Morelli said.

"There's preseason hockey tonight if you want to come over and share a pizza."

"Sounds good. I'll bring the pizza."

"Game is at eight o'clock."

I watched Morelli drive away, and I went into the bus to tell Connie and Lula that we had permission to sort through the office remains.

"I can't go climbing over all that junk in my Louboutins," Lula said. "I'm going to the hardware store to get boots."

"I'm okay in my sneakers," I said.

"I've got running shoes in my tote," Connie said, "so I'm okay too, but as long as you're going out you can get some big plastic bins."

"And air freshener," I said. "Something to get rid of the dead-mouse smell."

Connie changed her shoes and we stood on the sidewalk and looked at the mess in front of us.

"Vinnie had a safe in his office," Connie said. "We want to make sure it's secure. I don't know what he had in his desk drawers, and I don't want to know. I want the gun from my desk. Beyond that everything would be easier to reach from the alley."

"I'll walk around to the back and start looking for the file cabinets. You can start looking for your gun," I said.

The Rangeman SUV was parked behind my Whatever. The two men got out of the SUV and walked over to us. I recognized one of them. Raul. The other man was new. His name tag said he was Bek.

"Are you looking for something?" Raul asked.

"We need to salvage what we can from this wreck," I said.

"We can help."

"That would be amazing," I said. "Bek can go with Connie. She's working in the front of the office, and you can come with me. I'm going to walk around to the back so it's easier to get to the items we took in as security."

By five o'clock we had everything from the file cabinets in bins, plus we had assorted larger items that we found in the rubble. The gun safe was located and cleaned out. The guns were all packed off to Rangeman for storage. Connie had her desk gun, and we were waiting for the safe company to finish hauling Vinnie's safe through the debris to their truck. This would also go to Rangeman.

I was standing by the bus with Connie and Lula, watching the Rangeman guys stuff the bins in our cars.

"It's a good thing we had Raul and Bek

helping us," Lula said. "We couldn't have done this without them."

"We would have been done a half hour ago if your skirt wasn't so short," Connie said. "Every time you bent over Raul's eyes almost fell out of his head."

"I didn't know you could see something," Lula said.

"Everybody could see everything," Connie said.

"Not everything," Lula said. "I'm wearing undies. I'm covered up as much as when I'm on the beach."

I'd seen Lula on the beach, and it was something not easily forgotten.

An hour later, the safe was trucked away, and we put the crime scene tape back in place. The bus was parked at the curb for the night, and we felt comfortable that there wasn't a lot left to steal. We formed a caravan with our cars, drove to Connie's house, and unloaded everything into her garage.

We thanked Raul and Bek and they went back to their SUV.

"Good thing we're done," Lula said. "I couldn't pick up one more thing or carry any more bins anywhere. I feel like my back is broken. We should have let Bella make that stupid bomber poop himself again."

"Opportunities missed," I said.

"Fuckin' A," Lula said.

Connie's mother was standing watch at the edge of the garage. "I heard that," she said. "We don't allow that kind of language in this house."

"Sorry," Lula said. "I wasn't thinking it might be offensive. It seemed like an appropriate comment for what we were saying about the poop spell."

"We don't say that P-word either," Mrs. Rosolli said.

"You mean 'poop'?" Lula asked. "What do you call it?"

"We call it plops," she said.

Lula and I looked at Connie.

Connie rolled her eyes and gave up a sigh. "Plops and pleeps," she said.

"That's just wrong," Lula said. "I can see where it's coming from, but I don't want to admit to making a plop. Maybe men make plops. My experience is they don't care what they do."

I had my hand clapped over my mouth. I was trying not to laugh out loud, but squeaking sounds were escaping from between my fingers.

"For God's sake, just go ahead and laugh before you pleep yourself," Connie said.

Mrs. Rosolli made the sign of the cross

and asked forgiveness for her daughter. "We don't take God's name in vain," she said.

CHAPTER SEVENTEEN

I drove back to my apartment, said hello to Sir Lancelot, thanked him for guarding my life, and told him he could go home to his bride. I liked that these guys wanted to pitch in and help, but I worried about their abilities if they came up against armed kidnappers. I didn't want them hurt.

"Are you sure you're going to be okay? I don't mind staying," Lancelot said.

"I'm friends with the man who owns Rangeman Security, and he has men watching out for me too. Tell Benji and Carpenter that I appreciate your help, but I think I'm safe now."

"Cool. I'll let them know and if anything changes you can call us."

I went inside and ate a tablespoon of peanut butter and five olives out of the jar because I was too tired to make a sandwich. I tapped on Rex's cage and said howdy. He stuck his head out of his soup can, gave me a once-over, and went back into his can.

I thought it would be nice if I could do that. I felt like crawling into a can and sleeping until my life improved. I shuffled into the bathroom and stood under the shower until the water turned cold. I halfway dried my hair, got dressed in my comfy jeans and a Rangers jersey, and called ahead to Pino's for a pizza, extra-large with the works, extra cheese.

I was feeling better after the shower, and I was looking forward to the pizza. I couldn't get overly excited about a preseason game, but I knew it would take my mind off Vinnie. I didn't want to think about Vinnie because I had no way to help him. He was in a horrible place.

We'd called Vinnie's father-in-law and the owner of the bail bonds business, Harry the Hammer, but Harry and Vinnie's wife, Lucille, were in the process of leaving for Aruba with some of Harry's business associates. I didn't think I could go to Aruba if my husband was missing, but that's just me. Okay, let's be honest, I couldn't go if my hamster, Rex, was missing.

I grabbed a sweatshirt and my messenger bag and went downstairs and got behind the wheel of my Whatever. Raul and Bek were parked nearby but I didn't wave to them in case I was being stalked by the bad guys. No bad guys showed up, so I called Ranger.

"I know you're trying to keep me safe," I said, "but we need the kidnapper to make a move, and he's not going to make a move as long as I have a big, black, shiny SUV following me. I'm totally wired with the necklace and whatever other illegal devices you've planted on me. I have your gun, loaded and handy. I'm going to Pino's to pick up a pizza and then I'm going to Morelli's to watch the Rangers game. I think you should retire the SUV escort. At least for the night."

What I didn't say was that it would feel creepy to have the Rangeman SUV sitting outside Morelli's house while I was inside with Morelli, probably spending the night.

"You have a red button on your dash, next to the ignition. If there's a problem, press the red button."

I looked at the dash. Sure enough there was a red button next to the ignition.

"What does the red button do?" I asked him.

"Your lights flash, an alarm goes off, and a signal is sent directly to my control room."

"Good to know," I said.

The Rangeman SUV followed me out of

the lot. I chugged off to Pino's, and Rangeman peeled off in a different direction. I relaxed with a deep breath and enjoyed the luxury of being on my own. I guess if you're royalty or a movie star you get used to having security 24/7. I was neither of those, and security felt okay at first but claustrophobic after a day.

Pino's lot was packed at this time of night. At the bar there would be medical workers and cops coming off rotation, families would be in booths, and people like me would be getting takeout.

I knew almost everyone who worked at Pino's. And I knew a lot of the people who ate there. I parked, went inside, and sat close to the kitchen at the end of the bar. Sonny Mancuso looked up from his workstation, waved at me, and pulled my ticket off his counter. I went to grade school and high school with him and now he was married to my friend Jeannie and working as a line cook. He gave me a sign that meant *five minutes,* and I gave him a thumbs-up.

I looked around the room. Connie's car had been parked in Pino's lot. Impossible to know if the kidnapper was passing through and found the lot convenient or if he lived in the neighborhood. There were a couple men in the room who fit the description. Stocky, middle-aged. One of them lived across the street from my parents. Probably he wasn't the kidnapper, although I wasn't willing to totally rule him out.

Another chunky, middle-aged guy walked in and sat at the far end of the bar. Wavy black hair cut short. Balding. Two-day beard. Gray hooded sweatshirt. He said something to the bartender, and the bartender got a large takeout bag from the kitchen. The sweatshirt guy dropped some money on the bar and got off his bar stool. He looked my way and stared for a moment too long. He smiled and nodded and walked out.

I made communion with the bartender. He was Sonny's cousin Boomer. I caught his eye and called him over. "Do I know the guy who just left?"

"Doubtful," he said. "He's not a regular. Comes in maybe once or twice a month and pays cash. Doesn't talk to anybody."

"He smiled at me."

"No crime there. He probably thought you were pretty. We all do."

Now I smiled. "You're just saying that because I'm a big tipper, but I like it anyway."

Sonny came out of the kitchen and handed

me my pizza box. "Is Boomer hitting on you again?"

"He said I was pretty."

"I can't argue with that," Sonny said. "I put the pizza on Morelli's card, and I gave myself a tip."

"Perfect."

"You watching the Rangers tonight?"

"How could you tell?"

"You got a ninety-three on your back," Sonny said. "Good choice."

I grabbed my extra-large pizza with two hands, pushed the dining room door open, and walked out into the lot. It was a perfect night. Clear sky with a sliver of moon. Cool enough for a sweatshirt. I got to my car and couldn't open the door while I was holding the giant pizza box. I was about to set it on the roof of the Whatever when I heard a footfall behind me. I turned in time to see a guy in a hoodie reach out with a stun gun. He tagged me but he only got my oversized jersey. He reached out again with the stun gun but I smashed him in the face with the pizza box and kicked him somewhere in the private area. He doubled over and staggered back a couple steps and I hit him again with the pizza. I pulled Ranger's gun out of my messenger bag, but the guy tackled me before I could aim. We both went down to the ground and the gun discharged, kicking back into my face. I was momentarily stunned, and when my vision cleared, he was getting into a car on the other side of the lot. I grabbed my cell phone and snapped a picture as he was leaving. I was tempted to take a shot at the car but what if it wasn't the right car? That would be embarrassing.

I picked the pizza up off the ground and put it back in the box. I closed the box and saw that it was partially soaked in blood. I checked myself out. It didn't seem to be my blood. I used my cell phone flashlight to follow the blood trail. Either I had given him a bloody nose when I hit him with the box or else I had accidentally shot him.

I sucked in a couple breaths to calm myself and I went back to Pino's. I took the same seat at the end of the bar, and I put the pizza box in front of me. I was impressed with myself because my hands weren't shaking.

Sonny came over and looked inside the pizza box. "I guess you need a new one," he said. "Aside from the gash between your eyes and the bruise that's forming you look okay. I'm thinking you look better than the other guy. The one who bled all over this box. Do we need to go scoop him up?"

"He got away," I said. "Afraid there's some blood in your parking lot."

"Happens all the time," Sonny said. "Not a problem."

Boomer set a glass of red wine in front of me and handed me a towel with ice in it. "Rangers scored an early goal," he said.

I drank some wine and put the ice on my forehead. I looked at the picture I had taken of the car. It was a Camry. You could clearly see the license plate. It didn't have a JZ, but it had a J7. I sent the picture to Ranger.

A minute later I got a phone call.

"Babe," Ranger said.

"Long story short, he got away, but I might have shot him. I'm waiting for my pizza and then I'm going to Morelli's."

"My office first thing in the morning," Ranger said.

I finished my wine just as my new pizza was placed in front of me.

"Do you want an escort out?" Sonny asked me.

"An escort out would be lovely," I said.

Sonny grabbed a chef's knife from the kitchen and went to the door with me. "Have you ever thought about a different line of work? Something less dangerous, like getting shot out of a cannon or being a lion tamer."

We got to my car without getting shot or zapped, and Sonny didn't have to stab anyone with his chef's knife. I put the pizza on the backseat, and I got behind the wheel.

"Thanks," I said to Sonny. "Say hi to Jeannie."

I drove out of the lot, looked in my rearview mirror, and saw Raul follow me out. So much for security liberation.

Morelli came to the door to help with the pizza box. I handed it over and Bob rushed at me, giant paws on my chest, giving me Bob kisses.

"The Rangers already made a goal," Morelli said. "I think this is going to be a good year."

"I heard when I was at Pino's. Sorry I'm late. There was a problem with the pizza."

He put the box on the coffee table. "Guard this with your life," he said to me. "Do you want wine or beer?"

"Wine."

Bob was instantly on high alert the minute the pizza box was set down. Bob ate everything. Shoes, upholstered furniture, underwear, anything wooden, and he especially loved pizza.

Morelli returned with wine for me and a roll of paper towels. He took a piece of pizza and looked at my face.

"You have a gash in your forehead just above your nose and you're getting two black eyes."

"It was one of those accidents," I said.

"Un-hunh."

I ate a piece of pizza and gave Bob my crust.

Morelli opened a bottle of beer. "Do you want to tell me about the accident?"

"No," I said. "It would be boring."

Truth is, it was embarrassing, and I didn't want to talk about it.

"Un-hunh."

He chugged some beer and looked at me. "You hit yourself in the head with your gun again, didn't you?"

"How would you know that?"

"Sonny called me. He was worried about you. He said he thought he heard a gunshot, but it was when the Rangers scored and there was a lot of noise, so he wasn't sure until you walked in."

"He ratted me out! That's the last time he gets a tip."

"He always puts it on my tab anyway," Morelli said.

I pointed to my forehead gash. "Occupational hazard."

"Un-hunh."

I was really getting annoyed at hearing *un-hunh,* so I gave him my narrow-eyed *don't mess with me* look.

"You're such a cupcake," he said. "I perfected that look. I made plainclothes because of that look."

"Okay," I said, "but my look is still pretty good."

A strand of hair had come loose from my ponytail. He tucked it behind my ear and very gently kissed me on my nose.

"Have another piece of pizza," he said. "I'm going to get some ice for your eyes. If they get any more swollen, you're going to miss the game."

CHAPTER EIGHTEEN

Morelli was gone by the time I woke up. I went into the bathroom and was horrified but not surprised by what I saw. The bruises around my eyes were black and purple and green. My eyes were swollen but thankfully not swollen shut. All because of a stupid gun. No one should ever give me a loaded gun. The only one worse with a gun was Lula. Maybe Grandma. Of course, if it weren't for the gun, I might be chained to a chemical toilet in a dark room with Vinnie right now.

I went into the bedroom, picked my clothes up off the floor, and got dressed. I made my way to the kitchen, I said good morning to Bob, and I downed a cup of coffee. It was almost eight o'clock when I left Morelli's house.

Ranger would be in a state of disbelief that I thought this was *first thing* in the morning. His first thing in the morning was night-time. I pulled away from the curb and found a Rangeman SUV in my rearview mirror. No surprise there.

I did a detour to my apartment, took a fast shower, and changed out of my Rangers jersey. My hair was still wet when I ran out of my building and got into my Whatever.

I bypassed the school bus office and went straight to Rangeman. The black Rangeman SUV was on my bumper the entire time and followed me into the underground garage. I gave the security camera at the elevator entrance the finger and stepped inside. It took me to the fifth floor.

Ranger met me at the elevator and ushered me back inside, and we went to his apartment.

"Have you had breakfast?" he asked.

"No," I said. "Just coffee."

He called down to Ella for breakfast and he moved me into his office.

"Talk to me," he said.

"About what?"

"The eyes for starters. I had the short version, now I want the long version."

I gave him the long version and he was silent for a beat. "So, you accidentally discharged the gun and knocked yourself out?"

"Not knocked out! It was more like I was stunned for a second or two," I said. "Anyway, the important thing is that I got the license plate and I actually saw this guy."

Ella came in with a tray of food and a coffeepot. She set it on Ranger's desk, smiled at me, and left.

I really like Ella. She irons Ranger's sheets, supplies him with bath products that make him smell amazing, and doesn't shoot people. At least none that I know about.

"We enhanced the picture you got of the plate, and it was obvious why we couldn't trace it," Ranger said. "The photo we had from the DOT camera was distorted. It wasn't JZ. It was J7. The car is registered to Marcus Smulet. Forty-six years old, lives on Karnery Street. Divorced. Long-haul independent trucker. Doesn't seem to own a truck. Has a spotty work history. Nothing recent. No traffic violations. The only interesting thing we found was an arrest six years ago for human trafficking. He claimed it was a humanitarian effort and he got a slap on the wrist." Ranger pulled up a photo. "Is this the guy?"

"Yes!"

"I have people watching the house. So far there's been no activity. The Camry isn't on the property."

"Jeez. I hope I didn't kill him."

"It would be convenient if you did, but it's unlikely. He was able to drive away. There's been no police chatter of finding the Camry or a body that fits Smulet's description. He didn't check into any of the local ERs for treatment."

"Now what happens?"

"You eat your breakfast while I make some phone calls and then we take a look at Smulet's house."

Karnery Street was less than a mile from Pino's. It wasn't in the Burg, but it felt like the Burg. Small two-story houses on small lots. Single-car detached garages.

Ranger parked his Porsche Cayenne two doors down from Smulet's, and we sat for a moment, taking the pulse of the area. I knew Ranger had men watching behind the house and in front of the house, but I didn't see them.

We left the Porsche and walked to Smulet's front door. Ranger rang the bell once and knocked twice. There was no answer, so Ranger did his magic, unlocked the door, and we went inside. We pulled on gloves and methodically went through each room.

The furniture was basic. A couch and two armchairs upholstered in beige. Coffee table. Area rug, also beige. Medium-sized flat-screen television facing the couch. Walnut dining table with six chairs. Kitchen with brown granite counters and ivory cabinets. Standard appliances. Everything neat. No clutter. No houseplants. Condiments in the fridge but not a lot of food. No dirty dishes in the sink. Several takeout boxes and fast-food bags in the kitchen trash. There were three bedrooms and a bath upstairs. Two beds were made. One had been slept in. Men's clothes in the one closet and dresser. Men's toiletries in the bathroom.

"He sleeps here, but he doesn't live here," Ranger said. "He probably spends a lot of time on the road. Maybe spends time at a girlfriend's house."

"There wasn't a Pino's bag in the trash. He got takeout but he didn't bring it back here."

"He'll come back here eventually," Ranger said. "He'll need clothes. He owns this house. He's not going to walk away from it. Not yet. As long as he has hopes of getting his eleven million, he's going to hang around. I'll switch to electronic surveillance tonight."

"What about relatives?"

"None in Trenton. There's a brother in El

Paso. A sister in Massachusetts with his parents. The brother is also a trucker. The sister works for a bank. Parents are retired."

"It was stupid of him to try to kidnap me in Pino's parking lot," I said.

"He saw an opportunity," Ranger said. "And he underestimated you."

"I'm a killer with a pizza box."

The bus was still parked on the street, and a thick orange extension cord tethered it to an electrical outlet at the rear of the property. Lula and Connie were inside. Connie was setting up a new computer and Lula was on the couch, surfing on her phone. She looked up and grimaced when I walked in.

"Holy crap," Lula said. "What happened to you?"

"I was sort of aiming my gun and it kicked back and got me between the eyes."

"Again?" Lula said.

"Who were you aiming at?" Connie asked.

I took a doughnut from the box on Connie's makeshift desk. "Marcus Smulet. He attacked me in Pino's parking lot. I smacked him in the face with the pizza box and then I think I might have shot him. Anyway, he got away, but I was able to get a picture of his car."

"Was it a Camry?" Lula asked. "I just know it was a Camry. Damn, girl, you're good. Did you get the plate?"

"Yep. I got the plate," I said. "I sent it to Ranger, and he traced it. We went through Smulet's house but didn't find anything useful. Smulet wasn't there."

"Where's he live?" Lula asked.

"Karnery Street."

"That's a nice neighborhood," she said. "You wouldn't expect a kidnapper to be living there."

"Knock, knock," Grandma said from the sidewalk.

She was standing at the open door, holding a grocery bag and peering in at us.

"What happened to your eyes?" Grandma asked me. "They look terrible."

"I was jumped in Pino's parking lot," I said.

"She got off a shot and hit herself in the head with her gun," Lula said.

"Again?" Grandma said. "What about the jumper?"

"He got away," I said.

Grandma stepped inside.

"I heard about the mobile office at the deli so I came to take a look. I always wanted one of these. It's got everything you need and it's on wheels so you can go

329

wherever you want. If I had a driver's license, I'd get one."

"It needs some fixing up," Lula said, "but it has potential."

"It has no potential," Connie said. "It's rusting out from under us."

"Yeah, but it has temporary potential," Lula said.

We all agreed that it had temporary potential, especially since we had no other alternatives.

"I don't want to go scouting new office locations without Vinnie or Harry getting involved," Connie said. "And neither of them is available."

"This isn't so bad, short-term," Lula said. "I found my stash of *Star* magazines this morning. And you can't hardly smell the mouse anymore."

"Are you taking it on the open road?" Grandma asked.

"It won't go on the open road in its present condition," Lula said. "It has a leakage issue."

"Leakage is a bummer," Grandma said.

"We have to at least move the bus to the back of the property," Connie said. "The city won't let us stay on the road."

"Let's do it," Grandma said. "I want to go for a ride."

"I'm all about it," Lula said.

"Will it make it around the block?" Connie asked.

"I drove it here from the junkyard, and I only had to add motor oil once," Lula said.

I jumped out and pulled the plug on the electric and Lula added motor oil. Grandma and Connie sat at the small built-in table, and Lula got behind the wheel.

"Here we go," Lula said.

There was a lot of grinding noise and the bus inched forward. We turned the corner, and the bus coughed a couple times and stopped. We all got out to take a look. Motor oil was running in a steady stream from under the bus.

"This isn't good," Lula said. "I used all my cans."

The Rangeman SUV pulled up behind us and two Rangemen got out. I knew both of them. Hal and Rodriguez.

"What's up?" Hal asked.

"We're trying to move the bus to the back of the property, but it's sprung a leak," Lula said.

"We'll give you a push," Hal said. "Get behind the wheel and make sure it's in neutral, brake off."

We got the bus situated in the small lot, and I got out to thank Hal.

"No problem," he said. "There aren't parking spaces back here now that the bus is in place. We're going to have to hang on the street, but we'll still be able to see you."

We were all going to have to park on the street and then we would either have to pick our way through the debris or walk around the block. There was no parking on the side street. It wasn't ideal but it wasn't at the top of my list of things freaking me out.

I pulled the monstrous orange electric cord over the jumble of roof shingles and collapsed ceiling and plugged it into the bus.

"We got power," Lula yelled. "It's all good."

I was glad Lula was happy, but I didn't think it was all good. I was officially on overtime in my attempt to rescue Vinnie. He was being held hostage by men who were increasingly desperate, and I had two black eyes and a dubious future.

"That was fun, but now I need to get my groceries home," Grandma said to me. "I was hoping you'd give me a ride. You need to pick up your laundry anyway. Your mom has it all folded and ironed."

"She's going to go nuts when she sees my eyes and the gash on my nose."

"That's a fact, but you might as well get it over with. Your face isn't going to improve for at least two weeks."

I drove Grandma home and followed her into the house. My dad was still out with the cab. My mom was in the kitchen knitting. She looked up when I walked in. She shook her head and threw her hands in the air, still holding tight to her knitting needles.

"You hit yourself in the head with your gun again, didn't you?" she said. "Who did you shoot this time?"

"I think it was the kidnapper, but I'm not sure I shot him."

"Omigod," she said, "the kidnapper. He's after you? How do you get into these situations? No wonder no one wants to marry you."

"People want to marry me," I said.

"Who?" my mom asked.

"Remember the butcher, what's his name? He wanted to marry me."

"You shouldn't have passed him up," my mom said. "He was a good man."

"He gave us rump roasts and lamb chops," Grandma said. "All the best cuts."

A shiver ran down my spine, thinking about the butcher. He spent his day stuffing giblets up turkey butts and he had big drooly lips like a giant grouper.

"Anyway," I said. "I'm fine, and I just came for my laundry."

"You don't look fine," my mom said. "Did you put something on that cut? You should have gotten stitches."

"I didn't need stitches. It's mostly a bruise."

"This never happens to your sister," she said. "She's married. She has children. She lives in a house with two dishwashers."

I loved my sister, but honestly, she was a baby-making machine. I had lost count of the babies. And what does a person do with two dishwashers?

I thanked my mom and carted my laundry out to my car. I put it in the backseat and returned to the office. My Whatever was small, and I was able to squeeze most of it behind the bus. As long as a garbage truck didn't come down the alley, I'd be okay.

Connie was on her feet when I rolled in.

"I need to bail someone out," she said. "Text me what you want for lunch. I'll stop at the deli on my way back."

"Did the kidnapper call?"

"Yes. Short message for you. 'Tell Plum to live in fear. We want our money.' And they sent a picture. I texted it to you and Lula."

"It just came in. I haven't had a chance to look at it."

"It's disgusting. And it brought the whole horrible ordeal back to me," Connie said. "I hear that voice and I get heart palpitations. I'm having trouble sleeping at night. I sleep with the light on."

"That's terrible," Lula said. "I tell myself not to hate anyone, but I hate these kidnappers. It's hard to find my zen with all this going on."

Connie left and I opened the photo she'd sent. It had been taken in a dark room. There was a black object in the frame.

"I can't make this out," I said to Lula.

"We had the same problem," Lula said. "I thought it was a giant bat at first. You know how they hang upside down with their wings folded around them. When you enlarge it a little you can see that it's Vinnie. I figured it out because of his tight pants. See, at the top are his pointy-toed shoes."

"Is this upside down?"

"No," Lula said. "Vinnie is upside down. They got him trussed up and hanging from some kind of hook."

I went light-headed and nauseous. I sat down, bent over, and told myself to breathe.

"I don't think he's dead," Lula said. "I think he's just hanging there. You can sort of see his face, and he looks angry. You know how he gets all squinty-eyed when he's really pissed off."

My phone rang and I saw that it was Ranger.

"We enhanced the picture," he said. "It looks like they've got Vinnie in some sort of industrial building. The wall behind him is grainy. It's the sort of concrete wall that you might see in a commercial garage. They have him bound with duct tape and hanging from a hook that you would find in a restaurant freezer or a meatpacking plant. They also use hooks like that in certain conveyor systems."

"Do you think he's okay?"

"He's dangling upside-down from a hook," Ranger said. "I don't think he's happy. I'm going to send someone out to scout around some industrial areas. In the meantime, you need to be careful. Hal said the bus got moved to the alley. We have a camera back there and I have a car on Hamilton, but there's still more risk for you parked in the back lot. I wouldn't want you there at night."

"Understood. Is there anything I can do to help?"

"Yes. You can learn how to shoot a gun without knocking yourself out. I don't have any time today, but Tank has an hour to give you instruction. Meet him in my rifle range at three o'clock."

Ranger and Tank were in Special Forces together. Ranger was point and Tank watched his back. This is still their relationship. I've seen pictures of Tank when he was a kid. He was built like a tank when he was four years old, and that's always how he's been known. Tank. I suppose he has another name, but I don't know what it is. He's big and tough and he has a cat named Fluffy.

Lula looked at me when I hung up. "What?"

"I'm getting firearms instruction at three o'clock."

"From Ranger?"

"From Tank."

"Hah!" Lula said. "Poor Tank. You're one of those hopeless gun people. You haven't got good gun juju. Some people have it and some don't. I'm lucky I've got it. I naturally take to guns. I don't need instruction. I let my instincts take over and I point and shoot. I've got instincts up my gazoo."

I've seen Lula miss a target that was three feet away. Probably one's gazoo isn't a good place to store instincts.

Connie hustled into the bus with bags of food from the deli. "I've got pastrami on rye for Lula, grilled cheese with bacon for Stephanie, and a bunch of extras. Coleslaw, macaroni salad, some chips, they threw in some extra pickles, and there's three-bean salad that Gina made fresh this morning."

There was only room for two people at the dining table, so I ate standing up at the sink.

"Who did you bond out?" Lula asked Connie.

"Some guy who caused a scene at the coffee shop on Third. He was barking like a dog, and he bit a couple people. His eighty-year-old mother was in court with him. She signed for the bond. She said he got rambunctious when he didn't take his meds."

"I like it," Lula said. "We need more crimes like that instead of the same old rape, murder, and armed robbery stuff."

"Anything interesting happen here?" Connie asked.

"Stephanie's getting shooting lessons this afternoon," Lula said.

Connie stopped eating. "Really?"

"Ranger set it up with Tank," Lula said. "Remember when Stephanie decided to clean her gun in the dishwasher?"

Truth is, I still don't know how to clean a gun, but I know enough not to put it in the dishwasher.

I finished my sandwich and grabbed my messenger bag. "I'm heading out for the day. I need to go home and get my Smith & Wesson. Let me know if there's any news, horrible or otherwise."

I drove down the alley and waited at the corner of Hamilton to let the Rangemen catch up to me. I couldn't shake the image of Vinnie hanging from a meat hook. It was ugly awful. If Tank was willing to take the time to teach me how to use my weapon, I was going to pay attention. And I was not going to lose my escort. Ranger was working to find the kidnappers and we were inching our way closer to that goal. I had to do my part to stay safe.

Benji was sitting on the floor in front of my door when I got to my apartment. He got to his feet and gave me a bag.

"This is for you and Lula and Connie," he said. "Housewarming gift for the bus. I haven't seen it yet, but Beedle told me about it. He said it's being guarded by guys dressed in black, so I thought I'd give this to you here."

"They're friends of mine," I said. "You can visit anytime you want."

I let us into my apartment and opened the bag. It contained a stack of superhero comics and the Thor action figure Lula wanted.

"This is great," I said. "Thanks."

"I decided not to go to Hawaii," he said. "I have a bunch of friends here, and I like selling comics and stuff. Anyway, as soon as I got the money, I used it to buy the comic store and I couldn't get my money back. I renamed the store and I'm having a grand opening on Saturday, if you guys want to come."

"What's the new name?"

"Benji Land."

"That's perfect!"

Benji left, and I took my S&W out of my brown bear cookie jar and put it in my messenger bag. I read a couple comics, brushed my teeth, retied my ponytail, and drove to Rangeman.

Ranger's gun range is in the basement, next to the garage. I met Tank in the first-floor lobby, and he walked me down the back stairs to the soundproof room. We sat at a table, and I took my two guns out of my bag.

"Let's start with the basics," Tank said. "Name the parts of the gun."

Turned out that I didn't know many parts. I was pretty much lost after *trigger* and *barrel*.

"We only have an hour so we're going to concentrate on the Glock 42," Tank said. "It seems like that's the one you use because that's the one that's loaded."

"Ranger gave it to me that way," I said.

"How many magazines do you have for it?"

"This one."

"No extra ammo?"

"No."

"Any ammo for your S&W?" he asked.

"No."

"Oh boy."

"I'm not really a gun person," I said.

"You will be after today," Tank said. "Both these guns are thirty-eight caliber. The S&W is a revolver, and the Glock is a semiautomatic. Ranger gave you the Glock 42 because of the size and the recoil. Even though it has the least possible recoil you still managed to knock yourself out."

"There were circumstances," I said. "We were scuffling on the ground, and I didn't knock myself out. I was momentarily stunned."

"That's encouraging. The Glock 42 is equipped with the 'safe action' system. It's a fully automatic safety system consisting of trigger, firing pin, and drop safeties, which sequentially disengage when the trigger is pulled and automatically reengage when the trigger is released. It gives you six rounds in a flush-fit magazine."

"I don't know what any of that means."

"Okay," Tank said. "Moving on. Release the magazine and reload."

"I don't know how."

"Oh boy."

"Look," I said, "I know I'm stupid about guns. I don't like guns. I'm afraid of them and I don't want to shoot anyone. But I'm in a bad situation and I have an opportunity to learn something about my weapons, and I'm going to make the most of this opportunity. So just try to be patient and I'll try to pay attention."

"Deal," Tank said.

Twenty minutes later I knew all the parts of the gun. I knew how to load it and safely carry it. Ranger had tried to teach me all these things a couple years ago, but we'd ended up naked on the floor. There was no danger of this happening with Tank. I liked Tank a lot, but naked? No. And besides, Ranger might kill him.

"Okay," Tank said, "let's see you shoot. I've set up three targets at different distances. Try the closest target."

I two-handed the little gun and squeezed off a shot.

"You'd have more luck hitting the target if you didn't close your eyes," Tank said.

"I know," I said. "It's one of those reflex

342

actions."

"Well, we have lots of ammo and we're going to stay here and shoot until you keep your eyes open. If your eyes aren't open after ten minutes of shooting, I'm using duct tape on your eyelids."

"Jeez. You're tough."

"I lied about the duct tape."

He adjusted my grip and after about twenty rounds I started keeping my eyes open.

"This is better," he said, "but you're making a scrunchy, slitty-eye face that's creeping me out. Pretend you're Ranger and you have no emotion."

"Ranger has emotion," I said.

"He doesn't show it when he's shooting."

I took a moment to channel Ranger, then I fired off a round and almost got a bullseye.

"Wow!" I said. "Did you see that? Look what I did!"

Tank was smiling. "You have a good eye. Your problem is attitude."

I shot for the rest of the hour and Ranger came in.

"How's it going?" he asked Tank.

"She's a sharpshooter," Tank said. "I might marry her."

"That doesn't work for me," Ranger said,

"but I'm glad she can shoot."

"We only had time to spend with the Glock," I said. "I'd like to come back and learn how to use the S&W."

"We'll set something up," Ranger said. "I want you to come upstairs with me to look at the photo."

I thanked Tank, took my guns, and followed Ranger up the stairs, into the elevator, and into his apartment. He closed the door and pushed me against the foyer wall. He leaned into me and kissed me. The first kiss was soft and serious. The second kiss was all passion.

He broke from the kiss and our eyes met.

"Let me guess," I said. "You get turned on by sharpshooters."

"Not all sharpshooters," he said. "Tank is obviously a better instructor than I am."

"Yes, but I wouldn't marry Tank," I said.

"Would you marry me?"

"Is that a proposal?"

"No."

"Testing the waters?" I asked.

"Curious," Ranger said.

"I honestly don't know the answer. The fast reply might be negative, but there's Ella to consider."

"You'd marry me to get your sheets ironed, your clothes folded, and gourmet food in the kitchen?"

"It sweetens the deal."

"Something to remember," Ranger said. "Let's go into my office. I want you to see the kidnapper's photo in high definition."

We went into his office, and he pulled the photo of Vinnie up on his monitor.

"The first thing that I see is that they've used duct tape to hang him on the hook," Ranger said. "This suggests that they don't intend to keep him there for very long. I think this is a setup to scare you."

"It worked," I said.

"I don't see any sign of real torture on Vinnie. He's still fully clothed. He doesn't look tortured. He looks angry. I don't think these are sadistic people. They probably killed Paul Mori, but I don't think they're professional killers. I think they're just desperate for their money. They were able to capture Connie and Vinnie, but they screwed up twice trying to get you."

"Amateurs," I said.

"Yes, but dangerous amateurs. And determined. You don't want to underestimate them. You can't see much of the room because the photo is so dark. Is there anything about it that looks familiar to you?"

"No."

"Marcus Smulet is a long-distance truck

driver who somehow managed to acquire eleven million dollars. I'm guessing he didn't do it by hauling toaster ovens."

"Maybe he was hauling humans."

"Or drugs, or both."

"What about his ex-wife? Does he have kids?"

"No kids. The ex-wife lives in White Horse. Do you want to go for a ride?"

"Sure."

CHAPTER NINETEEN

Ranger drove his Porsche Cayenne out of the Rangeman garage. He cut across town to Route 29, and from there it was a straight shot to White Horse. Ranger isn't usually a music guy when he drives. He wears an earbud and talks to the control room when necessary. Today there was minimal conversation, and he was in the zone.

When we got to White Horse, Ranger left Route 29 and followed the GPS directions to Susan Smulet's house. She was now Susan Crane and she lived in a white Cape Cod–style house with blue shutters and a blue door. It was in a pleasant neighborhood filled with basketball hoops in driveways and toddler Big Wheel bikes on front lawns. Ranger parked in front of the Crane house. We walked to the door and rang the bell.

A pretty, brown-haired, brown-eyed woman in her late thirties to early forties answered.

"We're looking for Susan Crane," I said.
"That's me."

"You were married to Marcus Smulet?"

"Yes. What's this about?"

"We're looking for him," I said. "We just have a few questions. We thought you might be able to help us."

She stepped outside and closed the door behind her. "It's been a long time. Why are you looking for him?"

"We know about some money that might belong to him."

"That sounds like Marcus. He was always scheming to get money."

"Do you know where we might locate him?"

"Sorry. I haven't seen him in a long time. We were only married for two years. Marcus and his brother had this idea to build a trucking company. His brother, Luther, would live in El Paso and Marcus would live in Trenton and they'd haul all sorts of things from Mexico to the Northeast. It sounded good on paper but the reality of it was that Marcus was never home. And when he was on the road he would fool around. So, I divorced him." She turned and looked at her closed door. "I have a really nice family now. A good husband and two kids. They don't know a lot about Marcus. I'd like to keep it that way."

"Understood," I said. "Thank you for sharing this with us."

"The plot thickens," I said to Ranger when we were back in the Porsche.

He called his office and asked them to get information on Luther Smulet.

Ranger has four spaces reserved for him in the Rangeman garage. One space is set aside for his Porsche 911 Turbo S. This was currently empty. His badass pickup occupies another. The third space is for the Cayenne. The fourth space doesn't have a car assigned to it, so this is where I'd parked my Whatever. The Whatever looked ridiculous.

"I might have to give you a car," Ranger said.

Add that to the plus side of the marriage list, I thought. A shiny new car and Ella. Not that Ranger needed anything more than himself. If Ranger were penniless and homeless, he would still be totally desirable.

We went to his fifth-floor office, and he pulled up the information on Luther Smulet. Two years older than Marcus. Divorced. Two kids. His wife had custody and lived in Austin. Luther had a house in El Paso. Also, a house in Chihuahua, Mexico. Sole proprietor of Acut Trucking. Owned two tractor trailers. One purchased ten years ago. The second purchased five years ago.

"Let's see if Luther is in El Paso or Chihuahua," Ranger said.

Ranger called someone in his control room and told him to find Luther. He disconnected from the control room and his phone buzzed with a text message.

"It's Ella," Ranger said. "She's asking if you're staying for dinner. Do you have other plans?"

"No plans."

Yes, she's staying, Ranger texted back. *We'll eat in the conference room.* He stood at his desk and disconnected his MacBook Pro. "There's more room in the conference room," he said. "I want to look at a map."

We moved to the conference room. Ranger opened his MacBook and brought a map up on the large monitor that was mounted on the wall.

"This is a section of Trenton that includes Smulet's house on Karnery Street, Paul Mori's dry-cleaning business, and Pino's," Ranger said, moving a pointer around on the map, depositing a red X on each location. "They're relatively close to each other. A long walk or a short drive."

He went from a street map to a satellite view.

"Are we looking for something in particular?" I asked.

"We're looking for a place to park an eighteen-wheeler. And we're looking for a building that would lend itself to hanging a man on a hook."

"I can't see an eighteen-wheeler parked anywhere in the Karnery Street neighborhood," I said. "Driveways aren't long enough to accommodate one and residents wouldn't tolerate one on the street. There are several blocks around Mori Dry Cleaning that have alleys behind them. In theory you might be able to park a tractor trailer in one of those alleys, but they're only one lane, so a big truck would shut down the alley. And you couldn't leave it there on garbage day."

"I sent Manuel out to scout the area and he came back with the same conclusions, but I thought it was worth seeing it on satellite with you. You already know those streets."

"That whole area is residential with mom-and-pop businesses sprinkled in with the houses. I don't see a big rig getting parked there. And I don't know of any buildings with concrete walls and meat hooks suspended from the ceiling. There are a couple butcher shops that might have meat hooks, but they wouldn't have concrete walls. If you drive past Pino's and cross Broad there are some more commercial buildings. There's an auto body repair shop with a parking lot surrounded by chain link. You might be able to make arrangements to park a truck there. I'm not super familiar with the other businesses."

Ella knocked and came into the room with a serving cart. She set out placemats, linen napkins, silverware, water glasses, and wineglasses at the end of the table. She added a large bottle of water and a bottle of red wine.

"We have New Zealand lamb loin, wild rice, and mixed fresh vegetables tonight," she said. "I brought a fruit plate for dessert, but we also have fruit sorbet."

She set the plates of food on the table, removed the domes, and set the domes on the cart.

"Would you like anything else?" she asked.

"No, this is perfect," Ranger said. "Thank you."

Ella rolled the cart to the far end of the room and left.

The silverware didn't have smudges of peanut butter. The white linen napkins had been ironed. The glasses were elegant and stemmed and didn't have water stains. The plates of food looked like they came from a three-star Michelin restaurant. I've never eaten at a three-star restaurant, but I've seen pictures.

"This is why I might consider marrying you," I said.

Ranger reached for the bottle of wine. "I can give you some other reasons if you want to spend the night."

"Not tonight," I said. "I don't want to get overwhelmed with reasons. And I should stick to water. I have to drive home."

"I have two men riding your bumper twenty-four/seven. You can leave your car here and go with them."

"What about using me as bait to catch the kidnappers?"

"That ship sailed. I'm just trying to keep you alive and unharmed until we find them."

"What about Vinnie?"

"I'm having a hard time getting emotional about Vinnie."

I held out my wineglass. "Fill it up."

I ate every crumb on my plate and was tempted to lick it clean, but I didn't want to be gross in front of Ranger. I drank two glasses of wine and was feeling incredibly mellow and moderately sexy. Okay, I'm going to be honest. I was feeling moderately mellow and incredibly sexy. Let's face it, the man was more delicious than the lamb, and the lamb had been freaking amazing.

Ranger finished eating and pushed back from the table. "I want to check with control to see if they have any information on Luther Smulet."

I poured myself half a glass of wine and followed him back to our seats at the computer.

He went online and dialed into his system. He found what he was looking for and scanned through the report.

"We're making progress, babe," Ranger said. "Luther left El Paso three weeks ago, driving one of the trucks to Trenton. He hasn't returned."

"How do you get information like this so fast?"

"Luck. Michael Ortega is my IT specialist. He has relatives in El Paso."

A photo of Luther Smulet appeared on the screen.

"He resembles his brother," I said. "Same chunky build. He could easily be the second kidnapper."

"Luther has a tattoo on his neck. It doesn't

show in this picture, but the intel report lists it."

"What sort of tattoo?"

"Scorpion."

"Ugh."

I looked at my glass. It was empty. Someone drank my wine. I suppose it was me.

"Now what?" I asked Ranger.

"We keep looking for the rig. And we watch for the Smulet brothers. We know they're here."

"Yes," I said, resting my head on the table, closing my eyes. "But what about Stephanie?"

Ranger turned in his chair and looked at me. "Babe, how much wine have you had?"

"Not even four glasses."

"Two is your limit. You're a lightweight."

"Yes, but I was having such a good time with the lamb and the fruit and also, you're looking very sexy."

Even as I was saying this, I knew the tragic truth. Two glasses of wine and I'm fun Stephanie. More than two and I'm a total snoozer.

CHAPTER TWENTY

I woke up in luxury. Ranger's bed. The room was dark and cool. The linens held the faint scent of Bulgari Green shower gel. There was no Ranger next to me. I found the bedside clock and checked the time. Seven o'clock. Practically the middle of the day for Ranger. I put the bedside light on and looked at myself under the covers. I was wearing my panties and a Rangeman T-shirt. Crap.

I took a shower using Ranger's shower gel and dried myself off with one of his fluffy towels. When I returned to the bedroom the bed had been made and my clothes were laid out for me. They were clean and folded and Ella had added new lingerie.

I got dressed and went to the kitchen. Breakfast was waiting for me on the small dining table. Fresh fruit, yogurt, Ella's house-made granola, smoked salmon with capers, a whole wheat bagel, and a carafe of coffee. I knew it was my breakfast and not Ranger's because a single luscious chocolate doughnut had been added to the mix. Ella probably had to smuggle it into the building.

I finished eating, hung my messenger bag on my shoulder, and went in search of Ranger. I found him studying a blueprint in his fifth-floor office.

"I'm heading out," I said. "Thank Ella for a wonderful breakfast." I looked at the blueprint. "Is this a new account?"

"Yes. An office building going up in Hamilton Township."

"About last night," I said. "I'm fuzzy on the details. I woke up in your bed, and I was wearing a Rangeman T-shirt."

"You had three-plus glasses of wine and crashed."

"I passed out?"

"No. You kept falling asleep. It seemed like a lot of effort to take you home, so I tucked you in here."

"That's sort of embarrassing. How did I get out of my clothes and into the Rangeman T-shirt?"

"It was a joint effort. I would have just rolled you into bed, but you had gravy on your T-shirt."

I looked down at my T-shirt. No gravy.

Ella was a laundry guru.

"Did we . . . you know?"

"Not even a little. Trust me, you would have remembered. Do you want to ride with my men today? Or do you want to drive yourself?"

"I'll drive."

I took the elevator to the garage and gave up a sigh when I looked at the cars in Ranger's reserved spaces. No Whatever.

I called Ranger. "I'm in the garage, and my car isn't here."

"It ruined my color scheme. I replaced it with a Discovery Sport. The key is on the driver's seat. You had a Superman gift bag in your Whatever car. Raymond put it in the Discovery."

The Discovery was a great-looking car, and there was no doubt in my mind that it was equipped to report my every move to the control room. It probably had sensors in the steering wheel to take my pulse and alert Ranger if my heart rate went too high.

I drove out of the garage and went to the office. I cruised down the alley, stopped at the yellow bus, and realized the Discovery wasn't going to fit in the Whatever's parking space. I drove around the block and parked in front of the demolished office. I took my messenger bag and the Superman gift bag, and I picked my way along the narrow path that had been created to get to the back lot.

Lula and Connie were already in the bus. A new coffee machine and four coffee mugs had been placed on the kitchen counter. The essential box of doughnuts was on the table serving as Connie's desk. Lula was dressed in sneakers and spandex camo fatigues.

"Sneakers?" I said to Lula.

"I got tired of walking around the block to get here and I'm not ruining my collection of fine footwear by trying to make my way along that half-assed path we got going over what used to be the office."

"It's a good look for you," I said. "And I like your camo-colored hairstyle."

"The thing is you gotta put it all together," Lula said. "When you're a fashionista like me, you have to be top to bottom. Like you can't use a red thong with desert camo outerwear. That would be all wrong."

"Are you wearing a camo thong?" I asked her.

"I decided to go with khaki on the thong. It's a good accent piece, and it complements my skin tone, but it's still in keeping with the overall theme."

I put the Superman gift bag next to the doughnut box. "I saw Benji yesterday. He brought this as a new office gift, and he invited us to his grand opening tomorrow. He bought the comic book store and renamed it Benji Land."

Lula pulled the comics out of the bag and shrieked when she saw Thor.

"It's the Thor action figure!" she said. "It's the exact one I wanted. It looks just like Thor in *Ragnarok* before he got his haircut. Don't get me wrong, Thor is a hot god no matter if he's got long or short hair, it's just I prefer the long version. He's got his mighty hammer with him too, and you can move his arms." She set Thor on the couch next to her. "We've gotta go to Benji's grand opening so I can thank him," Lula said. "We're all going, right?"

"Right," I said.

"Right," Connie said.

"How long is Harry going to be away?" I asked Connie.

"He's supposed to be home on Wednesday."

"Does he know about the office? About Vinnie?"

"He knows about the office. The insurance adjuster is supposed to look at the property today. I have the plans from when we rebuilt the office last time it got destroyed, so it should be easier this time.

Harry hasn't mentioned Vinnie, and I haven't brought him up. I don't know what to say about Vinnie."

"About all you can say is that he's missing," Lula said. "Unless you want to add that he looks like a big bat hanging from a meat hook somewhere. Problem is that inspires conversations we got no answers for."

My mom called. "It's raining and I need some things at Giovichinni's. Your father is out with the taxi and my car is in the shop. Something's wrong with the starter."

I looked out the window. Sure enough it was raining.

"Send me a list," I said.

"I thought we'd have pot roast tonight for you and Joseph. Eddie, the butcher at Giovichinni's, is holding a nice rump roast for me. And I know Joseph likes chocolate cake. I thought we'd have that for dessert."

"Sounds great."

I hung up and texted Morelli. *Are we on for dinner at my parents' house tonight?*

Yes, he texted back. *I'm on call but hopefully I won't be needed.*

"I have to make a deli run for my mom," I said to Connie and Lula. "I'll be back."

"We'll be here," Lula said. "We're just

hanging out waiting to hear from kidnappers."

I put the hood up on my sweatshirt and kept my head down walking through the rubble. I got to the sidewalk and had a moment of confusion when I couldn't find my car. I realized my car was a new black Discovery, and I did a mental head slap. Duh.

I drove to Giovichinni's, parked at the curb, and ran inside. I went straight to Eddie and got the rump roast.

"It's a beauty," he said. "I picked it out first thing this morning when your mom called. Are you still seeing that cop?"

"Joe Morelli? Yes."

"Too bad. Come see me if it doesn't work out."

I assured him that he would be the first to know, and I started working my way through my mom's list. What is it with butchers and me? It's like I'm a butcher magnet.

I got everything on the list and wheeled my cart to the checkout. Mary Ann Giovichinni was working the register. She looked at me and then her attention shifted to the door.

"Oh crap," Mary Ann said on a whisper.

It was Bella.

"Look at this," Bella said, focusing her

squinty eyes on me. "It's the slut. You let the slut shop here?"

"Hello, Bella," Mary Ann said. "Haven't seen you in a while."

"I'm under house arrest," Bella said, "but I snuck out. I need macaroni salad. My daughter-in-law knows nothing."

"Tell Eddie and he'll scoop some fresh for you."

"You good girl," Bella said. "I not give you the eye."

"Holy hell," Mary Ann said when Bella went to the back of the deli. "She scares the bejeezus out of me. She's freaking creepy."

I helped Mary Ann bag, and I rushed out of the store before Bella returned with her macaroni. I sat in the Discovery and I looked around. There were no other cars parked at the curb. Bella came out of the deli and opened an umbrella. She was going to walk home in the rain. Damn.

I rolled the window down and yelled at her. "Bella! Do you want a ride?"

She walked over to me and looked in. "You try to get on the good side of me?"

"Do you have a good side?" I asked her.

"Hah!" she said. "I let you give me a ride."

It was a short trip and neither of us spoke. I stopped in front of her house, and she got out. "You a slut but you know to do the right thing," she said.

Grandma and my mom were at the kitchen table when I brought the groceries in. They were having coffee and crumb cake because that's what you do in the Burg when it's a rainy morning. I put the groceries away and joined them at the table.

"Bella was at Giovichinni's when I was there," I said. "She told Mary Ann that she was under house arrest, but she needed macaroni salad."

"Sometimes I almost like her," Grandma said.

I took a piece of crumb cake and smeared some butter on it. "The butcher at Giovichinni's hit on me."

"Eddie?" my mom said. "What did you tell him? Are you going out with him?"

"No," I said. "I'm going out with Morelli."

"You could do worse than Eddie," my mom said. "I like Morelli, but he comes to dinner, and I don't see a ring on your finger."

"Do you want me to marry Eddie?"

"I want you to marry *somebody*," my mom said.

"How about Ranger?" I said.

My mom froze with her coffee cup halfway

to her mouth and she made the sign of the cross. Grandma choked on a piece of crumb cake.

"Did he ask you to marry him?" my mom finally said.

"No," I said. "It was a hypothetical question."

"Oh, well, goodness," my mom said. "Okay then."

"What's wrong with Ranger?" I asked her.

"I don't know exactly," my mom said. "He's very mysterious. He feels dangerous."

"He's hot," Grandma said. "I'd marry him in a heartbeat."

I couldn't argue with either of them.

"I'm looking for someone who lives on Karnery Street," I said. "His name is Marcus Smulet."

"I don't know anybody named Smulet," Grandma said, "but Grace Lucarello lives on Karnery Street. She's lived there forever. What's this Marcus guy done?"

"He might be associated with the kidnapping," I said. "He's more of a person of interest right now than a suspect."

"I can ask Grace if she knows him. Karnery Street isn't that big. It's only a couple blocks."

"Call her and ask if we can come over. I want to ride by Smulet's house anyway."

Ten minutes later we were in the Discovery, heading for Karnery Street with Rangeman following us.

"This is a beauty of a car," Grandma said. "I guess I know where you got it. I know your mother thinks Ranger is dangerous, but there's lots of good things to say about him, too. Did you ever find out where he gets all his new cars?"

"No. That's one of the mysteries of Ranger."

"Probably better that way," Grandma said.

A while ago, Ranger had said they were part of a business arrangement. I thought that was sufficiently vague to still qualify as a mystery.

I did a slow pass by Smulet's house first. No action there. No lights on. No car in the driveway. Grace lived on the corner, three houses away from Smulet. Lights were on and a VW Taos was in the driveway.

"Grace's husband passed a couple years ago," Grandma said. "She's fixed pretty good, so she was able to keep her house, but she still watches what she spends. She only plays two cards at bingo."

Grace came to the door before we rang the bell. "Come in," she said. "Such a rainy day. Do you want tea?"

"Tea would be wonderful," Grandma said.

I placed Grace as in her seventies. She was wearing slacks and sneakers and a light-weight flannel shirt. Her hair was gray and cut short. Her house was stuffed with furniture. We followed her into the kitchen, and Grandma and I sat at the kitchen table while Grace put the kettle on.

"It's interesting that you want to know about Marcus Smulet," Grace said. "Nobody knows what to make of him. Even his next-door neighbors don't really know him. He lives alone mostly. His brother comes to visit sometimes. The brother stays for a couple days and leaves. Word is that they're both truck drivers and they're on the road all the time. A couple times there was a gigantic truck parked in front of the Smulet house. Nobody raised a fuss because the truck never stayed long."

"Have you seen him lately?" I asked.

She brought three mugs of tea to the table and sat with us. "No," she said, "but that's not unusual. He's a real loner."

"Does he have a girlfriend?" Grandma asked.

"Not that I know about." Grace leaned forward over the table and lowered her voice. "Why do you want to know about Marcus? I know you're a bounty hunter. Is he a fugitive? Is there a reward on his head?"

"No," I said. "Nothing like that."

Grandma leaned forward and lowered her voice like Grace. "He's a person of interest. We can't say more. It's very hush-hush."

Grace looked overjoyed to hear this. "I knew it!" she said. "Don't worry, I won't say a word to anyone."

We finished our tea and said goodbye to Grace. She promised to keep an eye out for Marcus and his brother and call us if she saw anything.

"Do you think she'll keep this quiet?" I asked Grandma when we were in the car.

"Not a chance," Grandma said.

I took Grandma home and drove to the office. The insurance adjuster was poking around in the debris when I parked at the curb. It was raining buckets and he was holding a big black umbrella in one hand and a cell phone in the other. It looked like he was taking photos and videos with his cell phone. I didn't want to disturb him, so I parked and walked around the block.

Connie's car was parked behind the bus, and Lula and Connie were next to it, standing under a single umbrella. Connie was holding her tote and a black garbage bag. Lula was holding her huge purse and Thor.

"It's raining inside the bus," Connie said to me. "We moved everything we could to the dry side, and we're closing up shop. I'm going to work from home. I'll call you if I hear from the kidnappers."

"Ditto," Lula said. "Me and Thor are going home, too. I promised him we could watch *Aquaman.*"

I was soaked by the time I got back to Hamilton Avenue. I didn't want to ruin the seats on Ranger's Discovery, so I hitched a ride with the Rangemen. They dropped me at the back door to my building. I ran inside and dripped all the way to my apartment.

I kicked my shoes off in the kitchen and my phone buzzed. It was a text and a photo forwarded from Connie. *This is just the beginning,* the text said. The photo was a bloody hand missing two fingernails. I went light-headed and threw up in the sink. Thank heaven for garbage disposals.

I felt better after a shower. There was still anxiety about Vinnie but at least my stomach wasn't churning. I got dressed in a soft blue V-neck sweater and my nicest jeans. I dried my hair, swiped some mascara on my lashes, and applied lip gloss. I looked at my reflection in the mirror. "It's important to give the illusion of normalcy," I said to reflected Stephanie. "That's how you keep going when things are tragic." I had two black eyes and I was finding it hard to smile. I couldn't do anything about the eyes, but I could make more of an effort at smiling. If I allowed the horror of Vinnie's nails to overwhelm me, I would be useless at tracking down the kidnappers.

I grabbed my messenger bag and a sweatshirt, went downstairs, and crossed the small lobby to the back door. The Rangeman SUV drove up to the building when I stepped out. I asked to be taken back to the Discovery and fifteen minutes later I was in my car and on my way to my parents' house. The rain had cut down to a misty drizzle. Hopefully the bus was drying out. I arrived ahead of Morelli. I said hello to my dad but I'm not sure he heard me. He was in front of the TV, slumped in his chair, eyes closed. The dining room table was set and the smell of burned rump roast was overwhelming. That was my mom's secret. Cremate the rump to get super-dark gravy. Some people might have thought the gravy tasted a tad burned, but we were Plums and we liked it that way.

"Can I help?" I asked.

"Drain the potatoes," my mom said. "I'm ready to mash them."

I took the huge pot to the sink, poured the potatoes and boiling water into the colander, and returned the potatoes to the pot. When I stepped back my face was bathed in steam and my hair had frizzed. My mom took over adding milk and butter. Lots of butter.

I heard Morelli at the door and went to greet him. He gave me a quick kiss and stepped back to take a look at me.

"Steam bath?"

"Potatoes," I said.

The six o'clock news came on and my dad woke up and stood. "Where's dinner?"

"It's on the table," my mother said, setting the carved pot roast in front of his seat.

Grandma brought the potatoes and gravy. The vegetables and wine followed. Dinner was a perfectly orchestrated event that had occurred every night for as long as I could remember. Grandma was a relatively new addition, and my sister, Valerie, had her own family meals now in her own house, but the basic ritual here was still the same. It was both comforting and disturbing.

"What did you do today?" Grandma asked Morelli. "Did you arrest a killer?"

"No," Morelli said. "I almost never arrest killers. In this town they're usually killed by other killers before I get to them."

"The circle of life," Grandma said.

Everyone thought about that for a moment. The moment was broken by my dad yelling for gravy.

"Jeez Louise," he said. "Pass the gravy. My meat's getting cold."

Morelli poured a glass of wine for himself and one for me. I took a sip and put it back on the table. Best not to guzzle wine two days in a row.

"How about an autopsy?" Grandma asked. "Have you seen any of them lately? I'd like to see an autopsy. Especially the part where they weigh the brain. It's a shame you have to be dead before you can find out how much your brain weighs."

My mom chugged half her Big Gulp of iced tea, which we all knew to be whiskey. I couldn't blame her.

"How's your knitting going?" I asked my mom.

"I started a new skein today," she said. "Purple."

"I bet it's pretty."

"It's not as vibrant as I hoped it would be," she said. "It knits out to be more lavender."

I didn't know where to go from here. I'd just made my best stab at polite conversation, and now I had nothing. It was easier eating with Rex. I ate over the sink, and he didn't expect a lot from me.

"How's Bob?" Grandma asked Morelli.

"He's good," Morelli said. "He's out in the car. I thought Stephanie and I could take him for a walk after dinner if it stops raining."

"Are you sure he's okay in the car?" Grandma asked. "I thought you weren't supposed to leave kids and dogs in the car."

"The windows are cracked and the temperature is okay," Morelli said. "He's comfortable."

"You should bring him in," Grandma said. "I'd like to see him. He would make it a party. I could give him a bowl of water."

My dad didn't say anything. He was shoveling in mashed potatoes and gravy. My mom raised her glass and smiled. "To Bob," she said.

"It's okay with me," I said.

Morelli left the table and came back with Bob. Bob was beside himself, doing his happy dance. Bob was a people dog. Bob made his way around the table, sniffing everyone. He got to my dad, gave him a sniff, and snatched two slabs of rump roast off his plate.

"Hey!" my dad said to Bob. "That's rude. What the hell!" He looked over at Morelli. "Don't you feed this dog?"

My mom and Grandma were laughing,

and I was having a hard time keeping a straight face. Morelli looked conflicted between thinking Bob was cute and being completely mortified.

"Sorry," he said to my dad. "I should have kept him on the leash. Bad, Bob!" Morelli said to Bob.

Bob came over and settled down between Morelli and me.

"Well, don't everyone just sit there like a bunch of dopes," my father said. "Someone pass me the meat."

My mom brought the chocolate cake to the table and Morelli's phone buzzed.

He looked at the number and stood. "I have to take this," he said, moving into the living room. He returned a couple minutes later and sat down. "I need to go to work but I'm not leaving until I have cake."

"Is it someone dead?" Grandma asked.

"I'll know when I get there," Morelli said.

He finished his cake and left. I stayed to have a second piece. Bob didn't get any because dogs shouldn't eat chocolate.

I helped clear the table and put the food away, and Bob positioned himself in the kitchen. Grandma hand-fed him chunks of rump roast and gave him a bowl of vanilla ice cream since he couldn't have cake.

It had stopped raining, so I clipped the

leash on Bob, and Grandma and I took him for a walk. The Rangeman SUV crept along behind us.

"I feel like a movie star," Grandma said. "They have bodyguards following them everywhere just like this."

I felt like an idiot. I felt conspicuous. When the walk was done, I collected my bag of leftovers, including half the chocolate cake, loaded Bob into the Discovery, and went home to my apartment. I texted Morelli that Bob and the cake were with me. Morelli texted back that he was going to be late. Save him some cake.

CHAPTER TWENTY-ONE

I fell asleep on the couch and woke up at midnight. I shuffled off to my bedroom and crawled under the covers. When I woke up in the morning, Bob was sprawled next to me, and Morelli was on the edge of the bed next to Bob.

I got up and took a shower. I got dressed and went to the kitchen for coffee. Morelli came in a couple minutes later.

"I smell coffee," he said. "How long have you been up?"

"Not long," I said. "When did you get home last night?"

"Around three o'clock. Bob was in my spot in the bed and wouldn't give it up." Morelli got a mug and filled it with coffee. "What's for breakfast?"

"Chocolate cake."

"That works for me."

We stood in the kitchen eating cake and drinking coffee.

"I have to go back to work this morning," Morelli said. "I need to follow up on a couple things from last night, and then I'm taking my rotation at babysitting Bella."

"Must have been a riot last night."

"Pretty much. It started out as an organized smash-and-grab and turned into a bloodbath. There were a lot of people involved. Some didn't walk away." He rinsed his plate off in the sink and put it in the dishwasher. "What are you doing today?"

"The bus was leaking water yesterday. I'm going to check it out. See if any real damage was done. And then I'm going to Benji's grand opening. He bought the comic book store and renamed it Benji Land."

"Clever," Morelli said. "Where do you suppose Benji got enough money to buy the store?"

I shrugged. "Do you have any ideas?"

"I have one or two. How about you?"

"I have one or two."

He kissed me and the kiss lingered.

"I'm definitely not on call tonight," he said. "I think we should go out to a fancy dinner and then come home to my house and get naked."

"I like it," I said.

"And if we finish up early enough, we can catch the end of the ball game."

"You're such a romantic."

Morelli grinned. "I have to go home to change clothes. I'll take Bob with me. Thanks for letting us spend the night. Do you have anything you want me to tell the Rangeman guys parked in your lot?"

"Tell them I'll be out in a couple minutes."

When Morelli asked about my plans for the day, the unmentioned elephant in the room was Vinnie. Neither of us had been able to make any progress at finding Vinnie. I can't speak for Morelli, but I was exasperated that I couldn't go more proactive. Surely there was *something* we could do to find him.

The sun was shining, and the air had a chill in it. I drove to the office, parked behind Connie's car, and walked to the school bus. The door was open, and I could hear a fan going inside.

I looked in at Connie. "Trying to dry things out?"

"It could be worse, but it's obvious we need something better. It'll take at least a year to rebuild, and we can't conduct business in this."

"What if there is no business?" I asked her. "What if there's no Vinnie?"

"Harry will find someone else. Harry

378

needs this business. It's part of his corporate image."

I didn't want to ask about Harry's corporate image. There are things about Harry best left unknown.

Lula stumbled in. "I don't know how anyone can walk in sneakers. My balance is all whackadoodle. When I'm in heels my boobies and booty are compensating for each other. They're all synchronized. There's just nothing happening when I'm flat-footed. None of my voluptuous body parts knows which way to swing."

I didn't have this problem. My body parts were a lot less voluptuous than Lula's. They didn't swing anywhere.

"Anything new going on with the kidnappers?" Lula asked.

I shared the fingernail picture with her.

"That's disgusting," Lula said. "I'm not happy to see this. Okay, so he's an annoying jerk, but that don't mean I'm gonna stand around and let some kidnapper torture him. This is something else. If anyone tortures him, it should be us. Or at least someone we hired to torture him."

Connie and I agreed.

"So, what are we going to do about this?" Lula asked. "I think we should entertain the possibility of raising the money."

"It's eleven million dollars!" I said.

"Yeah, but we might be able to get *some* of it," she said. "We could buy a bunch of scratch lottery tickets. And we could start a GoFundMe page. You always have to start with something that gets people's attention. We could tell people we want to save the highly endangered pointy-toed weasel."

"I guess I could try to bargain with them next time we get a phone call," I said.

"Omigosh," Lula said. "I've got it! We could put up Lost posters. My neighbor did that when their cat disappeared. A lot of people called her saying they saw her cat. Maybe someone saw Vinnie get snatched. Or they might have seen him get dragged into a building."

"The Lost poster might work," Connie said. "We could offer a reward."

"I'll make the poster," Lula said. "I always got a good grade in art when I was in school. First thing, I'm going to need a picture of Vinnie."

"I don't have any on hand," Connie said. "I'll get one tonight. I should be able to find something online. Right now, I'm going out with a Realtor to look at office space. It would be great if you two could look for a storage unit for the files. They can't stay in my garage. It isn't secure."

"What about the grand opening?" Lula asked. "When are we doing that?"

"How about after lunch?" Connie said.

"Do you have anyplace special you want us to look for storage?" Lula asked Connie.

"Find something cheap and convenient," Connie said. "It doesn't have to be climate controlled, but it has to be secure."

Lula looked at the box of doughnuts on the table. "What about the doughnuts? Are we leaving them here? It would be a shame to leave them here to get stale if nobody is here eating them."

"Take the doughnuts," Connie said.

Lula and I walked back to Hamilton Avenue and got into the Discovery.

"It's a pleasure riding around with you in this car," Lula said. "It even smells nice."

"It smells like doughnuts," I said.

"It's the happiest smell in the whole world," Lula said.

"I don't know anything about storage units," I said. "See what you can find on your phone."

"I'm suggesting that we start with the closest ones first. There are two on Broad. Then there's one on Chambers."

The first one on Broad didn't have any available units. The second one was too expensive. The one on Chambers had been turned into condominiums.

"There are a bunch in Hamilton Township," Lula said. "That's not so far away."

After two hours of searching, we came away with three possibilities, and we went back to the bus to rendezvous with Connie.

"Pino's is delivering," Connie said. "I went with meatball subs. What did you find out about getting a storage unit?"

"We have three possibilities," I said. "They're all in Hamilton Township and they're all about equal." I gave her two brochures. "The third one didn't have a brochure," I said. "New ownership."

"But they were real nice," Lula said. "They liked my camo gear, and they didn't have any rats or anything."

"Did the others have rats?" Connie asked.

"We didn't see any," I said.

"There were droppings in one," Lula said. "I know rat droppings when I see them, and they were rat droppings."

"How'd you do?" I asked Connie. "Did you find an office?"

"No. I didn't think it would be this difficult. We're going out again this afternoon. The Realtor is picking me up at Benji's."

"Suppose we got one of those already-made houses," Lula said. "I see them riding down the highway all the time. They got curtains on the windows and everything."

Pino's grandson Zak yelled, "Knock knock," and stuck his head in the door. "I got subs," he said. "Grandpa threw in macaroni for free because he made too much for the people at table number four."

"I like macaroni," Lula said.

Connie took the bags, paid for the subs, and gave Zak a tip that made him smile.

The couch was still too wet to sit on so we huddled around the tiny table.

"This is like camping out," Lula said. "I never camped out, but I bet it's like this."

"I camped out once," Connie said. "It sucked. Nature isn't what you see on television. I had bug bites all over me and there's nothing to do. You're just out there in the woods."

"Didn't you have television?" Lula asked.

"No. We were in a tent. No electricity. No toilet."

"I wouldn't do that kind of camping," Lula said. "I gotta have television and a toilet."

We finished lunch and left the bus. Everyone got into the Discovery, and I drove to Benji Land. Carpenter Beedle's Mercedes was parked in front of the store. There were a few people wandering around inside. One of them was Sparks in his Sir Lancelot costume.

Benji came over to us. "There's a food truck out back," he said. "It's all free. Wieners and soft drinks."

"That was nice of you to give us Thor," Lula said. "It's the good Thor, too."

Sir Lancelot came over. "What do you think of Benji's store? It's wonderful, right? There's a whole Tolkien section now. Plus, he's added D&D, Magic: The Gathering, and Pokémon gameplay nights."

"I gotta go see Tolkien," Lula said. "Point me in a direction."

Beedle ambled over. "How's it going?" he asked. "Benji said you didn't need our help anymore, so I guess everything got resolved."

"Unfortunately, nothing is resolved. A friend of mine is in the security business and he's running protection for me."

"Rangeman," Beedle said. "We've been seeing the cars."

"How's it going with you?"

"It's good. I'm in start-up mode with the finance business, so it's slow, but it'll pick up. I have a couple clients. I see the bail bonds office is operating out of a retired school bus."

"It's temporary. Connie is looking for something more substantial. Lula and I are looking for a storage locker for some of the stuff we were able to salvage."

"Did you try Susan Dippy Storage?"

"No. It didn't show up in Google."

"Yeah, it's under the radar. I keep some stuff there. It isn't fancy but it's convenient. It's a couple blocks from here on Cord Street. If you go out the back door it's a three-minute walk. You turn left down the alley and right on the first cross street."

I found Lula in Superheroes, checking out the Thor action figure with short hair.

"I might need this," Lula said. "It would be good to have both Thors."

"I was just talking to Beedle, and he told me about some storage units a couple blocks away. I thought we could take a look at them."

"Sure, but I need a free wiener first. I haven't been to the food truck yet."

We went out the back door to the food truck. I got a soda, and Lula got a hot dog and a soda.

"They've got all the good condiments here," Lula said. "This is a first-class free wiener. And the bun is just right. Not too big and not too small. Plus, the slit is on the top."

We walked down the alley and turned right on Cord Street. Traffic was sporadic.

Houses were set back on large lots. There were lots of trees. We came to the second block and didn't see Susan Dippy Storage. When we reached the third block, I saw a car turn out of the alley that ran behind the houses.

"Bingo," Lula said. "I just got the same idea you got."

We took the cross street to the alley and found Susan Dippy. It was a small cinder-block strip mall of storage units that had been built into the alley and stretched the length of a block.

"I don't see an office," Lula said. "Must be at the other end."

We walked halfway down the alley and a car came at us from behind at high speed. It screeched to a stop and four men in ski masks jumped out and tackled Lula and me. We were all rolling around yelling and kicking and clawing. Lula got to her feet, one of the men stunned her, and she crumpled to the ground and lay there lifeless. A second car came in from the other direction and two men also in ski masks got out, scooped Lula up, and stuffed her into their car. A moment later someone gave me a bunch of volts, and I went scramble brain.

CHAPTER TWENTY-TWO

I'd been stun gunned before. This was nothing new. I knew the recovery process. Tingling in my fingers. Buzzing in my head. Disoriented. I tried to relax and concentrate on breathing. I couldn't see anything, and it took me a while to realize I had a sack over my head. My hands were tied behind me. Felt like a plastic zip tie. The fog was lifting. I was cramped into a fetal position, getting pushed along in some kind of cart. Wheels on concrete, I thought.

I was finally alert enough to be scared. I was sightless with the sack over my head, but there were horrible visions stuck in my mind. Connie's burns, Vinnie hanging upside down, bloody fingers without fingernails. My heart was racing, and I think I was drooling. Or maybe my nose was running. Hard to tell when you're in a sack and your hands are tied. I heard a door swing open, felt the bump of my cart being rolled over a threshold.

I was working hard to calm myself. I was telling myself I had to be smart. I had to watch for my moment. Panic was the enemy. Suddenly the cart was tipped, and I rolled out onto a hard floor. Deep breaths, I told myself. Don't show fear. Don't show pain.

"Now what?" a male voice said. "You want me to beat her up? Get her attention?"

"Not yet." Another male voice. "She's probably still stupid from the stun gun. Take the sack off her so she doesn't suffocate. She's no good to us if she's dead."

The sack was pulled off, and I still couldn't see a lot in the dark room, but I could see enough to recognize Marcus and Luther. Not a good sign that they were letting me see their faces. I took it to mean that they weren't expecting me to leave the building alive. I didn't look beyond them. I lay on the floor with my eyes unfocused and my mouth open. Impaired. Thinking I was pretty good at looking stupid.

"She's breathing kind of fast," Marcus said.

"You'd be breathing fast, too, if you just took fifty thousand volts," Luther said. "Let's get lunch. She's not going anywhere."

The door slammed shut and I got myself into a sitting position. I was in a room about the size of my parents' living room. Cement floor. Cement walls. Cold and damp. My eyes adjusted to the dim light, and I saw a dark blob in the corner. The blob moved and I realized it was Vinnie.

"Are you okay?" I asked him.

"Yeah," he said. "I'm having a great time here."

"We were wondering about that," I said.

"Funny. Very funny."

"Is there a way out?"

"You mean if I wasn't chained to a chemical toilet that's bolted to the floor?"

I scanned the room. One door. Looked solid. Probably metal. No windows. Low ceiling for an industrial building. Nine or ten square feet I was guessing. Large vent of some sort in the ceiling over the toilet.

"Do you know where we are?" I asked Vinnie.

"No clue. I was stun gunned and bagged. Came around in this room. How did you get here?"

"I was stupid. I went to look for a storage unit with Lula and I didn't check for a tail. I should have known they were watching me, waiting for a chance to capture me."

"Why were you looking for a storage unit?"

"The office got bombed. Long story. I'll

tell you some other time."

"That's a real pisser."

"Yeah. It was upsetting. Not as upsetting as the picture of you hanging from a meat hook."

"They walked me down the hall and two stairwells for that. Never saw the light of day. Always cement walls or some kind of stucco. Bad light. Peeling paint. I'm guessing this used to be a factory and now it's abandoned. They wanted a photo op. I hung there for about an hour while they fiddled with their cell phones. These brothers aren't smart. Luther and Marcus. I heard them talking. Sounds like you've got a lot of money that they want."

"I don't have it."

"They think you have it and that's what matters."

"What about your fingernails?" I asked him.

"What about them?"

"They sent a second picture of someone's bloody fingers that were missing some fingernails."

"Not mine," Vinnie said.

I looked up at the vent. "That's how we're getting out of here."

"Do they have you in flexi-cuffs?"

"Yep."

"Amateurs," Vinnie said.

"They were counting on me still having scrambled neurons."

Flexible nylon disposable restraints serve a purpose. They're inexpensive and they take up no space. They're a good substitute for metal bracelets unless you put them on someone who knows how to get out of them. And one of my first lessons from Ranger had been how to get out of them.

If I'd been cuffed in front, it would have been relatively easy. Being cuffed behind my back made it more difficult.

"Get over here," Vinnie said. "Let me do it. I'm chained in front. I can work with my hands better than you."

He got the cuffs open, and I studied his chains. They weren't attached to the toilet. They were attached to a rusted eyebolt that was screwed into the floor next to the toilet. I tried unscrewing the bolt, but it wouldn't budge. The concrete around it was cracked and crumbling but not enough that I could work the bolt loose.

"I need to give this bolt a good whack," I said to Vinnie.

"They keep a flashlight by the door."

I looked at the door. "I don't see it."

"It's there. It's so freaking dark in here

it's hard to see. It's probably lying on its side."

I ran over and found the flashlight. It was a monster Maglite. I tried the door. Locked, of course. I ran back to Vinnie and gave the rusted eyebolt four whacks with the Maglite, and the bolt cracked open.

"We're in business," I said to Vinnie.

He was no longer attached to the floor, but he was still bound by the chain. I checked my watch. Time was ticking away for us. "I can't figure out this chain system," I said. "They've got them twisted around your wrists."

"Let me do it. I'm good with chains. Sometimes Madam Zaretsky goes on to another client and forgets about me, and I have to let myself out."

"I wish I hadn't heard that."

"Hold the end of this chain while I work at the other end. I've almost got it unraveled."

"We have a decision to make," I said. "We can hide behind the door and take them by surprise and beat the crap out of them. Or we can try to escape through the overhead vent."

"I'd like nothing better than to beat the crap out of them, but, more often than not, there are more than two. There are at least six people involved in this."

"Then it has to be the vent. I hope it goes somewhere."

Vinnie stood on the toilet. "I can alley-oop you up to the vent. The hard part is getting myself into it."

I climbed up Vinnie, sat on his shoulders, and removed the rusted vent.

"We're in luck," I said. "This is part of a huge air duct. We can easily slither along in it."

I climbed off Vinnie and into the air duct. I was flat on my stomach, but I had enough clearance to belly crawl. Vinnie was tiptoes on the toilet, trying to pull himself up into the duct, having no luck.

"What about the laundry cart they used to get me into the room?" I called out to Vinnie. "It had a bar across the top. If you could stand on the bar, you might have a better chance of getting into the duct."

"Good thought," Vinnie said.

Seconds later I heard the cart roll across the room and bang into the toilet.

"Are you okay?" I asked him.

"Yeah. I had to ram the cart against the toilet to hold it steady. This is going to work."

He climbed up the cart and pulled himself into the air vent.

I was already on the move. I was being careful not to make noise, and I was looking for a vent that led to a hallway. I didn't want to drop into another locked room. The first vent looked into a room similar to the one we'd just left. The second vent opened to a room that appeared to be littered with sleeping bags thrown on the floor, empty water bottles, and crumpled fast-food bags. All the rooms were windowless and lit by a single low-watt bulb. I wasn't surprised to see the sleeping bags and trash. Abandoned buildings were used by runaway kids and druggies. I was surprised that it was so close to the room where the brothers were imprisoning their captives. And I was surprised that there was electricity in a building used by squatters. It meant that the building wasn't completely abandoned.

"We need to get out of this air duct," Vinnie whispered. "They're going to come after us, and we don't want to be trapped here."

I crawled up to another vent and looked into another room filled with sleeping bags. Too many sleeping bags. Almost wall to wall. Dormitory. What exactly was this place?

The air duct branched off to the left and I took the left turn. Finally, a vent that didn't open to a room. I got to the edge, and I heard voices. The brothers and another man. Talking about baseball. Mets fans. I held my breath when they passed underneath me. They continued down a hall and I could no longer hear their voices. They were probably on their way to our cell.

I worked the vent loose and grabbed it before it crashed to the floor. I passed it back to Vinnie. I eased myself out through the hole in the hall ceiling and dropped to the floor. Vinnie did the same. We quickly moved down the hall in the opposite direction of the three men. We came to a stairwell and carefully entered, listening for voices or footfalls. The number 5 was painted on the door. It appeared to be the top floor.

We reached the fourth-floor landing and the sound of machinery carried through the door. I cracked the door and looked out. It was a large, brightly lit room filled with women at sewing machines.

"Sweatshop," Vinnie whispered. "The women are kept in the dorms upstairs."

"In Trenton? Are you kidding me?"

"There are men in there too. Supervisors."

We hurried down the rest of the stairs to the cavernous underground garage. The stairs were next to a freight elevator. A Sprinter van and four cars were parked close to the elevator.

An Acut eighteen-wheeler was parked a distance away.

"That's Luther's truck," I said. "It's Acut Trucking and it's got Texas plates."

"That's how they bring the women in," Vinnie said. "Luther and Marcus are running a trafficking operation. Long-haul traffickers."

"Horrible."

"Yeah. Not my problem. We need to get out of here."

"I can't go," I said. "Lula is here. They took Lula."

"And that's a bad thing?"

"Yes! It's a bad thing. Now that I have the lay of the land, I'm going back to find her."

Vinnie growled.

"Do not growl at me," I said. "That is unacceptable behavior."

"I've been in the same clothes for four days and I've been doing my business in a chemical toilet. I'm not in a good place. Call Ranger. He'll come find her."

"He's on his way."

"How do you know?"

"I know."

"How are you going to find her?" Vinnie asked. "There are five floors to this building. And it's a big building. It was probably some sort of factory."

"I'm thinking she's on the fifth floor. It seems to be the hostage floor."

"If she's in one of those fifth-floor rooms you'll need a key to get to her. It's not like you're gonna get her out through the air duct. She'll never fit. And it's not just those two idiot brothers," Vinnie said. "There were supervisors in the room with the women workers. They were armed."

"There were only three of them," I said. "It's not like there's an army here."

"Hello. You're talking crazy. There are six of them. There are two of us. They got guns. We got nothing. We're not even big and scary looking."

Vinnie wasn't very big, but he was definitely scary. His hair wasn't slicked back anymore. It was sticking out like it belonged to a cartoon cat that had just been electrified. He had a four-day beard going, his clothes were stained and wrinkled, and he didn't smell great.

"I'm going back to get her," I said. "You don't have to go with me."

"This sucks," Vinnie said. "I can't let you go back alone. I'd look like a pussy. God will repossess my nuts."

I nodded. "True."

"If we're going to do this, we need to even the playing field. We need guns. We're gonna have to kill someone and get their gun."

"I'd rather not kill anyone," I said.

"You're making this difficult."

"Maybe you could just injure someone instead of killing them. And you could make sure it's a really bad person."

"I'm thinking if they're in this building, they're really bad," Vinnie said. "Nice people don't keep women locked up in cement bunkers."

We stopped talking and turned toward the garage entrance. A truck was approaching. There weren't a lot of places to hide but the lighting was dim and there were dark corners and stacks of wood pallets. We ran to a stack of pallets and crouched down.

The truck rolled in and parked. It was the second Acut truck with Texas plates. The freight elevator opened and Marcus and two men with assault weapons stepped out. One of the men grabbed a large pushcart dolly that was beside the elevator, and they all walked to the truck. A man and a woman swung down from the truck's cab, stretched, and walked to the back of the trailer. The doors were unlocked and opened. The male driver climbed into the truck and offloaded about a dozen boxes that were stacked on the dolly. Women were offloaded after the boxes. Most were in their late teens and early twenties. There were three children with the women. I would guess ten to thirteen years old. Everyone looked exhausted. I couldn't see much of their faces from that distance. They each carried a single bag that I assumed was filled with clothes and a few essentials.

"How long do you think they've been in that truck?" I asked Vinnie.

"If it came from Texas, they've probably been in there for about thirty-five hours. Two drivers could make a nonstop run in that time. Maybe a little longer if they were avoiding checkpoints. Most likely these women were picked up in Mexico and then the trip would be closer to two days."

Nine women and the three children were put in the Sprinter van and driven out of the garage by the two truck drivers. The remaining women were put in the freight elevator with Marcus and one of the armed men. That left one man to unload the rest of the truck.

He lounged against the truck, smoked some weed, and surfed around on his cell phone. He was wearing a sidearm. His rifle was propped against one of the back wheels.

Vinnie looked pretty happy about all this. I knew Vinnie was thinking taking this guy would be a slam-dunk. At first glance Vinnie looks like a sneaky-eyed member of the weasel family. No bones. No muscle. A brain the size of a walnut. The reality is that Vinnie is a nasty street fighter. He's smart. He's stealthy. He's fast. He's surprisingly strong. And he has no problem going for the jugular.

The armed guard threw his butt on the ground, put his phone in his pocket, and climbed into the truck. As soon as he was out of sight, moving boxes around, I cut across the garage and Vinnie ran to the front of the truck. I was in deep shadow at the exit ramp, and I could partly see into the truck. He had a bunch of boxes lined up at the tailgate. He jumped down and started transferring the boxes to the pushcart.

I waited for him to get a few feet away from the truck and I stepped out in full view. "Hi," I said. "My dog ran away. I thought he might have run in here."

"There's no dog in here," he said. "This is private property. You have to leave."

Vinnie was directly behind the guard. Vinnie tapped him on the shoulder, and when the man turned around, Vinnie sucker punched him in the throat and kicked him in the privates. The man doubled over, and Vinnie gave him a chop to the back of the head that sent him to the ground.

I ran to the truck and looked down at the guard. He wasn't moving. "Omigod," I said. "Is he dead?"

Vinnie toed him. "Nope," Vinnie said. "I can see him breathing."

Vinnie took the assault rifle, and I took the sidearm. It was a Glock. Much larger than mine, but I knew how to make it go bang. I searched the guard's pockets, found a key ring, and slipped it into my back pocket.

"You're sure Ranger is coming," Vinnie said.

"Absolutely sure."

We ran to the stairs and went one flight at a time, listening for footsteps or voices. I could see a bar of light shining under the third-floor door. I cracked the door and peeked inside. The new women were gathered in there. Luther was speaking to them in Spanish, and Marcus and two armed guards were standing watch. The room had long tables and folding chairs. Laundry carts were scattered around the room. Impossible to see what was in them. I carefully closed the door.

"This is good," Vinnie said. "Marcus and Luther are in there organizing the latest batch of workers. That means they aren't going to be on the fifth floor."

CHAPTER TWENTY-THREE

We ran up to the fifth floor and discovered that a large part of the space was unused storage. It would have made an amazing loft but currently it was a depository of mouse droppings and cobwebs. The open storage backed up to a hallway that contained the windowless rooms being used as dorms and cells. The freight elevator was positioned in the middle of the long hall and there were stairs at either end.

We started at one end of the hallway. I tried the keys on the guard's key ring and found one that opened the door to the first room. No one there. The key worked on all the other doors, but Lula wasn't in any of the rooms.

"Now what?" Vinnie asked.

"We try the other floors."

We went into the stairwell and heard shouting and people running up the stairs.

"They're looking for us," Vinnie said.

We exited the stairwell and ran down the hall to the stairs at the other end. We burst into the stairwell and stopped and listened. Nothing.

"I vote we go to the garage and get the hell out of here," Vinnie said. "We'll get the Marines and the cavalry and come back for Lula."

"Agreed!"

We bolted down the stairs. I was behind Vinnie, and Vinnie was flying with a ten-foot lead on me. I reached a landing, a door suddenly opened to the side of me, and I was grabbed and yanked inside. It was the room with the long tables and laundry carts. The women from the truck were huddled together at the far end of the room. One of the armed guards stood next to them. Luther had wrestled me into the room, and he kicked the door shut and threw me onto the floor like I was a rag doll. I hit the concrete hard and the Glock flew out of my hand and slid across the floor.

Luther came at me, grabbed the front of my sweatshirt, and dragged me to my feet.

"In the beginning I just wanted my money," he said, "but now I hate you." He made a fist and pulled his arm back to hit me.

"Not in the face!" I said. "My eyes are

still black and blue from when I tried to shoot you."

"I want my money."

"I keep telling you. I don't have it. I don't know where it is. I was lucky to find the coin. I had no idea it was associated with a lot of money."

"Where did you find the coin?"

"I got it from one of the street vendors on Wheaton Street. It was just dumb luck."

"You're lying. It's not even a good lie. I know you have the money. You're driving a brand-new Discovery."

"My boyfriend gave it to me."

"Your boyfriend is a cop. He doesn't have that kind of money. He drives a crappy green SUV."

"It was my other boyfriend."

"You have two boyfriends? Sweetheart, you aren't that hot. You're lucky the cop likes you."

"I know," I said. "I can't figure it out either."

"Where's Jimbo?" Luther yelled at the guard.

"He's in the kitchen icing his gonads," the guard said.

"I need someone to take Miss Plum upstairs," Luther said.

"I'll take her," the guard said. "I was going upstairs anyway. I was going to show the girls their room."

"Cuff her," Luther said. "And shoot her if you have to but try not to kill her."

The guard pulled out flexi-cuffs from his back pocket.

"Use the bracelets on her," Luther said.

The guard switched to metal handcuffs.

Crap. I held my arms out and he clapped the cuffs on me. Score one for Plum. At least I had my hands in front of me.

We all marched into the service elevator and got out at the fifth floor. No one said anything. The women were ushered into one of the larger dorm rooms and the door was closed and locked. The guard motioned for me to walk to the end of the hall. He opened the door to the last room and told me to go in.

"What about the cuffs?" I asked. "Can they come off?"

"No," he said. "The cuffs stay on until Luther wants them off."

"What if I have to go to the bathroom?"

"This room doesn't come with bathroom privileges," he said, smiling, looking like this was an enjoyable part of his job.

He closed and locked the door, and I was alone. The room was like the room Vinnie had been in but without the toilet. My first thought was about Lula. Worst-case scenario was too horrible to consider. Best-case scenario was that she'd managed to escape. I looked up. There was a vent in the ceiling, but I had no way to get to it. I had keys in my pocket, but the doors had blind locks. They only locked and unlocked from the outside.

I paced for a while. Occasionally listening at the door. I was wearing Ranger's necklace so I knew he could find me. The tricky part was getting him to start looking. The men sitting in the SUV outside Benji Land had to first realize I was missing. No telling when that would happen.

A half hour went by, and I heard noise outside the door. Someone shouting. The door was wrenched open, and Luther stood in the doorway. His face was red and blotchy, and he was sweating. "Get out," he said, pointing a gun at me. "Move!"

"What's going on?"

"We're leaving. You can cooperate and live or you can die. The only thing keeping you alive right now is our lost eleven million. Marcus and I sold our souls and worked our asses off for that money. It's our retirement ticket. You're either going to give it up or you're going to die. And it's not going to be a nice death."

"What about this building and the workers? Are you just going to walk away from this?"

"Marcus and I transport. We've got two trucks. That's it. This hellhole is someone else's problem." He shoved me in front of him. "Run," he said. "We're taking the back stairs."

I ran down the hall and entered the back stairwell. *Bang. Bang.* It sounded like a couple of small explosions. I started to go down, and Luther grabbed me by my ponytail and yanked me back. "We're going up," he said. "The stairs aren't safe."

"There aren't any stairs going up."

"There's a ladder. Go up the ladder. We're going to the roof."

I climbed up the ladder and shoved the hatch open. Not the easiest thing to do wearing handcuffs. The sun was glaring bright after the darkness of the building. There was a slight breeze. I looked around and recognized some landmarks. I was in the industrial area by the button factory.

I couldn't see the street in front of the building, but I could hear activity there. We were at the back of the building. There was a small patch of dirt and gravel and then there was the back of another building. Lots of windows in the other building. Half of them broken. Three stories high. There was a narrow walkway and another building.

"We're going to the street," Luther said. "Marcus will be waiting with a car."

I crept closer to the edge, looked down at the ground, and felt some vertigo. The way to get to the ground was by a fire escape ladder attached to the building.

"I can't do this," I said. "I'm not good with heights, and I can't go hand over hand wearing handcuffs."

"There's enough slack between the bracelets for you to manage. Get over the edge."

I was debating whether it would be better to get shot and take my chances at dying on the roof or choose falling to my death from the fifth-floor ladder.

"If you don't go now, I'll shoot you. I swear to God," Luther said. "I'm running out of time and patience."

I sucked in some air and grabbed hold of the handrails as best I could. I swung a leg over, made sure I had good footing, and I swung the other leg over.

"I'm coming down right on top of you," Luther said. "I'm going to be watching you, so don't try anything stupid."

I thought attempting to go down the ladder was at the top of the stupid list, but I was doing it anyway because I believed him when he said he would shoot me. Halfway down I was sweating from the exertion of hanging on to the ladder. I reached the second floor, and my legs were shaking. I looked up at Luther. He didn't seem to be having any problems. It was obviously a lot easier when you weren't wearing handcuffs.

"Don't just hang there," Luther said to me. "We haven't got all day. Move!"

I was almost to the bottom. I missed a rung and crashed to the ground.

Luther swung down after me. "Get up."

"I'm getting," I said.

I was on all fours, trying to stand. He grabbed hold of my arm and pulled me to my feet. I took a step and went down to one knee.

He pointed the gun at me. He had his finger on the trigger. His teeth were clenched. "Get up."

My peripheral vision caught a flash of white and the sun glinting off silver. I turned in time to see Sir Lancelot do a twirl maneuver and slash out at Luther with his sword. There was a clang of metal, Luther's gun sailed off into the air, and three fingers dropped onto the ground.

It was as if we were all frozen in time for several beats.

"Fuck," Luther said, grabbing the hand

that was short fingers.

There was a lot of blood and for a second, we all stared at the fingers that were lying in the dirt and gravel. Sir Lancelot's eyes rolled back in his head, and he fainted. Luther stumbled back and sat down hard on the ground. I scrambled across the yard and grabbed the gun. My hands were shaking, but I managed to fire several shots into the air.

Marcus ran out of the alley on the other side of the yard. I saw him coming at us, gun in hand, and I fired off a shot at him. He aimed and attempted to shoot back but the gun misfired. He dropped the gun, turned, and ran for the street. After what he'd done to Connie, Vinnie, and me, not to mention all the women and kids he'd sold into slavery, no way was he going to get away. I crossed the yard and chased him into the alley. I was struggling to run with my hands cuffed in front of me, but he was no athlete. Too many hours sitting in the cab of a truck, popping gummies to stay awake.

I caught up to him as he was getting into his car. I hit him in the back of the head with the butt of the gun. He turned and I hit him square in the face. He went down to the ground, and I kicked him. I was still kicking him, calling him really vile names, when someone wrapped their arms around me and wrestled me away.

It was Ranger. He was holding me tight against him, and I could swear he was laughing. This is sobering because Ranger doesn't laugh a lot.

"Babe," he said. "I hope you never get that mad at me. I'm not sure I'd come out the winner."

"He was *not* going to get away," I said.

"And he won't," Ranger said. "We'll take it from here. I'm pretty sure he's got a couple broken ribs and his nose is no longer in existence, but I think he'll live." He looked down at me. "And you did all this damage while you were handcuffed. That's impressive." He took a universal key from his pocket and released the handcuffs. "We have the building secured, and I brought the police in. This is a major drug operation."

"And human trafficking," I said. "There are women locked in rooms on the fifth floor."

A fire truck and an EMT screamed down the street, lights flashing, and stopped in front of us. Two cop cars followed.

Two Rangemen brought Luther out to the street. He was partly walking and mostly getting dragged. One of the Rangemen was holding Luther's arm up to slow the bleeding.

Ranger and I returned to the yard behind the factory. Sir Lancelot was still on his back. Hal was with him, talking him back to consciousness.

"Luther was going to shoot me," I said to Ranger. "Sir Lancelot came out of nowhere and knocked the gun out of Luther's hand with his sword and lopped off three fingers."

A med tech came out of the alley and walked over with a small Igloo cooler. "I'm told there are fingers back here."

I pointed to the bloody patch on the ground. The med tech picked the fingers up and dropped them into the cooler. "Thanks," he said. "Anybody need help?"

"Nope," I said. "We're okay."

Sir Lancelot was on his feet, walking around. I waved and smiled at him, and he came over to us.

"I fainted," he said.

"Anybody would," I told him. "You're my hero. You saved my life."

"Gee whiz," he said.

"How did you know I was here?"

"We went looking for you. Connie came back to the store and wanted to know where you were. Carpenter said you were looking at the storage units, but you and Lula didn't come back, so we all went to the storage units and saw your drink cups on the ground. And we found your messenger bag and Lula's purse in some bushes. So, we told the Rangemen in the SUV. And they made a phone call right away, and then they took off. We thought they might need help, so we followed them. And eventually they came here. We were out front trying to stay out of everyone's way, and I wanted to see what was in the back of the factory. And that's when I saw you in trouble."

"Omigosh," I said. "I forgot about Lula."

"We found her in the garage," Ranger said. "I think they put her in the trunk and forgot about her. Or maybe they didn't want to deal with her. We heard her pounding on the trunk lid and yelling when we cleared the area. Vinnie was there too. He said you were behind him on the back stairs but when he reached the garage you weren't with him. He couldn't make it to the exit ramp because there were men unloading one of the trucks. He was hiding in a corner behind the stairwell. I had one of my men take him home."

Connie, Lula, Benji, and Beedle came out of a back door and hurried over to us.

"What's going on? What did I miss?" Lula asked.

"Sir Lancelot smote Luther," I said. "It was awesome. If it wasn't for Sir Lancelot I'd be on my way to Mexico now."

"How bad did he smote him?"

"Chopped off three fingers," I said. "The paramedic came and collected them."

Everyone gave Sir Lancelot two thumbs up and some *dilly dilly*s.

"I would have liked to smote someone," Lula said. "I was left in the trunk of some smelly car like I was a used tire. These people got no couth."

"I'm sorry I didn't get a chance to do some damage," Connie said, "but at least the nightmare has ended, and I'll get a chance to testify. And I can guarantee you that the Smulets will not make bail."

We all went back into the building and walked to the front lobby.

"Vinnie and I never explored the first and second floors," I said to Ranger.

"They aren't being used. They were locked when we got here."

"But you got them open?"

"We blasted them open. I didn't want to waste time getting in," he said. "I knew you were here. I didn't know anything beyond that. I didn't like what I saw when we went

414

into the garage."

We left the building and walked out into the sunlight. There were Rangeman SUVs, cop cars, fire trucks, and EMTs. A satellite news truck rolled into the small parking area. I saw Morelli pull in.

"This is going to turn into a circus," Ranger said. "Every three-letter agency is going to have a piece of this. I'm going to pull my men out and let the feds take over."

"Thank you," I said. I put my hand to my necklace. "Do you want this back?"

"Keep it," he said. "I'll turn the tracking function off. Let me know if you want it back on."

He was standing close enough that I could feel the heat from his body and smell the faint scent of Bulgari. Our eyes held for a long moment before he turned and walked away.

Lula was standing behind me. "Holy hell," she said. "Holy crap. He wasn't even talking to me, and I got all verklempt."

"What's *verklempt*?"

"I don't know exactly. When I was a ho, I had a steady customer who got verklempt. I'd be doing my job, and he'd be saying, 'I'm verklempt. I'm verklempt.' I think it might be like an orgasm of the brain. Like a good aneurism, or something. I figured it was on account of I was an excellent ho. If anybody was gonna make a man go ver-klempt, it was Lula."

Morelli made his way through the chaos of cops and cars and flashing lights. Bella was scuttling after him.

"I was taking Bella to Aunt Choochi's house, and I heard the call go out for a major drug bust at this address. Dispatch said Rangeman had the building secured, and I got instant heartburn. I knew in my gut you were involved."

"Only tangentially," I said.

"Huh," Bella said. "Slut knows big word."

The guard who had taken me upstairs and locked me in my cell without bathroom privileges was cuffed and waiting with several other guards for police transport.

"Do you see the men standing by the police car?" I asked Bella. "They're all hand-cuffed."

"I see them. So?"

"I was talking to them, and the one with the brown ponytail and red shirt said he hated Italians. Especially Sicilians. He said they're all stupid and smell bad."

"He say this?"

"He said he'd rather kiss a pig than kiss a Sicilian."

Bella straightened. "I give him the eye. I

416

give it to him good."

Bella marched off to the handcuffed group of men.

"You're evil," Morelli said to me.

"I have my moments."

"Are you okay?" he asked. "No hidden injuries?"

"I'm good."

"Are you going to be arrested for anything?"

"Nope. Not today."

"And the kidnappers?"

"In custody."

"Then our date is still on for tonight?"

"You betcha."

ABOUT THE AUTHOR

Over the last twenty-six years, **Janet Evanovich** has written a staggering forty-two *New York Times* bestsellers. In addition to her #1 bestselling Stephanie Plum novels and many other popular books, Janet is the author of *The Recovery Agent,* the start of a blockbuster new series.

The employees of Thorndike Press hope you have enjoyed this Large Print book. All our Thorndike, Wheeler, and Kennebec Large Print titles are designed for easy reading, and all our books are made to last. Other Thorndike Press Large Print books are available at your library, through selected bookstores, or directly from us.

For information about titles, please call:
 (800) 223-1244

or visit our website at:
 gale.com/thorndike

To share your comments, please write:
 Publisher
 Thorndike Press
 10 Water St., Suite 310
 Waterville, ME 04901